Praise for *Heiress for Hire*

"If you are looking to read a romance that will leave you all warm inside, then *Heiress for Hire* is a must-read." —*Romance Junkies*

"McCarthy transforms what could have been a run-of-the-mill romance with standout characterizations that turn an unlikable girl and a boring guy into two enjoyable, empathetic people who make this romance shine." —*Booklist*

"Amusing paranormal contemporary romance . . . Fans will appreciate Erin McCarthy's delightful pennies-from-heaven tale of opposites in love pushed together by a needy child and an even needier ghost." —*The Best Reviews*

"One of McCarthy's best books to date . . . *Heiress for Hire* offers characters you will care about, a story that will make you laugh and cry, and a book you won't soon forget. As Amanda would say: It's priceless." —*The Romance Reader* (5 hearts)

"A keeper. I'm giving it four of Cupid's five arrows."—*Bella Online*

"An alluring tale." —*A Romance Review* (5 roses)

"The perfect blend of sentiment and silly, heat and heart . . . priceless!" —*Romantic Times* "TOP PICK" (4½ stars)

"An enjoyable story about finding love in unexpected places, don't miss *Heiress for Hire*." —*Romance Reviews Today*

continued . . .

A Date With the Other Side

"Do yourself a favor and make A Date With the Other Side."
—Bestselling author Rachel Gibson

"One of the romance-writing industry's brightest stars . . . Ms. McCarthy spins a fascinating tale that deftly blends a paranormal story with a blistering romance . . . Funny, charming, and very entertaining, *A Date With the Other Side* is sure to leave you with a pleased smile on your face."
—*Romance Reviews Today*

"If you're looking for a steamy read that will keep you laughing while you turn the pages as quickly as you can, *A Date With the Other Side* is for you. Very highly recommended!"
—*Romance Junkies*

"Fans will appreciate this otherworldly romance and want a sequel."
—*Midwest Book Review*

"Ghostly matchmakers add a fun flair to this warmhearted and delightful tale . . . an amusing and sexy charmer sure to bring a smile to your face."
—*Romantic Times*

"Offers readers quite a few chuckles, some face-fanning moments, and one heck of a love story. Surprises await those who expect a 'sophisticated city boy meets country girl' romance. Ms. McCarthy delivers much more."
—*A Romance Review*

Praise for the other novels of Erin McCarthy

"Will have your toes curling and your pulse racing."
—*Arabella*

"Erin McCarthy writes this story with emotion and spirit, as well as humor."
—*Fallen Angel Reviews*

"Both naughty and nice . . . sure to charm readers."
—*Booklist*

Bled Dry

Erin McCarthy

BERKLEY SENSATION, NEW YORK

THE BERKLEY PUBLISHING GROUP
Published by the Penguin Group
Penguin Group (USA) Inc.
375 Hudson Street, New York, New York 10014, USA
Penguin Group (Canada), 90 Eglinton Avenue East, Suite 700, Toronto, Ontario M4P 2Y3, Canada
(a division of Pearson Penguin Canada Inc.)
Penguin Books Ltd., 80 Strand, London WC2R 0RL, England
Penguin Group Ireland, 25 St. Stephen's Green, Dublin 2, Ireland (a division of Penguin Books Ltd.)
Penguin Group (Australia), 250 Camberwell Road, Camberwell, Victoria 3124, Australia
(a division of Pearson Australia Group Pty. Ltd.)
Penguin Books India Pvt. Ltd., 11 Community Centre, Panchsheel Park, New Delhi—110 017, India
Penguin Group (NZ), 67 Apollo Drive, Mairangi Bay, Auckland 1311, New Zealand
(a division of Pearson New Zealand Ltd.)
Penguin Books (South Africa) (Pty.) Ltd., 24 Sturdee Avenue, Rosebank, Johannesburg 2196, South Africa

Penguin Books Ltd., Registered Offices: 80 Strand, London WC2R 0RL, England

This book is an original publication of The Berkley Publishing Group.

This is a work of fiction. Names, characters, places, and incidents either are the product of the author's imagination or are used fictitiously, and any resemblance to actual persons, living or dead, business establishments, events, or locales is entirely coincidental. The publisher does not have any control over and does not assume any responsibility for author or third-party websites or their content.

First edition: May 2007

Library of Congress Cataloging-in-Publication Data

McCarthy, Erin.
    Bled dry / Erin McCarthy.—1st ed.
        p.   cm.
    ISBN 978-0-425-21515-9
    1. Vampires—Fiction.   2. Stripteasers—Fiction.   3. Las Vegas (Nev.)—Fiction.   I. Title.

    PS3613.C34575B59   2007
    813'.6—dc22   2006103250

PRINTED IN THE UNITED STATES OF AMERICA

10   9   8   7   6   5   4   3   2   1

One

"Well, it's not the flu."

Brittany Baldizzi watched her general practitioner tuck her hair behind her ear as she stepped back into the room. Perched on the edge of the examination table, Brittany was seriously confused. "An ulcer then? I've felt this awful nausea for weeks."

"Not an ulcer." Dr. Hopkins smiled. "You're pregnant."

"Excuse me?" The room went stark white and a buzzing rang in Brittany's ears. "Pregnant? I can't be pregnant!"

There was no way. It wasn't possible.

"Have you been practicing abstinence?" Dr. Hopkins asked with a rueful shrug.

"Yes, I've been totally abstinent." How in the hell could she be pregnant?

Dr. Hopkins raised her eyebrows. "Really?"

Okay, so that wasn't completely true. "Well, mostly. I've only had sex once in the last six months." But that had been with Corbin Atelier, and that didn't count because he was a vampire.

"Once is all it takes."

Normally. When you were having sex with regular, mortal men. "But . . ." Brittany rubbed her head. "He can't have children." She didn't think. Of course, he had never really said he couldn't have children. But neither had he suggested birth control.

"I'm sorry this is such a shock, Brittany, but obviously he can have children, because you are definitely pregnant."

"Well, I had no idea." That vampires had sperm.

Which was a stupid assumption on her part. After all, hadn't her brother-in-law sworn to her up, down, and sideways that her own biological father had to be a vampire? But she hadn't put two and two together when she and Corbin had been talking that night.

Though to be totally honest, it wasn't like she and Corbin had devoted a whole lot of time to conversation when he had climbed in her bedroom window and asked for blood. She'd given him her blood and her body, and now he had given her a baby.

Holy crap.

It really would have been nice if he had warned her his boys could still swim.

"You're what?" Her sister, Alexis, just stared at her.

Brittany threw herself down on Alexis's leather couch and groaned. That appalled look of disbelief on Alexis's face must have been what she had looked like in the doctor's office. "You heard me. I'm pregnant. And before you ask, I made the doctor do the test twice."

"Well. Gee. Shit. This is unexpected." Alexis rubbed her hands through her hair. "A baby. You're going to be a mother. Wow. Okay. Well, that's exciting. I think. No, I'm sure, it is, babies are always good. But damn, for the first time since Ethan turned me, I think I actually regret being a vampire. I'm not exactly going to have a normal relationship with my niece or nephew, am I? Though you know I'm happy if you're happy."

Tears popped into Brittany's eyes. Alexis was the closest thing to a mother she had, since their mom had overdosed when Brittany was thirteen. It was hard sometimes to accept that Alexis was now a vampire, married to a really old vampire and living in his Las Vegas casino. Her sister had a whole different life from Brittany's mild-mannered existence as a suburban dentist.

A suburban dentist who happened to be knocked up by a French vampire. Oh, God.

"I'm happy about a baby, yes, but Alexis, I'm scared."

Alexis popped up off the easy chair and came over to her. "Oh, honey, don't be scared." She hugged her, which made Brittany feel better. She may have been nearly a foot taller than Alexis, but it still felt good to be cosseted. "It will work out. We'll help you out."

"Help her out with what? What's wrong?" Alexis's husband, Ethan Carrick, current president of the Vampire Nation, strolled out of their bedroom in pajama pants and no shirt.

"Did I wake you, Ethan? I'm sorry." Brittany hadn't been

able to wait a minute past six o'clock, which was really early for vampires to be getting up for the night, but she had desperately needed to hear Alexis tell her everything was going to be alright.

"It's fine. What's wrong, Brit?"

"She's pregnant," Alexis told him.

"Oh." His mouth opened, closed, opened again. "So, uh, congratulations. That's fabulous! A baby. I'm sure you'll be a brilliant mother."

"Absolutely," Alexis said stoutly, patting her leg. "This is one lucky baby."

While Brittany had always imagined she would have several kids, and had looked forward to that time in her life, she had never once thought she'd be having a baby alone, without a man anywhere in the picture. Not to mention she was a touch concerned about the health of two-hundred-year-old vampire sperm. That seemed a little past the expiration date.

"I've always wanted to have a baby, and I'm sure once the shock wears off, I'll be really excited. It was just a . . . surprise. Really unexpected."

"I didn't even know you were seeing anyone," Alexis said. "Who is the father? Do you think he'll want to be involved with the baby?"

Whoopsie. She'd left that little tidbit of info out, hadn't she? Brittany pulled away from Alexis and looked down at her jeans. She commanded her tongue to speak, but it didn't cooperate. Alexis was going to freak when she heard Brittany's very embarrassing answer.

"I'm not sure if he'll want to be involved, but I suspect the answer is no. I haven't seen him since the one night we slept together eight weeks ago." Brittany looked up, locking eyes with Alexis, hoping like hell her sister would put two and two together so she wouldn't have to say it out loud.

Alexis stared back. Then suddenly she jerked on the couch like she'd been electrocuted, her jaw dropping, head shaking. "Brit . . . oh, no, don't tell me. Please tell me that the baby's father is not Corbin Atelier."

"It is," she said in agony, feeling like a total idiot. Why had she even slept with the charming, good-looking, arrogant idiot in the first place?

Because he was charming, good looking, and arrogant. And the sex had been hot.

"It is what? Corbin's baby?" Alexis said, like she was trying to convince herself she'd heard wrong.

"Yes! It's Corbin's baby."

"The Frenchman got you pregnant?" Ethan's voice was outraged, his hands on his hips. "Didn't he use birth control?"

Now that was a little personal.

"Ethan." Alexis glared at him. "That's not really any of your business."

"It is," he insisted. "Vampires aren't supposed to sleep with mortal women without using birth control. While the odds of pregnancy aren't as great as copulation with a mortal man, there is still that risk. It's irresponsible to mate with a mortal woman and impregnate her with a half-vampire, half-mortal child."

Copulate . . . mate . . . impregnate . . . could he make it sound any grosser? Next he'd toss out *breeding* and *bitches in heat.*

And she was not about to tell her by-the-book brother-in-law that Corbin had not used birth control. That they had gone from discussing Corbin's scientific experiment to body slapping in about a blink. There hadn't been time to grab a good breath for moaning, forget finding a condom. They had been there and done before you could say ovulate.

"Corbin and I may have been irresponsible, but that's irrelevant at this point, Ethan. I'm having a baby. Alone, apparently, since I haven't seen Corbin since we conceived this child." Well, she had thought she'd seen him the night she'd been so sick, but Alexis had assured her she must have dreamed that Corbin had showed up, hauled her off the bathroom floor, and put her to bed. "I have no idea how to get in touch with him."

Brittany would be mortified to actually have to face Corbin and tell him she was having his child, but it made her uncomfortable to realize that he wasn't going to know. Whatever he wanted to do with the knowledge of impending fatherhood was fine with Brittany—he could be involved or not—but it only seemed right that he have the opportunity to make the choice himself.

But she couldn't tell him if she couldn't find him.

Rubbing her mildly nauseous stomach, Brittany bit her lip and worried. It took her a second to realize that Ethan and Alexis weren't saying anything. When she looked up, she saw them glancing at each other. Damn them. They were doing that vampire mind-reading thing with each other, leaving her out of their conversation.

"If you guys are talking about me, quit it. That is so rude."

Alexis swore. "Ethan . . ." she said in warning. "Let me handle this."

"I don't need to be handled," Brittany said, feeling a little irritated. "What are you keeping from me?"

"So handle it," Ethan said, sweeping his hand out gallantly. "I have utter confidence in you to do the right thing, Alexis."

Did they even notice she was sitting there? "What are you both talking about?"

"Brit . . ." Alexis tugged on the end of her shaggy blond hair. "Corbin is in Vegas if you want to talk to him."

Her breath caught. "He is?" A lump the size of a grapefruit seemed to be stuck in her throat. She was having trouble swallowing, and her stomach was grinding and twisting. "How long has he been here?" And why the hell hadn't he told her he was in town?

"Um, I'm not really sure," Alexis said, biting her fingernail. It was a clear sign she was lying. Apparently she decided to come clean. "But well, actually, I think he's kind of always here because he sort of has to be. I don't think he ever left. He, um, well, lives here."

Tears popped into Brittany's eyes, mortifying her. So no one had told her Corbin lived in Vegas, including Corbin himself. Big whoop. They were nothing to each other, an embarrassing little one-night stand, two minutes out of Corbin's two hundred years of life. Of course he hadn't put her at the top of the list of people to see when he was out and about. She wasn't even sure why she had assumed he was from out of town, except that maybe that had been wishful thinking, her mental justification for why he hadn't bothered to speak to her in the last eight weeks.

She was usually so much more rational about men. Brittany had always liked to live in the moment, to have fun, to meet new people, and she enjoyed sex for the pure physical pleasure. Never before had she felt this weird sort of melancholy and longing for a guy she wasn't dating, didn't really know, and who clearly had no interest in her. She had no problem admitting she had indulged in a one-night stand or two in her time, and she'd always walked away with a whistle, no regrets.

This was different, and she didn't know why. Definitely didn't like it.

And she was pregnant.

"Where is he?" Brittany blinked hard. She really needed to find Corbin, tell him the news, and retreat back to her corner to get a grip on her life.

Ethan cleared his throat. "I believe he's on the twenty-fourth floor at the moment."

"He's here? At the Ava?" Corbin was in Ethan's casino right as they were speaking in that very same casino? Her stomach roiled.

"Yes."

"Oh, I'm going to throw up." Brittany lurched forward and tossed her dinner into the sink adjacent to the bar with impressive velocity.

Bled Dry

A martini glass fell off the counter and crashed to the tile floor when she jerked back up, wiping her eyes and mouth. Brittany clutched her gut and ignored her sister and brother-in-law staring at her in horror. Shaking her hair off her face, she took a deep breath.

She had a fertile French vampire to see.

Two

Corbin Atelier stared out the window at the Vegas cityscape, feeling restless with his confinement. He'd been living in Las Vegas for nearly four decades, and never had he felt the yoke around him so tightly as now. There was no reason for it, but he longed to be able to leave the desert, to fly to the ocean, to the mountains, to smell the crisp air of Paris in late October.

A knock sounded on the door of the suite of rooms he had been staying in for the past two weeks as he oversaw Ringo Columbia's withdrawal from his drug blood addiction. Corbin made no movement to answer the door, staring, searching, wanting some kind of answer from the view in front of him.

"There's someone here," Ringo said.

Corbin turned and saw that Ringo was slumped on the divan with his eyes closed, legs stretched out in front of him. A cigarette dangled at his lips, and his cheeks were pale, skin sallow. His chest moved up and down laboriously, like ancient bellows. It was difficult to watch Ringo suffer through his withdrawal, but Corbin was confident he was through most of the physical trauma. Mentally, it was never a sure thing. Addiction waged war on its victim, the battle was never completely won, and Corbin wasn't entirely sure Ringo wanted to be free of his dependency.

The knocking came louder.

"Would you answer that?" Ringo asked, voice rising in irritation. "It's probably Kelsey."

Corbin didn't know what the relationship was between Ringo and Ethan Carrick's secretary, but her visits usually had a positive effect on the patient. However, this wasn't Kelsey.

"It's a mortal. I can sense it." Corbin moved to answer the door, suppressing a sigh. He had work to do and every day he spent stuck in Carrick's casino, forced into the role of part prison guard, part medical doctor to Ringo, the longer his research was delayed.

Brittany Baldizzi was standing in front of him when he pulled open the door. Corbin was so startled he said the very stupid and obvious, "Brittany! This is a surprise."

"Hi, Corbin." Her cheeks went pink, and her eyes didn't quite meet his.

"How are you feeling?" he asked. "Are you recovered from the flu?" Truthfully, she still didn't look one hundred percent healthy. Her skin tone was off, and she looked like she had lost weight. Corbin felt both worried and guilty. He should have checked up on her a second time, but he hadn't been entirely comfortable with his own feelings toward Brittany, so he had avoided her. Yet again. He had done plenty of avoiding as well following the night he had bedded her.

"How did you know I had the flu?" she asked, looking startled.

"I saw you. I came to your apartment one night when you were sick." The night he had heard her call him mentally, felt her suffering. Without thinking, he had gone straight to her and found her sick in her bathroom. He could have sworn at the time that she didn't have a fever, but she must have if she didn't even remember seeing him.

Her eyes went wide. "You were really there? I just thought . . ."

"What?"

"That I was dreaming."

This beautiful woman he had made love to thought he was in her dreams? That pleased Corbin more than it should. "No. I was there. I put you to bed."

"Oh. Well, thanks."

"You are welcome." Corbin suddenly remembered that he had manners. "Would you like to come in? Are you here to see Ringo?"

She shook her head. "No. I've actually never even met Ringo. I wanted to talk to *you* for a minute. Privately."

He couldn't possibly imagine what she wanted to discuss with him, but she looked so anxious Corbin didn't hesitate. He admittedly had a rather soft spot when it came to Brittany. Not to mention he'd been attracted to her since the first night they met, when she had thought he was a serial killer.

"Certainly. We can go into the other room." It was a bedroom, which wasn't the best place to be escorting a woman he thought was so beautiful, a woman he'd impulsively made love to in a moment of total sexual weakness. It had been a wonderful, madly erotic five minutes, and a bed was sure to remind him of that, but the only other option was the bathroom, and he was too much a man of the nineteenth century to speak to her by the commode.

He offered her a seat in the sleek gray suede chair next to the bed, but she shook her head.

"What is the matter?" he asked, unable to resist the urge to smooth her hair back from her forehead. She really looked ill, and he felt prickles of concern.

"Corbin . . . I'm pregnant," she blurted, locking eyes with him for a second, before dropping her gaze to the floor.

"Pardon?" She'd spoken so quickly, mostly to the carpet, that surely he had misunderstood.

Those dark eyes, which he found so innocently alluring, locked onto his. "I'm pregnant. I'm having a baby."

That was rather unpleasant news. Granted, he had not spoken to her since the night they had made love, aside from when she'd been ill, but he had foolishly thought she had felt the same way as him—knocked off his feet by their encounter. He had not so much as looked at another woman in those eight weeks, yet she had moved to another man's bed. He was not so memorable, it seemed.

"Ah. Zat explains the vomiting," he said, his English slipping as it always did when he was irritated. "Morning sickness, yes? Well, I wish you happy."

The last remaining bits of color in her cheeks leeched away. She frowned at him. "Is that all you're going to say?"

Corbin shifted uneasily. He didn't see how the situation called for him to say anything else. "Take care of yourself," he said politely.

"Uh!"

Tears came out of nowhere and rolled out of her eyes, scaring Corbin senseless.

"What ez the matter? Don't you want to have a baby?" And why was he the one standing there in complete discomfort patting her arm inanely? Where was the baby's papa?

"*I* want to have a baby. And I thought that it was only the right thing to do to come and tell you that *you're* having a baby, but it seems like I shouldn't have wasted my night. You could care less!"

Corbin listened to her words. Played them back in his brain. Was she saying . . . "*I'm* the father?"

"Duh. Of course you are!" Brittany swiped at the tears on her face. "Who else would be? You're the only man I've slept with in six months."

Well, that was pleasing—she hadn't found him so lacking as a lover she'd had to find another. But that also meant . . . "*Mon Dieu*, you're having a baby? Our baby?"

"That's what I'm trying to tell you."

Corbin needed to sit down. He needed a drink. He needed to

think this through. Good God. A baby? A small, crying, help-less, mortal creature. That was half his, half Brittany's biology. It didn't seem possible. There had only been that one night. But he had made no effort to use birth control or even withdraw at the precipitous moment. Quite the opposite. He had enjoyed ex-ploding deep inside Brittany. Just the memory had him shifting, manhood swelling inappropriately.

"You are certain?"

She sighed. "Yes, Corbin, I'm certain."

"We didn't use birth control," he said, trying to reconcile what she was telling him with what had happened.

"No. But I didn't think you had sperm."

Corbin frowned at her, feeling insulted. "Of course I have sperm. I am still a man. I still function, do I not? I have every-thing that is manly the same as a mortal."

Brittany couldn't stop a small smile from crossing her face. Corbin looked so outraged and French. "Yes, you still have everything." And then some. She would never forget how in five minutes he'd given her better sex than some guys had in six months of dating.

"Absolutely." He nodded up and down once.

Brittany couldn't tell how he was taking the news. He didn't look angry. He looked surprised, but nothing more. Damn, he was cute. She'd almost forgotten how adorable he was in person with his caramel-colored hair and rich, chocolate eyes.

Corbin rubbed his jaw. "And as such, I owe you an apol-ogy. This is my fault and I accept complete responsibility. I will marry you."

Brittany forgot how cute he was. "What!" Of all possible re-actions, she hadn't even considered that one. He was smoking something if he thought she was going to just marry him because he'd gotten her pregnant. And what kind of a proposal was that anyway? A sucky one, that's what kind.

"It is for the best." He nodded, like everything was decided. "We will marry and hire a nurse to care for the babe."

Someone had fallen back into the nineteenth century. "Why is getting married for the best? We barely know each other." Brittany sucked in quick, short breaths. Her stomach was churning again. "I don't want to marry you."

"You would have my child be born a bastard?" He looked outraged.

"This is Vegas! No one cares." Brittany took a step back. He was so close to her she was getting dizzy trying to talk to him. "My mother was a stripper, for God's sake!"

Corbin winced.

Brittany was offended. He didn't like that? Too bad. "I don't even know who my father was. My mother cheated on her husband with Mr. Anonymous. Alexis and I don't even have the same father."

She was blathering on in total panic, because while she was intrigued by the idea of maybe dating Corbin, or at the very least having an amicable relationship with the father of her child, she could not marry him. Jesus. What the hell did they have in common?

Just a bundle of cells that were dividing in her uterus as they were speaking.

"Brittany . . ." Corbin clapped his hand on his forehead. "You and I, we have forgotten something. Your father was a vampire."

"So?"

"So, you are half-vampire. I am a vampire. This baby you're carrying, it is a three-quarter vampire child."

"So?" she asked again nervously. Why did Corbin look like he was going to drop to the ground? His eyes were actually narrowing, darkening, turning almost black, and she could tell he was thinking hard.

"So, there has never been a three-quarter vampire child to my knowledge. Ever."

That didn't sound promising. "Why not?"

"Because vampires are not supposed to procreate. Some, of course, do anyway, when they inadvertently mate with a mortal who has the recessive gene for vampirism, which allows for conception, though fortunately their numbers are few. The resulting child is a mortal Impure. But never has a vampire mated with an Impure such as yourself, or if they have, there was no child, possibly because their mother did not inherit the gene from *her* mother. You clearly do have the gene, as do I, meaning the gene will most definitely be in our child. It is the most basic of biology, but there has never been such a child that I know of, one with a complete vampire gene."

He'd already said that, and he was starting to scare the crap out of her. "And?"

"And if there has never been one, there is no scientific precedent. What is it? Mortal or vampire? Day or night dweller?"

Breast milk or blood drinker. Corbin didn't say it, but Brittany knew he was thinking it.

"Oh, my God! You're telling me our child is going to be some kind of . . . mutant, or something? Is he going to have fangs?"

"Of course not!" But he didn't look convinced. Then he stood up straighter and his jaw locked. "Our child is not a mutant. He will be strong and intelligent, lacking mortal weakness. Yet he will not need the blood. I am almost sure of it, because it is the draining which activates the urge to feed, not the gene. Besides, I am Corbin Jean Michel Atelier, the most premier vampire research scientist, and I will correct my mistake, that I promise you."

Wow. How reassuring. Brittany burst into tears. Her baby was a bloodsucking demon. Instead of a Gerber baby, she was going to have an infant with fangs, pale skin, night vision, and the ability to read minds. Brittany pictured a fridge full of little bottles, prancing lambs on the outside, all filled with human blood. She would have to lock down her thoughts all the time so her baby didn't see her sexual fantasies about George Clooney or her mean unkind thoughts about her dental hygienist's butt and the way it looked in white pants.

This was panic time.

"Corbin, you can't experiment on our child! God, this is horrible, I'm going to be sick." She clutched her stomach. "We were both so stupid! I'm never having sex with you again."

"But it is not as if you can get pregnant a second time," he pointed out, looking a little mystified. "There would be no reason we'd need birth control if we lay together now."

"Arrgh!" How did you say *idiot* in French? *Idi-ote?* She turned to the window, tears blinding her. "I want to talk to my sister." Fumbling in her pocket, she pulled her cell phone out of her jeans and pressed number one to call Alexis.

"Alex?" she sniffled when her sister answered.

Alexis swore. "What did the bastard say to you? Where are you?"

"I'm still in the suite you told me to come to. Alexis, Corbin says our baby is going to . . . going to . . ." She choked on the words and dissolved into a fresh round of tears.

"I'll be right there."

When Alex hung up, Brittany let the tears take her over. She sobbed, overwhelmed, frightened, scared for her child. Totally flipping freaked out.

Suddenly Corbin was behind her, arms wrapping around her. "Shh. It is all right now, *ma chérie*. I did not mean to frighten you. Everything will be just fine, and we will have the most beautiful child. After all, look at his mother."

Corbin's voice was soothing in her ear, his embrace confident and strong. She shouldn't lean on him, should try to be strong, but she couldn't. And she had no right to place all the blame on Corbin. She had been there that night. She had encouraged him, enjoyed their time together, and she had never hesitated or considered that there could be ramifications of their actions.

She tried to stop crying. "I did always want to be a mother."

"Now you will be, and you will be *fantastique*. It will all work out."

"I hope so." Brittany relaxed a little. Corbin was pretty

damn old, and he was a scientist, after all. He had said he was really close to an antidote to revert vampires to mortal. If anyone knew how to deal with the situation, it was him. She closed her eyes and leaned back against him. Maybe this would be okay.

"And we will get married, yes?"

Her eyes flew open. "No!" Why was he stuck on that?

There was a pounding on the outside door. Corbin moved away from her. "We are not finished discussing this."

If he was talking about marriage, she was finished discussing. She was not going to bind herself to a man she barely knew. She didn't even really know how old Corbin was, let alone what his personal likes and dislikes were, whether he was neat or a slob. She'd never even seen him naked, and how sad was that?

She checked out his butt as he left the room. It was *very* sad.

Ringo wondered if they knew he could hear every word they were saying.

Since his voluntary entry into rehab to quit the drug blood habit, he had gotten really damn good at meditation and the other new age crap his pseudo-girlfriend, Kelsey, kept encouraging him to do. The end result was that he was way more comfortable sitting still, listening, than he had ever been in his life, and with his vampire hearing, he had caught most of Corbin and Brittany's conversation.

He had to admit, he'd had no clue vampires could knock

women up. That was good info to have, if he didn't want to create headaches for himself along the way.

And he also wondered if anyone would be interested in hearing that an Impure was carrying a three-quarter vamp bundle of joy. Like someone willing to pay for that information.

Like maybe his old drug pusher, now in New York awaiting his trial for treason.

Donatelli.

Brittany heard her sister's voice at the door and went to save Corbin. If she knew Alexis, she'd have Corbin on the ground in a karate maneuver before he could say *pardon*.

She got there in the knick of time. Corbin was shaking his head, protesting in French to Ethan, while Alexis was bouncing on the balls of her feet. Brittany knew that stance. It meant someone was about to be kicked.

"Alex, don't kick him!"

"Give me one good reason why not."

"Because he is the father of my child."

"That's the reason why, not why not."

"What?" Brittany tried to follow that logic, gave up, and settled for taking Alex's hand and giving it a squeeze to prevent a full frontal attack.

Ethan and Corbin went back and forth in French—which she had to admit was sexy, even as she resented the fact that they were excluding her.

"I didn't know Ethan speaks French," she told her sister.

"I didn't either." Alexis was glaring at her husband. "He told me he spoke a smattering of French. Does that sound like a smatter to you?"

"I have no clue what a smatter sounds like." Brittany looked around for a seat. She was exhausted and there were no comfortable seats in the suite. It was an artful arrangement of impractical, uncomfortable art deco furniture. She wanted a nice fat sofa with squishy cushions. Instead what she saw was a hard, squared-off set of chairs and a white sofa with a man lying on it.

It must be Ringo, and he looked uncomfortable, which any human being would when sitting on such crappy furniture. He was like an infant propped up in a seat, his shoulders and head drooping to the side, and his legs falling open. His back was taking the brunt of the awkward position, and Brittany had the urge to grab a sausage pillow and tuck it behind him.

"Can I get you a backrest or something?" she asked, feeling bad for him. "I'm Brittany, by the way."

He opened his eyes and glanced at her curiously. He had dark eyes, expressionless, and she thought maybe she'd woken him up, because he didn't speak.

Grabbing a throw pillow from the chair, she moved toward him. "Here, lean forward for a sec."

He did, and she tucked, bending the pillow in half so it would fill the space behind his lower back.

"Thank you," he said, his breath expelling on a sigh when he sank back. "And congratulations."

"What?" Brittany stopped, half-standing, half-bent. Their

eyes were almost level with each other, and he held her gaze without blinking.

"The baby. Congrats. You must be excited."

It was a perfectly inane nothing for him to say, polite conversation, but a cold disturbing shiver rolled down Brittany's spine. Ringo must have overheard when she and Corbin had been talking. It should have embarrassed her, to know that anyone had been witness to that bumbling debacle. But she felt an edgy unease more than embarrassment, and she stood up, moved back out of Ringo's space.

"Thank you."

"Brittany," Ethan said, striding into the room. "I need to speak with you, please. Back at our apartment. Let's go."

"But I don't think Corbin and I are done talking." At least she hoped not. They hadn't resolved anything. All they had really established was what they already knew—that Corbin had sperm, they'd had some romping good sex, and they were having a baby. Surely the conversation needed to go beyond that.

"I don't care. We need to leave."

Ethan could be just as stubborn as her sister, which made Brittany wonder how two such similar personalities managed to live together. Though she supposed it wasn't like they could kill each other, given that they were immortal. They just had to fight it out.

But knowing how to handle Alexis's stubbornness helped Brittany deal with Ethan now. "Okay, I'll be there in two minutes. You go ahead without me."

Ethan nodded. "Good."

But Alexis was on to her. "If you're not back at our place in five minutes I'm coming back for you."

Damn. The conversation with Corbin would have to wait after all. Alexis wouldn't play around. She'd be back in five minutes, karate kick at the ready. "Fine. I'll just come with you now."

She went over to Corbin, who was standing by the front door, arms crossed, looking annoyed. "So, if you think we still have some things to talk about, maybe we could get together in the next few days." She didn't want to pressure him, but she wanted to know how involved he intended to be so she could mentally deal with the logistics of raising a vampire baby, either alone or with his help.

"Of course we need to see each other. We have many, many things to discuss," he said, French arrogance back in place. "I will come to you tonight."

See, this was what had gotten her in trouble in the first place. When he did that whole appearing out of the dark sexy thing, she couldn't help but get a little excited. She should tell him no, but they did need to talk. "Fine. But knock on the front door instead of coming in my window this time."

He relaxed, uncrossed his arms, and cupped her cheek, stroking across her skin. Brittany stared into his pale green eyes, taking comfort in the strength and determination she saw there.

"Our baby will be fine, I am convinced of it. This child is not a mutant, or an aberration, or an accident, but a child born of passion, and I am honored that you will be his mother."

Now that was a sweet thing to say. Brittany felt some of the tension in her ease. "Thank you. And you really think everything is okay?"

"Absolutely."

"I'll see you later then." Brittany left, feeling much better.

Corbin watched Brittany leave with Carrick and her sister, and stuck his hand in his hair.

Mon Dieu, his child was going to be born a mutant.

A freak of nature, a bloodsucking baby. This was not good. And he had lied to Brittany. This was not fine, this was not okay, this was a complete and total genetic nightmare, and yet again he was to blame for such an act of total stupidity.

Nearly thirty years of mortal life, two hundred as a vampire, and he had never once gotten a woman with child. That he did now, with an Impure half-vampire/half-mortal woman, was a strange and cruel irony. Of course, skipping birth control in a century when it was available at every turn for less than a cup of coffee, was inexcusable.

Corbin had made mistakes before. Grave and unfortunate mistakes that had left one woman dead and his work in question.

But he was so close to finding a cure for vampirism. Success was just a few tests away and now this. He was such an idiot.

Corbin called in the guard who was standing in the hallway. "I must leave for a few hours. Keep an eye on Ringo."

The guard nodded even as Ringo said, "I don't need a baby-sitter. I'm not going to leave."

A determined but belligerent patient, Ringo had been dealing with the withdrawal symptoms fairly well, but Corbin knew drug lust drove vampires to desperate measures. He preferred having a guard keeping an eye on Ringo. Especially since part of Corbin's own punishment was essentially doing whatever the current government wanted him to do in exchange for being allowed to continue his research. Carrick was the head of that current government and Corbin didn't want to anger him and jeopardize his work. Of course, getting his sister-in-law with child probably hadn't endeared Corbin to Ethan Carrick.

He was such an idiot. He just couldn't say it enough.

"I know you are not going anywhere. You're technically under house arrest. He is just here to see to your comfort until I return. If you like, I can ask Kelsey to come and keep you company."

Ringo made a face. "I'm really not in the mood to listen to her babbling."

"Fine. I will be back later this evening." After he'd had time to gather his thoughts and mentally slap himself around a few times. After he'd had a chat with Brittany about how they were going to proceed, and how soon they could marry. He would not heap further mistakes on top of the first by allowing her to raise an illegitimate child alone. Of that he was certain.

"Take as long as you want. I get sick of you hovering over me all the time. You make me feel like a kid with a disappointed father, you know that? It's freaking annoying."

Corbin winced as he headed out the door. A father. Good Lord, he was going to be a father. To a mutant child.

It did not bear thinking on.

Instead, he would head to his lab, and he, Corbin Jean Michel Atelier, would fix this.

Eventually. Somehow. Maybe.

Three

"Okay, what was so important?" Brittany asked. She was exhausted, her stomach still hurt, and a giant pit of worry had lodged itself in her chest like indigestion that no Mylanta could cure.

Ethan had ushered her into his apartment and now he was pacing back and forth in front of the patio door. Alexis was biting her nail from her seat in a plaid easy chair.

"I want you to know that you are not the first."

"The first what?" Woman to get knocked up from a one-night stand? Of course she wasn't. That number could probably fill the UNLV stadium.

"The first to have a three-quarter vampire child. There was one before, that I know of. It was kept quiet, but I had personal knowledge of the situation."

Uh-oh. This could get dicey. While her sister knew her husband had a past—a very long one—Brittany still didn't think it was going to thrill Alexis to hear that Ethan had had a child with a mortal woman.

"Was the baby okay?" Regardless of Alexis's feelings, she had to know.

"The baby was fine and was kept hidden from her father. I do not believe he has knowledge of her existence to this day."

"You're not the father?" Brittany asked in confusion.

Ethan looked startled. "No. Why would you think that?"

"Can we just start at the beginning, please?" Alexis asked. "Before I get pissed off that you've kept yet something else from me."

"Alexis," Ethan said with a look of forbearance. "I have nine hundred years of existence to account for. There hasn't been time to tell you everything that's happened to me, let alone to other people I've known."

Brittany felt guilty. "Don't fight, you guys, this is all my fault. I'm causing problems for everyone." She felt close to tears again.

"This isn't fighting," Alexis said. "This is our form of communication. I get ticked, Ethan gets exasperated, we gripe at each other, then have sex. It works for us."

Well, that was too much information about her sister's marriage.

"*Any*way," Brittany said. "So who was the mother and what happened?"

"The mother is my sister, Gwenna."

Brittany had met Gwenna only once, at Ethan and Alexis's

wedding, and she had popped in, vampire style, said nothing to anyone, then left again. She had looked pale and fragile, and was a full vampire, not an Impure like Brittany was.

"I don't understand. Gwenna is a vampire, right?"

"Yes. I turned her when she bled to death after giving birth to her daughter. This was the eleventh century, you know, and childbirth was a risky, nasty business."

"I don't think this is the beginning," Alexis complained. "I had no clue Gwenna was an Impure. How was that possible if you weren't an Impure?"

Ethan's face hardened. "My mother was raped when my father and I were away at war. Gwenna is seventeen years younger than me, and when I became a vampire and eventually came home, I realized that her biological father had been a vampire, because I could sense her vampire blood. Unfortunately, by that time my father was dead, as were all my other siblings. It was just Gwenna, who was seventeen, and my mother in our castle. I had some issues to the north I needed to resolve, and against my better judgment I left the two of them there, with several of my vampire friends to watch over them. At that time, these were friends I trusted, who had shown me the way of the vampire, and they were staying with me. They assured me they would oversee my mother and sister's safety. By the time I returned ten months later, they were gone, one of them having betrayed me by seducing my innocent sister, who had just given birth to his child the day before. She bled to death moments before I arrived, and I found my mother with her body. My mother, who had buried everyone she had ever loved, and who assumed I was dead up north, given certain erroneous reports my betrayer had fed to her."

Ethan had been a warrior, Brittany knew that. But the way he stood now, fists clenched, jaw tight, she realized it wouldn't take much to strip away the civilized veneer of the British politician and discover that man inside him, who had fought for the safety of his family with his bare hands. It was a little intimidating at the same time it was comforting. Even if Corbin bolted, Ethan had her back because he considered her his sister now.

"So you turned Gwenna?" she asked carefully, her heart filled with compassion for him.

"Yes. I brought her back, though she was never the same as she'd been before. She was quiet, reserved, frightened. But she loved her daughter, and it was very worth it to me. My niece was born healthy and remained so."

Brittany sensed there was more to the story, but Ethan wasn't going to divulge it. It had obviously cost him a lot to talk about his mother and sister, and Brittany felt for him, for his pain, for his very long past and all that heartache. Squeezing his hand, she said, "Thanks for telling me, Ethan. That makes me feel better. Is there anything I should know . . . was the baby normal? No fangs or anything?"

"No fangs. Completely normal, and she was very strong and athletic. Tough both in body and character. She wound up becoming a warrior." Ethan smiled and glanced over at Alexis. "A bit like your sister, in fact."

"So I should plan on being a soccer mom then." It sounded so much better when she thought in normal, everyday terms. She would have an athletic, aggressive child. She could deal with that. After all, she'd lived with Alex for twenty years. "I really appreciate you telling me this, Ethan."

"You're welcome." He kissed the top of her head in a brotherly fashion that pleased her. "Everything will be fine, Brit."

"Thanks. Alright, I'm going to head home. Corbin is coming over to discuss 'ze situation,'" she said in an attempt at his French accent.

She blew them both a kiss. "Love you. Talk to you later."

Alexis looked at Ethan with a hearty dose of suspicion after her sister had left the apartment. Swinging her legs over the arm of the chair, she narrowed her eyes. "Alright, Carrick, what did you leave out of that story?"

"Some details." Ethan had his back to her, closing the blinds to the patio door.

"What details?" Alexis didn't like the sound of that at all. "Tell me the truth or I will seriously kick your ass. Who was the father of Gwenna's baby?"

Ethan's fist tightened on the blind cord and his jaw clenched. "Donatelli."

"What? I thought they got married like three hundred years later." Alexis was surprised. The way Ethan had made it sound, Gwenna had been seduced and abandoned, not lived happily almost ever after with the guy.

"They did get married in the fifteenth century, four hundred years after their original relationship. Gwenna was reclusive and I shunned Donatelli after his betrayal. He didn't even know she had been turned, and I admit, when they crossed paths inadvertently on a trip we took to Italy, I was surprised he even remembered her. Most womanizers don't recall all their conquests, especially not after so many years. But not only did he remember, he claimed that he, too, had been betrayed, that he had been forced to leave her, and that he had returned to search for her the following year, only to hear that she had died. Thank God the villagers had been told she died of a fever, because we didn't want anyone to know about the baby, at Gwenna's request. She was ashamed of her actions. But I blamed Donatelli, not her. I still do. He should have known better. And I blame myself for leaving in the first place. But when they met again, Donatelli fed Gwenna lie after lie, and she fell for it, sneaking around with him without my knowledge, and after a few months she up and married the bastard. It took her three hundred years to gather the courage to divorce the sorry sot."

"Oh, yikes. It's bad enough we all make mistakes with our first shot at love, but three hundred years?" The very thought of being stuck to her high school boyfriend, Bart Winslow, and his fart jokes, for all eternity made Alexis shudder. "Gwenna must be terrified to date." And she felt a little guilty for not reaching out to her sister-in-law more. Stuck in that nasty old castle in England, beating herself up for picking a crappy guy—like who hasn't?—with no one to talk to . . . Gwenna needed some girlfriends to hang with. Vampire girlfriends like herself and

Kelsey. And Cara, if she ever came back from Seamus's farm in Ireland.

"Maybe you should invite Gwenna to visit us. Or maybe we could go visit her."

"That's a thoughtful idea." Ethan looked surprised.

What? She couldn't be thoughtful without shocking people? Asshole. "I'm not a total bitch. I would like to get to know your sister better."

"We can't go over there until after the election, and I doubt she would visit. Coming here for the wedding was difficult for her."

"I can't believe the election got bumped back to February just because Donatelli dropped out. I think they should just give it to you." Alexis still couldn't believe Donatelli had just agreed to resign his campaign for the presidency. Granted, Ethan and Seamus had promised to kill him if he didn't drop out, but Alexis would have thought Donatelli would weasel around them somehow. Or at least try to. So far, he'd kept his distance, though.

"In all fairness, the other party needs time to choose another candidate and then campaign."

Alexis understood. She was all about fairness, being a prosecutor. When it worked in her favor. Or her husband's. But she was tired of the endless banquets and cheesy speeches. Most nights when she wasn't doing consulting work—daysleeping had killed her prosecutor's career—Ethan expected her to paste on a smile and a dowdy suit and play Laura to his George. But the problem was, Laura Bush was a nice woman, and Alexis wasn't. It taxed her patience to be pleasant to people she didn't like.

"Well, I still think it sucks. And what's up with you having to basically be nominated again?"

"In light of recent circumstances, it seemed wise to take another primary vote and ensure I am still the candidate with the most popular party vote."

He was so good at talking political BS. "I'm sure you are. And by the way, what happened to Gwenna's daughter? I got the feeling you were keeping something from Brittany."

Ethan turned away from her—one of his lie tells—and shrugged his shoulders. "It's probably irrelevant to Brittany's situation."

"What is?"

"That my niece went insane in her twenties and killed herself."

"Do you know who Brittany's father is?" Corbin asked Carrick, having cornered him in the casino several hours later. He had made sure Brittany was home, safely tucked in her apartment, and Ethan's wife was swimming laps in the casino's indoor pool, so they would not be interrupted.

Carrick looked at him sharply, before glancing back out over the casino floor. They were seated at a table in the casino's five-star restaurant, on a balcony that jutted out slightly into the action of the floor, yet kept them above the noise. They had drinks in front of them, since a vampire could digest liquids but not solids, and a serving staff that knew to leave the owner of the establishment alone.

"Why?" Ethan asked.

"Because it would be beneficial to know if he has a particular recessive gene I have run across in both mortals and vampires."

"So what if he does?"

Corbin tried not to feel frustrated. He realized Ethan was trying to protect Brittany, but Corbin didn't think he could explain one hundred years of research in genetics to Ethan. "It's complicated, but you know that vampires carry a virus for vampirism that is transmitted through saliva and blood, yes? Well, that virus lies dormant until a person is drained of blood. The virus is activated, the person feels the urge to replenish their damaged blood cells by drinking blood, and the change is complete. The question in my research has been if I can inhibit the virus even after a body has been drained, even after years of living as a vampire, and reverse its effects. In essence, return a vampire to mortality, with a dormant vampire virus. I believe the answer is yes."

"Okay. This is shaky territory, Atelier. You know as well as I do this sort of knowledge could split the Nation into two camps. As it is, there are plenty of Impures clamoring for vampire population growth."

"I know. And what none of them understand is that they are the very key to true vampire procreation because, statistically, a large number of them have the gene from their mother. Vampires can only mate and create a child if they or the mortal woman has the recessive gene I mentioned. Vampires without it who copulate with mortal women without it will never create a child.

But what happens when a half-breed Impure, like Brittany, mates with a vampire? I have the gene, and Brittany got it from her mother. I have the active virus, Brittany has the dormant virus. If Brittany has the gene from her vampire father as well, our child gets essentially a double dose of the virus and one whole reproductive gene."

"What the hell does that mean?"

Corbin looked out at the flashing lights of the casino, thoughts troubled, self-recrimination great. He had known the facts, but he hadn't done anything about them. He had been focused on the creation of a drug to inhibit the virus, not on reproduction. "It means that our child will be born immortal, with no need to feed on blood. Essentially, a superbaby."

"You've got to be kidding me. Bloody hell."

"This cannot be found out. No one can know this, or my child will be in danger, Carrick. Those who want growth, like Donatelli, they'll want this baby. They'll want to understand how to re-create him, how to generate a superrace, if you will, and that I cannot allow." Corbin shifted, uneasy, angry. "You know how Brittany is, what a wonderful woman she is. This child has every chance, and every right, to have a normal life with her as his mother. That is what I want, that is what Brittany and our baby deserve, and I cannot let anyone hurt either of them."

"You have my complete support, Atelier. I don't want Brittany or the baby hurt, either. But I don't know who Brittany's father is. Only her mother knew that, and she's been dead for fifteen years. I'm not even sure the vampire who slept with her knew there was a child. If he did, there is no evidence of it."

"I have a DNA database of about twenty percent of known vampires. I can run Brittany through it and see if we can find a genetic match." He would have to secure a sample from her. The night he had drawn her blood, the night they had conceived their child, he had actually left without taking the vial filled with her sample off her dresser. The whole reason for entering her apartment had been to ask her for a donation, and he had just left the blood sitting there. Utterly ridiculous.

"You have a DNA database? How the hell did you do that? Do you have my DNA?" Ethan looked outraged.

"Yes." Corbin shrugged, feeling just a little sheepish. "It's not difficult to collect, you know. A stray hair here or there, a glass left sitting there with saliva, skin, blood . . ." He trailed off at Carrick's expression.

"That is just wrong, Atelier. That's stealing."

"It is not. If you leave your DNA lying about, it becomes public property." He wasn't going to apologize for it. He wasn't a criminal or an evil scientist. He was conducting his research to give vampires *choices*. "The point is, I know who has the gene and who doesn't."

Ethan shook his head, leaned forward onto the table. "But what you don't know is that nine hundred years ago my sister gave birth to a child, just like yours will be. My sister was an Impure, though I don't know who her father was. I do know, however, who the vampire father of her child was. And I do know that my niece gave every appearance of good health, and no sign of ever needing blood."

Corbin stared at Carrick, disbelieving him. "There was a child? Who was the father?" He knew Carrick's sister had been married to Donatelli, who was interested in vampire population growth, and who had been Carrick's presidential opponent until he had suddenly dropped out of the race. But their marriage had been recent, only a few hundred years ago, he thought, not nine hundred.

"It doesn't matter who he was, because he didn't know about the child, and I know he's no longer active in the Nation. I told you to reassure you about the baby, but I respect my sister's privacy."

"I understand. Thank you for sharing what you have." It did reassure him, though he'd been certain his baby wouldn't need blood once he had thought through the biological repercussions.

"What happened to your niece? Did she have a normal life span?"

Ethan shook his head. "I'm sorry to say that my niece took her own life as a young woman. She did it thoroughly, through decapitation."

Corbin immediately regretted the question. "Good God, I am sorry, Carrick."

Ethan nodded. "Yeah, me, too. So how many vampires have this gene?"

"Of the twenty percent of known vampires I have tested, only ten percent have the gene. So allowing for a margin of error, I would suggest between one hundred and fifty to two hundred and fifty vampires out of our population of ten thousand. Each of those men are capable of producing innumerable offspring with women who carry the gene. I am one of them. You are not."

Carrick sank back in his chair, exhaling quickly. "Well, that's a relief. It's good to know I didn't scatter a bunch of kids around over the centuries and not know I was the culprit."

Corbin winced. "Reassuring for you."

"Sorry." Carrick made a face.

"Zat is all right. I am certain Brittany is the first woman to carry my child." Because generally speaking, Corbin wasn't intimate with women. He approached women, he charmed and flirted, he coaxed them into pleasure glamours and took their blood for research, but he did not seduce them wholly. Until Brittany.

"So what do you need me to do? How do we protect Brittany and the baby?"

This was the hard part, the dilemma that Corbin had turned around and around in his head because he didn't like it. But it was necessary and he knew it.

"No one can know the father of Brittany's baby is a vampire. Everyone must be led to believe she is having a baby with a mortal man, who has no interest in her or the child. Then the child is just a quarter of diluted vampire genetics, and nothing special. No one will care. Then later on, when I marry Brittany, the assumption will be that I am the stepfather, that we have fallen in love the normal way despite her carrying another man's child, and that I will adopt her baby. That way I am physically present in their lives to protect them both."

The thought that no one would know that she was having his

child, his flesh and blood, really bothered him, but Corbin didn't see that he had a choice.

Carrick's eyebrow shot up. "Atelier . . . what the hell makes you think Brittany will agree to marry you just for protection?"

Well, he wasn't, but surely she would see the logic in it. "She will want what is best for the child."

"Is it really necessary? It seems a little drastic."

"Yes, it's necessary." He was certain of it. "Do you know what they will do if they get ahold of this information? There are those who would raise this baby in a lab, testing its abilities, pushing the limits to see what he or she is capable of. The logical conclusions of this scientifically are that my child can lead a skilled team of scientists to the creation of a superrace, either through forced breeding or via cloning."

Carrick's face reflected the horror Corbin felt. "Oh, my God, this makes my head spin. It's a scientific nightmare."

"Zat is the double-edged sword, Carrick. In discovering how to reverse vampirism, I have also unearthed the means to propagate it." Corbin swished the liquid in his glass. "Now after tonight, I must stay away from Brittany. No one must have reason to suspect that I am the baby's father."

"What are you going to tell her?"

"Nothing. I don't want to frighten her. You will watch over her, yes? Keep her safe while I keep my distance?"

"Of course."

Corbin trusted Carrick and his crew of vampire security guards to protect Brittany, though he would have preferred to be with her himself. But he was convinced this was the best way to keep her safe and blissfully unaware of the potentially horrific consequences if anyone knew the real situation. "Then I would prefer she not know the dangers. She'll only worry."

Carrick shook his head. "Women don't like that, Atelier . . . it will turn around and bite you in the ass later. Besides, how do you know Brittany won't run around telling everyone you're the father?"

"She won't."

Because Corbin had a plan.

Ringo had a plan and it involved Kelsey cooperating with him. He pulled her onto his lap and gave her a smile.

She tried to shift away from him. "I'll crush you! You're still not healthy yet."

He rolled his eyes. "Kels, you weigh like ten pounds. If your bony ass can crush me, I deserve to die."

It was the wrong thing to say. Her lip quivered. "I don't want you to die."

"I'm not going to die." Ever. He still had trouble adjusting to his vampire status, the knowledge that he was around for the long haul, but there was no doubt about it. It would take a lot to snuff him out.

"And is my butt really bony? Is it gross?" Perched on the couch next to him, she felt up her ass, patting and rubbing the seat of her extremely tight jeans.

Ringo felt a hard-on stir to life. "Not at all, baby. But stand up, let me check it out."

Kelsey did, sticking her very tight booty just inches from his face. She peered back over her shoulder, clearly worried, hands still gliding around down there. Damn, she was so clueless, and yet she made him so hot.

"Very nice." Ringo put his hands over hers and squeezed her firm flesh. Her eyes widened in sudden understanding.

"You did that on purpose," she said, frowning at him even as she bent her knees slightly and rocked against his grip.

"Yep." Ringo bit her ass, letting his fangs puncture the denim and nip at her skin.

"Ouch!" She swatted at him with her pale hand and tried to wiggle away. "Stop it, that hurts."

"Then take your jeans off, let me have a real taste of you." He tugged her back so she landed in his lap, right on his boner. "Can't you feel that? I want you. I'm in pain."

She sighed, one of pleasure, yet regret. "I feel it. But not in here. The guard is right outside the door."

"So?" He thrust upward, and spread her knees with his hands. It amazed even him how much he really did want her. She was annoying, unpredictable, treated him like a problem child, and really did have a bony ass. Yet she was the only person whose company he could actually stand, and when he looked at her, he felt intense, biting desire, and the urgent need to protect her. He wasn't sure what it was exactly, or what it meant, but the sexual urges he knew how to act on, if she would just let him. "Who cares if the guard is in the hallway?"

She rubbed her butt against his erection. "I would be embarrassed if he heard us."

Said the woman who had gone down on him the first night they had met. Ringo was resigned to the fact that Kelsey's logic was never going to be clear to him. He would just use her reluctance in his favor. "Then let's go away somewhere together. Like a romantic weekend. No one around but you and me."

"You're still on house arrest. You can't leave Vegas."

Ringo supposed an apology for trying to assassinate the vampire president wasn't going to impress Kelsey or the tribunal. Not that he was interested in groveling, but he did resent having his freedom clipped. That's why he had a better plan. "Oh, come on, just a little weekend away. You know me. I'm not going to do anything. I just need to get out of this casino. I don't even need to leave Vegas. I just feel like I'm suffocating here, stuck inside all the time." He kissed her shoulder, brushing her long dark hair out of the way. "Don't you want to be with me? Don't you care about my mental health? Don't you want to make love to me somewhere private?"

Her eyes lit up as she turned to look at him over her shoulder. "I know, let's get married, Ringo, and get one of those really sexy romantic honeymoon suites with a whirlpool."

Married? Jesus, how had she pulled that out of her bony ass? While he had interesting emotions regarding Kelsey, the thought of marriage made him want to hurl up his blood breakfast.

"Okay," he said. Opportunity pops up, you take it. That was his philosophy.

"Really?" She spun all the way around. "You mean it?" Her arms came around his neck and she kissed him eagerly. "That's so cool."

"Way cool," he said, kissing her back, indulging in a little tongue. He needed the contact to reassure himself he wasn't going to regret this dumb-ass move. "So pack a bag, baby, and let's figure out how you can get the key to my ankle bracelet from the guard."

Four

Corbin knocked on Brittany's apartment door an hour later, determined that he would remedy the situation. What he suspected, based on simple biology, was that their child would be born immortal, with no urge to drink blood. At first glance, that had seemed a positive outcome to the situation, at least compared to the alternative. But what had concerned him was how an immortal child would mature, both physically and emotionally. That was something he could not predict, no matter how much research on vampire genetics he had garnered, but after talking to Ethan Carrick, he felt somewhat reassured. Carrick hadn't mentioned any complications from his niece's unusual genetics.

That left only the need to secure secrecy about the baby, which despite his aplomb with Carrick, Corbin had his doubts about. Brittany was a bit unpredictable, he had determined. Or perhaps *impulsive* was a better adjective to describe her. There was no guarantee she would want to marry him, but he was going to have to convince her of the obvious merits of such an arrangement.

Brittany answered the door with a smile. "Come in."

It struck him anew how beautiful she was, how sweet and pure of heart, honest and compassionate. That was what had attracted him to her in the first place, had made him forget himself. "Good evening, Brittany."

Corbin loathed the idea of lying to her. Hated that no one would know she was carrying his child, wouldn't know that she had opened herself for him, that he had taken her, blended his body, his DNA, with hers and created a child. It brought out all manner of feral urges he hadn't even realized he had.

Not to mention embarrassment.

"I knocked on the door," he said inanely, not at all sure what to say to the woman he had made love to with an appalling lack of finesse. That alone was cause for awkwardness, but added to his own bad handling of that night was the memory of her huddled in her pillow, so embarrassed she had refused to look at him. He could honestly say that had been a sexual first for him, leaving a woman writhing in emotional discomfort. Now that same woman was having his immortal child. There was not a greeting card for this particular occasion.

She laughed a little. "Yes, you did. Thanks." She led him to her living room and she sat down on a thick floral sofa.

Brittany's apartment was very white and pink with lots of competing floral patterns, china hung to the walls, and a profusion of pillows. It had a cottage feel to it that pleased him, even if it was excessively feminine. He sat down on the sofa opposite Brittany and was immediately enveloped by lacy pillows. It didn't feel like a position of power, to say the least, so Corbin leaned forward and put his forearms on his knees. He could do this. Had to do this.

"Aside from the morning sickness, you are feeling well?"

"Yes, I'm tired, but that's normal according to the doctor."

"When is your due date?"

"May twelfth."

Now what in hell did he say? Brittany was looking at him expectantly. "I am sorry if I have caused friction between you and your brother-in-law."

She shrugged. "Ethan is worried about me, but he's totally on my side."

And against Corbin. He heard the subtle censure. "I am also sorry for my irresponsibility. I have never before . . . created a situation . . ." He couldn't think of a delicate enough phrasing for what he meant.

"I'm the first girl you knocked up?"

He winced. So much for delicate.

"That does make me feel better, Corbin. I admit it would bother me if you'd had a kid every decade for the last five hundred years or something."

The very thought offended him. "This is not a habit for me. I do not normally succumb to passion and lose sight of all common sense. This was a first, and I have already apologized. Besides, I am only two hundred and ten years old."

Brittany looked amused. "Is that all? I'm twenty-six. And in case you were wondering, this is the first time I've ever gotten knocked up. So we'll just have to bumble through this first time for both of us together." Then her smile disappeared. "Unless you don't want to be involved. If you don't, I understand. I'm not expecting anything. I just need you to be honest up front and tell me so that I know what I'm dealing with. And it won't be fair to our child for you to pop in and out of her life whenever you feel like it, so I'm just going to be clear right here and now that I won't tolerate that 'I'll be a father whenever I feel like it' kind of mentality."

Surely her opinion of him was quite low if she thought him capable of such irresponsible selfish behavior. It occurred to him that they had certainly done this backward. They knew nothing of each other and yet they were having a child. He no longer got headaches, but he could swear he felt one now, throbbing at his temples.

Yet this would work out. He was determined.

"I have no intention of popping in and out, as you say. My intention is to marry you as soon as possible." After they were certain no one would suspect the truth. "We can live here if it pleases you, or we can live apart if you prefer. I will pay for the education and upbringing of the child. He can attend the same boarding school I did in France."

Brittany was sure he had no idea how absurd he sounded. "You want to get married but live apart?" What the hell was the point in that? All that would do was screw up her taxes and prevent her from ever dating in the future.

"If that is your preference."

Corbin was not making this easy. Brittany still had no real sense of how he felt about the situation. "What is *your* preference?"

"My preference is to ensure your happiness."

That was an artful dodge of the question. "Have you ever been married before?"

"No."

"And you're not going to be now. I'm not marrying you, Corbin. Just forget it. I am perfectly willing to give you visitation with the baby, though that could be dicey with the whole sleeping during the day thing, but we can work it out so you have plenty of time with the baby. I would like child support and a dialogue with you regarding major decisions. But I am not marrying you."

"You're being unreasonable."

And he was being ridiculous. "I am not being unreasonable. I just offered you shared custody. And sweetie, just to remind you, you are a vampire. How many women would be willing to leave their infant in the care of a bloodsucker? I think I'm being very reasonable under the circumstances."

"That is insulting. And if you were being reasonable, you would agree to marriage and we would not need to have this argument."

Brittany was trying really hard not to lose her patience. Normally, she almost never flew off the handle, and she was a real happy-go-lucky kind of woman. But she was tired, hungry, and nauseous, and he was pushing a bit hard against her patience. "So we should get married, live apart, each take recreational lovers whenever the mood strikes us, and send our child thousands of miles away to go to school. Why don't we just hire a wet nurse while we're at it." And move into a nineteenth-century gothic novel.

Corbin tilted his head. "Can you still find such a service? We should consider that."

The sad thing was, he was actually serious. "Sure, if we want our kid to be warped. You have no idea how children are raised in the twenty-first century, do you?"

He looked affronted. Corbin opened his mouth, snapped it shut, fell back into her couch cushions. "Perhaps not," he conceded.

The misery and horror on his face made her feel bad. It wasn't like she was an expert, either. "That's okay. I mean, you probably haven't been around kids much in the last two hundred years, have you? We just need to talk these things through, like we are now. See, we're doing so good at this already. We're communicating and working things out, which is so important when you're raising a child together."

"You do not know what in hell you're doing either, do you?" he asked.

No, but she was optimistic she could learn. "Not really. My experience with kids is kind of limited to *Nanny 911* episodes and the kids I see as patients in my dental practice."

But she knew a boarding school in France wasn't going to fly. And don't even get her started on the whole marriage-of-convenience thing.

"Brittany, tell me about your childhood."

"Oh, uh." Maybe they shouldn't go there. Brittany crossed her legs and cleared her throat. "Well, you know, I grew up here in Vegas."

"And your mother was a stripper?"

"Yes." She wasn't ashamed of that, not in the least, but it probably didn't mesh with Corbin's image of Mother Material. "My mom died when I was thirteen."

"I am sorry. How did she die?"

"She overdosed on painkillers."

"You were very young to be without a mother."

"I had Alex. She was eighteen and she took care of me, kept me on the straight and narrow, and put me through school. I'm normal and well adjusted, Corbin, I swear. My childhood wasn't a walk in the park, but it wasn't hell either. We had food and a roof over our heads, and our mom loved us in her way. We even had a stepfather for a few years who was fantastic and provided a positive male role model in our lives. I can be a soccer mom, I want to be a soccer mom, even if that's not the way I was raised."

"Soccer mom?" Corbin looked puzzled.

He really was out of the domestic loop. Too much night dwelling. "A suburban mother who drives a minivan full of her kids and their friends back and forth to soccer practice. It's sort of a general term for a suburban mom who spends a lot of time ferrying kids around."

"Ah," he said, but it didn't look like he was getting it.

"How were you raised?"

"My parents were very wealthy French landowners who es- caped to England during the Terror. I was born in London, but was sent to boarding school in France when we returned to the Continent after the defeat of Napoleon. My early years were spent learning to fence, learning to ride, and tending to my education. I did not spend much time with my parents, as it would have been unseemly for them to attend to my daily care."

Wonderful. They could just scratch using their own experiences off their parenting skills checklist. If they did that, Brittany would be popping Vicodin and Corbin would be too busy with his opera house mistress to ever see them. They were going to have to use common sense and do this their own way.

"Okay, if we're putting this in a nineteenth-century context, think of me as coming from a middle-class merchant family. How would a tradesman have raised his child?"

It was meant to get him to look at child-rearing in a more hands-on way, but Corbin merely stared blankly at her.

"How should I know?" he asked. "I was not a tradesman."

Brittany felt the urge to smile, but squeezed her lips together tightly. "Maybe we should hit the bookstore and get some parenting books."

That seemed to offend him. "I do not need to read a book to learn how to raise a child. Zat is absurd."

"I mean it as an information-gathering expedition. We should know our facts, see where we stand on the issues."

"I know the facts. You are expecting my child. That is the only fact that is relevant."

Yeesh, he was damn cute when he was being so French.

"Thank you," he said. "Though I am not fond of the descriptive *cute*."

"What . . ." Brittany felt her cheeks heat up. "Get out of my head, Corbin! Stop listening to my thoughts."

"They were wide open to me," he said with a twirl of his hand. "I was not fishing. They floated over to me."

That was so annoying. Brittany attempted to do a mental door slam on her thoughts. "*Anyway*. How do you feel about an epidural versus a natural childbirth?"

"I think that is entirely your decision since you are the parent giving birth. I would not presume to tell you what to do."

Score one point for Corbin. Brittany smiled at him. "Inducing labor? Cesarean sections?"

"I am not an obstetrician. We will discuss those issues with your doctor should they arise."

Geez, he was unshakable, with an answer for everything. He was looking stiff and determined, resigned to do his duty, and didn't look like he'd be curling up with a baby-naming book anytime soon. While she was grateful he wanted to do the responsible thing, she didn't want her child to have a father who resented his role.

"Do you think a baby can ever get too much love?" She wouldn't be able to stand it if Corbin was going to ride her for spoiling their child with attention. She was a cuddler, and she was going to cuddle the heck out of their baby while she had the chance.

His eyes narrowed. "Am I being interviewed for the role of father?"

"No!" Not really. "Of course not. I just think it's important we get to know each other's parenting style. See where the other one is coming from, so we can iron out any differences ahead of time before we're up to our ankles in diapers and bottles."

He continued like she hadn't spoken. "Because I am the father and zat is indelible. Unchangeable."

Next he'd be slapping her face with a glove and challenging her to a duel. He was so outraged in an old-fashioned way and she thought he was adorable. "I know. Chill out."

"I will not chill, as you say. I will answer all your questions, but then I demand the right to ask some of my own."

"Fine. Absolutely. So what do you think about the whole letting a baby cry thing?" Brittany wasn't sure about it herself. She saw both sides of the issue and figured it fell into the category of feeling her way through it.

Corbin frowned. "Babies cry. I don't understand how that is a question."

"Some people think you should pick them up right away, other people think you should wait five minutes and let them cry it out."

"I have no opinion at this time," Corbin said stiffly. "Though I would question what is the difference? If you can, you pick the babe up. If you cannot, you don't. What is the grand debate?"

Well, that certainly put things in perspective. "What about the family bed?"

"The what?" Corbin tilted his head. "I think perhaps my modern English is not very good, as I have never heard those two words put together."

"It's where the parents and the child sleep in the same bed every night." Brittany wasn't sure how she felt about it, having known friends who were happy on both ends of the spectrum. She was open-minded and willing to try whatever was going to work for her and her child.

But the look of horror on his face gave her his stance on that particular issue. *"Why?"*

"Um . . . for comfort and a sense of family, I guess. So a child doesn't feel abandoned." He didn't want their baby to feel abandoned, did he?

Corbin made a snorting sound. "I can tell you right now that if you and I are sharing a bed, there will *not* be a child in it with us. Ever. For any reason. If you and I are not living together, and you choose to have our child in the bed with you, I will not interfere, but never could I be convinced that such a thing is either necessary or appropriate. That is my final word on that topic."

Okay then. French vampire had spoken. Feelings of abandonment were not his concern. Duly noted.

"You are putting words in my mouth," he accused. "I would never, ever want our child to feel abandoned. As long as he is living, I will do my best to love and protect him."

His last words made her forget how annoying it was that he seemed to have no problem reading her mind. "Corbin . . . I just realized that you won't die. This baby and I, we'll get old, we'll die, and you and my sister and Ethan and Seamus and Cara, you'll all just go on and on and on." The thought made her unaccountably sad. They would all know entire centuries of living without her. "You'll be like that old lady from *Titanic* and I'll be Jack, a faded distant memory. You'll be young and sexy and dating some exotic South American woman or something and I'll be fertilizer."

Brittany started to sniffle. Damn, the business about hormones really was true. She couldn't stop tears from pooling up in her eyes.

Corbin swore, feeling guilty as hell. For getting Brittany pregnant, for making her cry, for war and poverty, for all human suffering, you name it, he felt guilty for it. A woman's tears did horrible, cruel, vicious things to his insides, and even more so with Brittany because she was normally so cheerful, so sweet. He had reduced her to this, he had made it obvious to her that her sister would live long after she was dead and gone.

He wasn't sure if now was the best time to tell her that the baby wouldn't die either, that Corbin strongly suspected this child would be born immortal—not vampire, since he wouldn't need blood, but not mortal either. Corbin expected the only one who would die in the equation would be Brittany herself and that thought was disquieting in the extreme. He had lost many people he had cared for in his early years as a vampire until he had isolated himself, focusing on his research, avoiding relationships.

Now he was in one up to his eyeballs.

"Brittany, hush, it is not so bad as all that." What the hell was he saying? It was a goddamn mess. And she was out and out sobbing now.

Corbin stood up, unable to sit still. "We will take things one day at a time, yes? Let's enjoy this blessing we have been given, and live in the now." Vampires were good at that. You had to be, or you'd go mad. Though he was lousier at it than most, and prone to melancholy. Perhaps he should keep that flaw to himself, though.

Conviction swept over him. He pulled her to her feet and wiped her tears. "And I will not be dating a South American woman because I will be married to you." That was the right thing to do. He knew it both intellectually and emotionally. It was the responsible, moral, and safe thing to do to ensure Brittany and the child's protection. He knew all that, had determined it was the proper course of action.

Plus he found the idea of being married to Brittany Baldizzi appealing in the extreme. He wanted the right to make love to her whenever the urge struck him, and he wanted to be there with her and his child through all the trials and triumphs. He had been given a gift. For a brief period in his long, long vampire life, he could live as a mortal man did, with a beautiful wife and a child. He wanted that with a fierceness that surprised him.

Her shoulders slumped and she looked nervous. "Corbin . . ."

"Do not protest. Let me show you how it can be between us." Corbin brushed back her hair, certain he had found the answer, the solution to all the confusion and guilt he'd been feeling. Yes, a marriage of convenience, but one that was passionate and comfortable. "Let me court you, Brittany, and show you that together we can raise our child, enjoy each other's company."

"Court me?"

Brittany was easy to read. Her face hid nothing, and she always spoke the truth. At the moment, she looked intrigued and pleased by his proposal. Her cheeks were pink, and she was a bit glassy-eyed.

It seemed a very natural thing to kiss her. To just close the space between them. "Yes, court you."

"I guess that would be okay," she said in a whisper, his mouth cutting off any further words.

Her lips were warm, plump, open for him, and Corbin savored the taste of her. He put his arms around her, drew her tight in to him, and took the kiss deeper. Brittany was delicious, felt so good against him, and that was why he had lost control the first time he had kissed her, and turned a simple touching of the lips into impending fatherhood. He wouldn't do that again—lose control, that is. But on the other hand, he could not get her pregnant a second time, and she felt so right, her soft sighs, her body flush against his spiking hot, eager desire. Surely he could indulge in a small taste of her charms.

She pulled her mouth back enough to murmur, "Corbin."

"Yes, *ma chérie*?" He buried his hand in that thick dark hair that flowed down her shoulders and back. That sigh she gave was very pleasing and he wanted to taste more of her, deeper. He kissed her again, sliding his tongue inside to mate with hers.

She groaned, echoing his own.

"Corbin, I . . ."

"Shh, I know."

"You're making me dizzy, it's too much," she said, her voice breathless.

"That is good." Corbin was wondering if it was much too

soon to make love to her fully. Surely not. After all, she was carrying his child, would soon be his wife. It was logical that they would be intimate again. Though he imagined logic was not what was driving him.

"We shouldn't . . ." she murmured, but there was a clear lack of conviction in her voice.

Corbin moved his lips over her long, pale neck, loving the scent of her dewy flesh, the hint of rich, strong blood pumping through her juicy veins. "We shouldn't have the first time, but we did and I do not regret it. This time there is nothing to stop us."

"I'm not normally easy."

"Of course not," he reassured her, hearing the doubt in her jumbled thoughts, but feeling the compliance in her body. He brushed his hand over her breast and reveled in the shiver she gave. "It is just you and I have something different, yes? We desire each other very much, have from the first day we met."

"That's true . . . you looked so sexy in your suit. But it was terrible of you to leave me on the roof like that."

He had left her on the roof because her cheerful acceptance of his vampirism had appalled him, but it *had* been uncalled-for behavior. Corbin kissed the corners of her mouth, slid his tongue along her bottom lip. "That was the second time we met, not the first. But it was bad of me, and I most humbly apologize. Perhaps you'll allow me to make restitution for my earlier rudeness, as well as for my rushed lovemaking."

Brittany gave a hearty sigh that veered into a moan when he rubbed his thumb across her nipple. "I'm definitely feeling like I could use a little restitution."

Corbin loved the way she reacted to him, the way her body leaned toward his, the way her fingers gripped the sleeves of his shirt. And he was well aware this might be his only opportunity for intimacy with her in several months. It suddenly felt akin to taking a last swallow before a long drought. "Then this is good timing, Brittany."

Eyes half-closed, she murmured, "I'm really, really tired lately. You know, since you got me pregnant. So I'm just warning you, you're going to have to do all the work."

Corbin felt his body—actually, a very specific body part—greet that information enthusiastically. "Of course. I am making this up to you, remember? All you need do is tell me what you like and what you don't like and leave the rest to me."

"Okay, then." She pushed his hand harder against her breast. "I like this."

Corbin never had to doubt Brittany's feelings. She never hesitated to share them, and he liked that. No guesswork.

The shirt she was wearing, a tight pink T-shirt, needed to disappear. Corbin lifted the bottom of it and dragged it off over her head. Brittany's bra matched her T-shirt, a vibrant, energetic pink satin. Her breasts were pale luscious mounds, pushed up and together by the magic of the modern bra. It almost matched the beauty of what a good corset could do, and had the added benefit of allowing her total movement, and him free access to her waist and navel.

Brushing his lips over her warm flesh, Corbin breathed deeply, enjoying the warmth of her dewy skin, the rush of her heated blood. She felt different to him, her waist tapered, ribs more prominent, skin pale, and it was clear she'd lost a few pounds. But in contrast, her breasts had swelled, were rounder and more robust than they had been before, and her scent was different.

The bra was cutting into her flesh, and Corbin traced his tongue between the fabric and her skin, feeling the groove it had left behind. "This has gotten too small, yes?"

"I know, but I've been too tired to go shopping." Brittany's hands rested on his shoulders.

Corbin raised his head and kissed her, strange feelings of compassion, guilt, desire rushing through him, running alongside something confusing and deep and strange. "Poor Brittany. This is all my fault. You should yell at me. Punish me for taking advantage of you."

She let him nuzzle her neck, her fingers digging into his flesh in a way that enflamed his desire. A slight smile crossed her face. "No one takes advantage of me. I wanted what you gave me, Corbin. And I want it again."

No, Brittany wasn't shy about revealing her feelings. Corbin swallowed, his mouth dry, his body taut with anticipation. "I am delighted to give it to you."

With that, he bent over, scooped her up into his arms, and started down the hall toward her bedroom.

She kissed him on the neck, the chin, the mouth while he strode faster and faster, not really seeing where he was going. At one point, he bumped against the wall, misjudging the door-frame. Instead of apologizing, he simply used it as a prop, a way to hold some of Brittany's weight, so he could kiss her back, fierce, hard, his fangs dropping down in his pleasure.

The swell of her breast was too close to ignore and Corbin licked her skin, suckled and kissed, before allowing his teeth to sink into her and then quickly withdraw. Just a little taste of her blood, just a tease for both of them.

Brittany groaned. "Why does that feel so good?" She swallowed hard, pushing his head back toward her breasts. "It's like . . . like almost as good as when your . . . goes into me. It's that same sort of . . . I don't know."

Corbin held her tighter, his erection throbbing, his control slipping, his mind going blank with desire. "It feels good because it is a joining, just the way it is when I thrust my manhood into you and you accept it with your body . . . this is the same."

"Manhood?" Brittany whispered. "Can you thrust something less icky-sounding into me?"

Corbin was tempted to laugh, but he didn't. He wanted Brittany to understand, to acknowledge and enjoy what was between them. "When I slide my teeth into you, we're feeling each other's pleasure, feeling the connection between us."

Moving his lips over her nipple, which had popped up out of her bra, he said, "You feel it, too, don't you? This bond between us."

"Yes. I definitely feel it." She stilled his movements, his casual brushing, by gripping his head. "Suck it, Corbin, please, you're torturing me."

This was why he could not resist her. There was no man with an ounce of testosterone who would refuse such a delicious and demanding invitation from a woman he desired. And he obviously had a reasonable amount of testosterone since he had in fact gotten her with child, which made him feel no small amount of pride and possessiveness.

So he tore off her bra with vampire speed, and covered her nipple with his mouth, drawing the taut bud fully into him and sucking hard.

She made a sound, sort of a growl low in her throat, that compelled him to set her down in the hallway so he could push his erection against her jeans as he moved from one breast to the other. The change in her body was even more apparent without the bra restraining her. Her chest was full and lush already, and clearly sensitive. Every move he made, every touch, every lick and suckle, had Brittany squirming, panting, gasping, and protesting when he so much as paused for a second.

Corbin undid the button on her jeans, slid his hand inside, and cupped her mound with his hand. She was very warm, and thrust forward to meet his touch. He pulled back, wanting all that denim gone, yet wanting to step back and slow down, so he could savor the experience, the taste of her.

"No," she murmured. "Don't stop."

"I am taking you to the bed," he murmured in her ear, nipping at the lobe.

"Oh, okay, then. Good plan."

Just to impress her, Corbin picked her up and moved to the bed with his undead speed, laying her down and discarding her jeans before she could so much as blink.

She licked her lips. "Cutting to the chase?"

"Yes." Corbin stood at the bottom of the bed and drank in the sight of her. She was amazing, delightful. Her full pouty lips were swollen from his kisses and her cheeks were flushed with color, two bright pink spots on either side. Her hair was spread out around her thick and lustrous, dark and exotic. Her legs were long and slim, going on and on, and he reached out and peeled her pink panties down a mere inch.

"Just don't cut too much to the chase, or I might miss all the action. I'm still mortal, remember? I don't want to blink and have the good stuff over with."

"That is not something you need to worry about. I plan to make love to you all night."

"Score."

Corbin paused, lips hovering right over her panties, unsure of her English. "What do you mean?"

"Nothing, it means that's a good thing that you're going to make love to me all night."

"It does?" He pondered that. He supposed it was a reference to sports and the winning of a point. "I am not well versed in modern slang."

"Okay, fine, I'll stop using it." She moved her legs restlessly. "Just stop talking and cut to the chase."

Corbin grinned, rubbing his lips over her panties, knowing it would torture her. "I thought you didn't want me to cut to the chase. And that is slang as well."

The groan of frustration she gave pleased him. "Corbin . . ."

"Yes?" He peeled pink satin down in front, holding it with his thumbs, and took his time studying her sex, taking in the scent of her desire, rubbing his mouth over her softness. "What is it, my dear?"

"Nothing." Her voice was breathy, her hips thrusting up toward him.

He pulled back. "Are you certain? I can stop if there is something you are uncomfortable with."

Eyes closed, her head went rapidly back and forth. "Don't stop."

"No?" Corbin moved his tongue over her sensitive flesh, closing his eyes to savor the taste of her, the triumph of her shudder, the pleasure of feeling her thighs relax, settle open farther for him.

"No," she whispered. "Don't stop."

Disposing of her panties, he traced her thigh, first one, then the other, with his tongue, enjoying the way she spread her legs, the way she arched to him, the way her fingers moved into his hair and gripped hard. When she was shifting back and forth, making little sounds of impatient distress, Corbin finally brought his mouth back to her, stroking his tongue over her clitoris.

Brittany groaned, her voice rising as he moved over her, tasting her thoroughly, stroking up and down with long leisurely licks, then pulling back to tease her. When she yanked at his hair, trying to drag him back, he gave her what she wanted, moving in with increased speed and intensity, nipping and sucking at her, plunging his tongue inside her warmth, pulling it back out. He knew she was going to orgasm, felt the tightening of her legs, her inner muscles, and he maintained his rhythm, his own desire hot and thick and hard as she exploded under him. Her cries were loud and unrestrained, her fingers fisting her bedsheet, hair spread out in all directions and tumbling over her cheeks and lips.

Her passion was beautiful. He loved that she wasn't insecure or shy about her body, about her desires.

"Oh," she said, eyes popping open, thighs settling back onto the bed. "That was hot. Take your pants off and give me another one."

No, Brittany wasn't shy. Corbin went up on his knees and unbuttoned his shirt and tossed it toward a wicker chair resting in the corner of her bedroom. "It would be my pleasure."

She pried at his belt buckle, obviously intending to speed up the process. "Take off your watch. It scrapes my skin," she said as she undid the belt.

Corbin paused, knowing he needed to tell the truth, but feeling a sense of shame. "It cannot come off," he told her bluntly, turning his wrist a little to show her the titanium-faced wristwatch. Most of the time he was not aware of it, but suddenly he felt its weight most acutely. "It is the way the Nation keeps track of my whereabouts while I am still under the terms of my punishment. To take it off would be essentially a parole violation."

Brittany frowned and lifted her hair up over her head, revealing cheeks and a chest still flushed pink from her orgasm. "You have an actual sentence?"

"Yes. Forty-five years I must remain in Las Vegas, visible to the government. I have served forty, with five remaining."

Her fingers still rested on his belt and he felt the sudden urge to shove them away. It was a mirage, his relationship with her. He was not entitled to happiness, as his wristwatch reminded him. Living as a normal mortal man was not his destiny, and he knew better than to think it ever could be.

"Because you killed a woman?"

Corbin flinched. "Yes. I did not realize she was emotionally unstable when I selected her to draw a blood sample from, and to bite to infect with the virus. In those days I was focusing on how the virus was transmitted. But she was unaffected by my glamour, and remembered what I had done. She followed me, offered herself up to me, and when I refused, I thought it was the end of it." Now was not the time to discuss this, but he knew, could read on her face, that Brittany was not going to let it rest. She was carrying his child, intending to be intimate with him yet again, and he knew she was entitled to the whole truth. "I did not realize she would cut herself open to entice me to feed, did not realize she would beg for the gift of eternity. I did not give it to her. Could not give it to her. So she died."

He swallowed thickly and looked over at Brittany's dresser, where she had framed pictures of her and her sister, Alexis. It was foolish to think he belonged here, that he could live a normal life. Not when he could still see that young woman's face, the desperation in her eyes as she begged him to make her whole, to make her a vampire, to drink her blood, all of it, even as he smelled and sensed she was pumped full of illegal drugs and antidepressants. He had been unable to turn her, had recoiled at the very thought, but she had gone wild, stabbing and slicing herself, her lifeblood bleeding out.

"I let her bleed to death, then I collected blood samples. It was a heartless, cruel thing to do." At the time, he had been so shocked by her behavior, that he had taken the blood almost automatically, as he had trained himself to do. But afterward, when he was in his apartment, her dead body left in the street, and he had called an ambulance anonymously, he had been appalled at how he had handled the situation.

Corbin had turned himself in to the Nation, disgusted with his useless, aimless life, knowing without a purpose he would go mad, slowly and certainly. Knowing that being vampire and watching so many mortal deaths had changed him, made him immune to the horror of suffering, the tragedy of death. He had even suspected he had grown cold to death because he himself yearned for it, had grown to despise his lonely and futile life. So he had committed himself to going beyond vampire viral transmission to actually finding a cure. The quest for mortality for the dozens of vampires tired of endless life.

And in his new purpose he had come to a new place of peace with himself, a tacit truce with his own eternity.

"I had removed myself so entirely from society that I forgot my humanity." The irony of his agreement with the tribunal was that he was allowed to continue his research, but he was not entitled to participate in vampire society. So he spent all his time moving among mortals, using charm and persuasion to collect blood samples from women when it was occasionally needed, never allowing himself to get emotionally involved. Until Brittany.

She wasn't looking at him with disgust, but understanding. "So you decided to pursue the cure to vampirism, didn't you?"

He nodded, surprised she had reached that conclusion.

Shifting her grip from his waist to his own hand, she squeezed. "I'm sorry. I can't imagine having to make that kind of decision, that choice, with no time to weigh the consequences. I think it was wrong of them to punish you. From a legal standpoint, you didn't do anything wrong, in my opinion. But I can see how it must have devastated you . . . I would have felt the same way. Someone can't possibly understand what they're asking for when they request eternity. It's not a decision you make lightly."

That was not the reaction he had expected. He'd thought Brittany would have argued that he wasn't responsible, that he was brooding for nothing. He had certainly heard that from fellow vampires. Then there were those, like the Committee for Fair Feeding Practices, who had condemned him for choosing his victim poorly, for his lack of a controlling glamour, and his poor handling of the situation. They had maintained that he should have wiped her mind completely clean so as not to jeopardize vampire security. Or if that was unsuccessful, turning her to vampire. Letting mortals die hysterical deaths was not something they could advocate without looking draconian.

He hadn't advocated it either. But Brittany was the first to understand why he hadn't been able to turn someone so obviously unstable to a vampire. He had felt a horror at the very thought, like the woman had no idea what it meant to walk the earth undead forever, nor had he thought she would be capable of following the rules of the Nation, given her behavior.

"It was not an easy decision, and it all happened so quickly. I just reacted. But that doesn't mean I'm not responsible for my own actions. I am. I initiated contact with her, and I did in fact infect her with the virus, and take her blood. That was not ethical."

"Yes, but if you had to live through the situation again, same circumstances, with forty years to reflect, what would you do?"

Corbin didn't really need to consider. He hadn't had a choice. The other options had been more abominable than the decision to refuse her his lifeblood. "I would do the same thing, though I would disarm her of the knife more quickly and call for medical help sooner. But even more to the point, I wouldn't have approached her in the first place." But that wasn't entirely the truth and he knew it. He still sought out unwilling donors to provide him with genetic material for his research, and he used both glamours and charm to achieve that. That was in fact precisely why he had originally approached Brittany—for her blood. The work was more important than worrying about taking one little vial of blood from someone, and he had to remember that, had to focus on the big picture. But the guilt ate at him.

He also knew that the real reason he wore the wristwatch and was banished from polite vampire society was because his research scared the powers that be. They had used the woman's death, and his clear remorse, as a convenient excuse to keep him in Las Vegas, to have him visible at all times. They didn't want him finding his cure or making any other genetic discovery, then taking it to the wrong vampire.

"You know what you believe is right, Corbin, and don't let them tell you otherwise. *I* think you did the right thing."

Looking down at her, seeing the conviction in her eyes, he believed her. Brittany and he had a lot in common, given that she was misunderstood the same way he was. Hadn't he heard her sister telling Brittany she was too trusting, too naïve? That wasn't the way Corbin saw it at all. What he saw was an intelligent, compassionate woman who stood behind her convictions. Convictions that were remarkably similar to his own.

He bent over, kissed her forehead. "Thank you. You are an amazing woman." Stroking her hair, he added, "Perhaps I should leave you, let you sleep." This may be his last chance to be inside Brittany for months, but he had ruined the moment with his confession, and she was fatigued anyway from the pregnancy.

Her eyebrow shot up. "Are you stupid? I don't think so! Take your pants off and let's do this thing."

"Do this thing?" He almost laughed.

"Yes. Do *me*."

Corbin felt his ardor immediately rise. He appreciated that she knew what she wanted, and just dove into it with her eyes open and heart on her sleeve. "Excellent suggestion. I will do this thing to you again and again until you are begging me to never stop."

Her eyes darkened. "Don't stop," she said, raising her hips, a smile playing on her lips.

Corbin scoffed. "That's not begging." He disposed of his pants and pushed himself inside her without warning, sinking his teeth into her shoulders.

She enclosed him, sending ecstasy sliding through his body, while simultaneously her blood sluiced over his fangs and rolled back into his throat. It felt amazing, delicious, but he forced himself to let go, to pull back out of her entirely, on both counts.

Brittany groaned. "Don't stop!"

"Closer," Corbin said, his own voice sounding tight, a sweat breaking out between his shoulder blades. "But not quite begging."

See, this was why Brittany had slept with Corbin the first time. He was a very polite, though brooding, vampire with mysterious green eyes. And when he touched her, he managed to obliterate any signs of rational behavior whatsoever. He was dominating and skilled, and both times within five minutes he'd had her at that point of no return, where she would willingly go just about anywhere sexually with him. Inhibitions? She had nada with Corbin.

"Please, put it back," she said, reaching down and grabbing hold of him, stroking his hard, slick flesh.

"That's not begging either. That's wheedling. That's flirting. That's you trying to get your way with your big beautiful brown eyes and your plump pouty lips." He bit the bottom lip she had admittedly shoved out.

Brittany closed her eyes, enjoyed that tingling, that tugging sensation of him pulling on her blood, drawing it into his mouth. It didn't hurt. It felt sexual, like having her finger sucked during passionate foreplay. She stroked him faster, trying to maneuver him between her legs.

"I don't know what you're talking about," she said, even though she did. She was used to pouting with her sister to get her way, even though she was a grown woman. It usually worked, so she kept doing it. But Corbin wasn't going for it, damn him.

Without warning he rammed his cock into her again, knocking her hand away. She barely had time to gasp at the full sensation, barely had time to enjoy the eye-rolling stretching of her inner muscles, when he left again, making her groan in frustration. "Stop doing that."

"Stop altogether?" he asked playfully, not seeming to be at the same point of desperation she was.

He was just suckling her nipple calmly, with no apparent hurry, while she was squirming and dying and tense. And she'd already come once. His control was to be admired.

Later.

Right now she wanted him to knock it off.

Locking her legs around his thighs, she tried to flip him on his back. He didn't even budge a millimeter. Damn undead strength.

Lifting his head, he gave her a very naughty smile. "Did you need something, my dear?" he said, sliding into her once more.

Trying to hold him inside her was futile. He was gone before she could dig her nails into his back. "Stop it."

"I believe the phrase is *don't stop*." He kissed her neck, her shoulder, her breasts, his fingers playing between her thighs, slipping and sliding, but missing the point for the most part.

Brittany gave up to the agony, every inch of her body screaming for satisfaction. "Don't stop, Corbin, please." She wiggled, trying to force his fingers inside her, but he eluded her again.

"Not quite right yet, but I'm feeling generous." He thrust deep inside her and rested there for a minute.

"Yes . . ." Gripping his biceps, she moved her hips, pleasure coursing through her.

He moved fast, hard, and pushed up into her over and over while Brittany panted and tried to keep up, ultimately giving up, collapsing back and letting him pound into her with delicious ferocity.

"Don't stop," she said, her voice warbling. "Don't stop."

And when she was going to come, when everything in her stilled and ripped up, when her mind was empty and pleasure painful, when she felt a breathtaking pause right before she burst over him, she said with everything inside her, "Do. Not. Stop."

Corbin locked eyes with her, and she watched his change to a deep forest green. "Never," he said.

She let go, and clung to him as they exploded together.

Five

"You care about your brother-in-law, yes?"

"Ethan? Of course. Alexis loves him and he's a good guy." Brittany snuggled up against Corbin, not really sure what place her brother-in-law had in the room when she was naked and postorgasmic. "Why?"

"I was just thinking that your pregnancy could have very negative repercussions on Carrick's reelection."

Brittany stopped playing with Corbin's chest hairs and looked up at him. What a mood kill. "What do you mean?"

"I mean that Carrick has campaigned on the side of population control. I am conducting very controversial research, not to mention that I have not completely served out my sentence. For you to be having my child, again a breach in vampire rules, will reflect very badly on Carrick. After the incident with Seamus

Fox turning Cara, it could well prevent him from being reelected president."

"I thought his opponent stepped down. And I don't understand why the election was pushed back. It seems like he should have just won automatically."

"It is meant to give the others time to replace Donatelli as an opposing candidate. And Carrick must still receive at least fifty percent of the popular vote within his own party to even remain on the ballot. It's democracy, doing its job."

Brittany was trying to get a grasp on vampire politics, but she had to admit she hadn't made a study out of it. She wasn't the vampire here. She was just a dentist, a normal day dweller. Until she had gotten knocked up by Corbin. Now she wasn't sure what she was, but it had honestly never occurred to her that her pregnancy could affect Ethan's career. "I don't want to mess things up for Ethan. But we can't change the facts. I am pregnant."

Corbin smiled at her, his hair still rumpled. "And delightfully so." He ran his fingertips over her arm, kissed her forehead. "But no one knows that I am the father of your child. No one even knows we are acquainted. Perhaps it would be best to keep our relationship a secret for a few weeks until the primary election is over. If any vampire discovered you were pregnant, they would assume the father to be a mortal. That would not be any cause for alarm."

"But this . . ." Brittany stroked Corbin's penis, loving the way his body immediately hardened at her touch. "Is cause for alarm? We're not supposed to be together? Does anyone really give a shit, Corbin? I think maybe you're overreacting."

He closed his eyes, his breathing heavier as she stroked him. Then to her disappointment, he reached down and held her hand still. "Zis es the reality, Brittany. I am a criminal. I am responsible for the death of a woman, however unintentional. I am on the verge of being able to offer a combination of medications, a vaccine essentially, that will inhibit the vampire virus, causing vampires to revert to a mortal physiology. There are vampires who hate me, who would like to see me dead. There are those who would like to steal my research, either to destroy it or to mutate it to their own purposes. Your brother-in-law is fighting with everything in his political power to ensure radical vampire politics don't overthrow the current government. Our one moment of weakness should not jeopardize the entire future of my race."

Well, he certainly had a way of sucking the romance out of the moment.

"Okay, God, when you put it that way. I can keep my mouth shut for a few weeks. But honestly, I had no idea things were as dire as you make them sound." Brittany felt a small bit freaked out. "We're having a baby, Corbin. Are you telling me rogue vampires are going to be after you all the time? I don't think bloodsuckers randomly dropping over to kill you is the best environment to be raising a child in." She was thinking bonnets and bottles, not draining blood and decapitation.

"Of course not. Once the election is over, and I present my findings to the UMA, then I intend to retire. We'll get married, move to a house, and we will be soccer mom and dad, yes?"

With his hand on her butt, and her breasts pressed against his chest, she could almost believe him that it would all work out, even if she had a hell of a time picturing Corbin sitting on the sidelines cheering from the bleachers. At night games. "So you're still going to court me? Try to convince me I should marry you?" she asked flirtatiously. She couldn't wait to see what his wooing entailed. It sounded fun and full of gifts. With any luck, it would also involve lots of sex and nights out on the town.

"Absolutely. But we will be discreet until the election is over."

"A secret courtship? Wow, we'll be like Romeo and Juliet. How sexy is that?" Brittany closed her eyes and yawned into his chest. A sharp stinging from the top of her head made her jerk back. "Ouch! Did you just pull one of my hairs out?"

"Sorry, it got caught on my watch." Corbin massaged her scalp and encouraged her to lie back down.

Not wanting to remind him of what his watch represented— his punishment—Brittany kissed his chest and teased, "But I haven't agreed to marry you, sweetie."

"You will marry me," he said. "That is what the courting is for . . . to show you how it will be between us, how we belong together."

Brittany shivered in delight. There was something really flattering and pleasing about his determination to be with her. "Court me hard, baby."

Apparently a certain nineteenth-century French vampire's idea of how to court a woman was different from Brittany's, and as far as she was concerned, his way sucked.

Eight weeks. Eight freaking weeks, and she had not seen Corbin. Not once.

Every week she got a bouquet of fresh flowers sent to her with a computer-generated note that said, "Thinking of you. Corbin."

Thinking of her? Big whoop. That was the equivalent of telling someone you thought about getting her a gift for her birthday, but didn't. The thought did not count in Brittany's book.

So Corbin had said they needed to be discreet until the election. She had heard him, known he meant it, but she didn't think that meant he was going to disappear into the frickin' night, never to return. She had thought he meant stealth sex, sneaking into her apartment at odd hours and whisking her away for romantic walks in the desert. Or something fun like that. Geez. Instead, she just felt like an abandoned pregnant woman stupidly waiting for a scrap of attention. Waiting for Corbin to get a clue.

"Brit, honey, just sit down. You're making me dizzy." Alexis squeezed her hand and tried to lead her to a patio chair, but Brittany shook her off.

"I don't want to sit, I'm fine." She leaned over the edge of the balcony to Alexis and Ethan's suite and stared out into the night like there were answers in the neon lights of Vegas's skyline. It all felt so ridiculous. She was bad poetry brought to life. She was like some forlorn chick in a vampire movie, desperate for the mysterious man of the night to return and bite her again.

She indulged in the moment, taking a good long wallow in self-pity. Where was the man who had made love to her with such feeling, such intensity, who had sworn they were going to be together? He was off doing who knew what and she was acting like a desperate loser.

Screw that. Brittany turned around and met the gazes of her sister and Cara Fox, Seamus's wife, and pulled her shoulders up. "I really am fine. Corbin said we should be discreet, and he's doing that. I respect and admire that." Even though it made her want to throw herself down on the carpet and scream. "But I thought tonight, since Ethan won the primary all over again, and we're having a party to celebrate, I just thought maybe he'd show up." Even as she said it, she realized she was veering right smack into pitiful again. And it was completely lame that they were out on the balcony when nearly fifty people were crammed into the apartment raising their glasses to Ethan's success.

Alexis should be in there, by her husband, but Brittany had felt hot and sick to her stomach in there, and she had wandered the room over and over, trying to catch a glimpse of Corbin. Finally she had needed to get out of the stifling crowd, away from the curious looks, and away from her own disappointment that Corbin hadn't shown up.

Fortunately, neither Cara or Alexis commented on how pathetic she and her hopes were.

"He can't come to this kind of stuff, Brit, you know that. He's a pariah."

"A pariah?" Brittany winced. Somehow she had thought Corbin was exaggerating when he always said he was banished from vampire society. And after hearing his story, she was further convinced he hadn't done anything wrong. "That's horrible!"

Cara uncrossed her legs and leaned forward in her chair. She was wearing a red cocktail dress, and her silky black hair was pulled up in a twist. Shooting a frown at Alexis, she said, "Maybe that's not the right word for it. But he is still serving punishment for what happened, and for the research he does. He doesn't get invitations to parties. It's just the way it is."

"Corbin isn't a bad man." Brittany was certain of that. She'd stake her life—okay, bad choice of words—on it. That was why she'd gone and indulged in sleeping with him a second time. "In fact, he only wants to help. He wants vampires to determine their own destiny, not have it decided for them."

"He's a weirdo," Alex said.

Trust her sister to say exactly what she was thinking. Alex didn't believe in white lies to make people happy, not even if she insulted the father of her sister's child.

"He's not a weirdo! He's just a little . . . out of the loop." Brittany sighed. He was actually very sweet. From the very first night she'd met him, when he had been drawing blood from a woman with a syringe, her face a mask of blissful pleasure, his lips on her neck, Brittany had been drawn to him.

His compassion, his desire to create a cure for vampirism, his obvious loneliness, all touched her heart, had made her seek him out several times, and when he had asked for her blood, she had given it to him despite her fear of needles. And even though he had run out on her both times they'd had sex, there were very legitimate reasons for that. The first time, she'd told him to go. This second time, Corbin had stayed away for Ethan's sake, which only further proved he was a good guy. Who couldn't be bothered to even call her, damn him.

Alexis stood up and tucked her blond hair behind her ears, fiddling with the diamond necklace she was wearing with her navy satin dress. "Look, I know he floats your boat, though I have no clue why. But Corbin Atelier is bad news. If you're going to get involved with a vampire, at least let me set you up with someone better."

That hurt Brittany's feelings. Alexis never trusted her to make important decisions for herself. "I'm already involved with a vampire! I'm *pregnant*." Though she seemed to be the only one who had a real grasp on that fact. Corbin hadn't even mentioned the baby once in any of his cursory, lame, click this box on the website for a greeting, floral offerings. "I'm not interested in dating random vampires, thank you very much."

Alexis gave her a sheepish look. "Okay, I'm sorry, that didn't sound right. I know you're pregnant, and I know you're worried about Corbin. But I'm worried about you, and your baby. I think maybe it's just time to concentrate on you. Maybe it's a good thing that he's keeping his distance and not dragging you into further complications."

Brittany felt tears in her eyes, which embarrassed her. She was not a weepy person. But she had been fooling herself. She had convinced herself that she was in charge, that she was merely going to explore a possible relationship with Corbin, but that she was perfectly rational.

Lie. That was a total lie. She hadn't been rational at all.

While she wasn't a person who cried, she was an impulsive person. She saw the best in most people, and gave her love easily. Alexis didn't understand that, but Brittany didn't see that as a flaw in herself. She had given herself to Corbin, and maybe that hadn't been the smartest thing to do, but she didn't regret it.

He had given her a baby, for which she was truly grateful.

If he did decide to pop back up out of nowhere, she would be more guarded this time, not so easily coaxed into anything. Like bed. And in the meantime, she had to buy some maternity clothes, since her pants were pinching, keep swallowing those horse-sized vitamins, and register at Babies "R" Us. That ought to keep her busy.

"I guess it's a moot point anyway, isn't it? He's not here, nor is he beating down my door. So I just need to get over that." Brittany touched her hair. She still couldn't believe how strange it felt. In a moment of impulse—big surprise—she'd gone and had it all hacked off. It now came only to her chin in a modified shag. It was meant to be easier to take care of when the baby was born, and she had to admit, while it was different, she liked it. It made her feel more grown up, edgier.

"Has anyone heard from Kelsey?" she asked. That was another mystery. Kelsey had vanished. Again. And no one had heard from her in close to two months.

"No," Alexis said. "And I'm sure she's with Ringo, so I doubt she'll be coming back. He knows he is basically on the run since he was under house arrest for shooting Ethan."

Cara frowned. "What I don't understand is why he took off.

I mean, I know he's not the kind of guy to enjoy imprisonment, but you think if he was looking to escape, he'd go it alone."

"Yeah, but he needed Kelsey to get him past the guard. You know he's not above using her like that." Now Alexis was the one pacing. "What I can't figure out is why she hasn't resurfaced. I would have thought Ringo would ditch her the first chance he got after they left."

"Maybe he really likes her," Brittany said, hoping that was the case. For Kelsey, and for herself. When she had first heard that Ringo and Kelsey were missing, she had remembered the look he'd given her, the fact that he knew she was having Corbin's baby. She'd been worried about Ringo telling someone and had wanted to discuss it with Corbin, but had no way to actually get ahold of him. Cell phones were not in his vocabulary, and when she had tried to mentally call him, he hadn't answered. No advice there. But it didn't seem like anyone in the vampire world knew Corbin was the father of her baby, and with this first step in the election over and done with, she had enough things to worry about without caring that Ringo knew the truth.

Eventually everyone was going to know she and Corbin had procreated anyway.

Alexis rolled her eyes. "He's using her."

"You don't know that." Brittany wasn't sure why she was arguing. It wasn't like she knew Ringo at all, and the one time she'd met him, he had given her the heebies. But it bothered her that Alexis always had to assume the worst. "You should give

Kelsey more credit than that. She wouldn't have gone with him if he was just using her."

"Brittany Anne, I swear, you can't really be this nice. Or this naïve."

Brittany bristled. She was not a child, she was *having* a child, and she wasn't naïve, she was optimistic. There was a big difference. One was dangerous, the other was zen. "Just because I don't walk around looking for the worst in people doesn't make me stupid."

"I never called you stupid!"

"This sounds like my cue to head back in," Cara said, standing up and adjusting the strap on her dress. "Seamus is probably wondering where I am."

"Absolutely," Brittany said, distracted from her sister's patronizing behavior. "I'm sorry I kept you out here for so long. Here you are just back from Ireland, you probably want to visit with everyone."

"Not me. I really don't know anyone but you two since we left for Ireland so soon after I was turned, but I think Seamus is enjoying seeing everyone. He won't admit it, but he misses the action of politics."

Alexis winced. "And don't tell him this either, because it will spoil the mutual disdain in our relationship, but I actually miss Seamus. Ethan can't keep his head straight from his ass without him, and if he asks me to show him how to create a spreadsheet one more time, I'll scream."

"Maybe you should move back," Brittany suggested. She wasn't sure she could live in the Irish countryside either. Where would she go to buy sexy underwear and lattes? Growing up in Vegas meant she had access to everything she could ever want, all the time. If you could afford it.

Cara leaned forward and whispered, "I think I actually like Ireland more than Seamus does. The dogs have all this freedom and everyone has been very nice to me. But Seamus just broods and he's now addicted to Free Cell on his laptop. It's pitiful."

"Speaking of pitiful." Alexis rolled her eyes and tilted her head to the left. "Brittany, I think you have company."

Brittany turned and looked past Cara, heart suddenly racing. There he was. Corbin. Lounging on the railing of the balcony next to them in a suit, feet dangling into open air, obviously not the least concerned that he could slip off and fall. The beauty of being undead—no need to exercise caution even when you were twenty stories high.

He looked crabby. Melancholy. His expression was black, eyebrows drawn toward each other, shoulders tense.

Brittany felt her compassion stir. She started toward him as Alex and Cara went in, wondering if Corbin even realized she was there. He didn't seem to be looking at her.

"I am well aware zat you are here," he said, his accent more pronounced than the last time she'd been with him. She noticed it seemed to thicken in direct relation to his level of irritation.

Now her own rose to match his, stomping on the concern she'd just been feeling. "Were you going to speak to me or should I just go back in and pretend like I never saw you?"

He turned and locked eyes with her. Without answering her question, he shook his head as he studied her, his expression horrified. "*Mon Dieu*, what the hell have you done to your hair?"

Given the look on Brittany's face and the loud gasp she gave, perhaps that wasn't the wisest thing to say. But Corbin had missed her most painfully, spent many, many sleepless days staring at the ceiling remembering the feel of her body beneath his, her thick long hair wrapped around his fingers, and he had broken his own vow to stay away from her by coming here tonight, just to catch a simple, secret glimpse. And he found her hair gone. Chopped. Shorn. She looked like his little brother Edgar after his nurse had given him a bath.

Her cheeks turned red. "I cut it, obviously. It will be easier to take care of this way after the baby is born."

Corbin swung his legs over, wincing inwardly at the error he had just made. Her chin was raised defiantly, her eyes flashing. He hadn't meant to give away his presence at all, or speak to her, but he had been unable to resist. He had been hovering on the rooftop so the other vampires wouldn't sense his presence, contemplating the best strategy to get a glimpse of her. He had been intending to actually wait for her at her apartment, but had been in the hallway when he had heard her getting off the elevator.

So he had been hanging around outside like a rather pathetic lovelorn Lothario when he had heard the door open and Brittany step out with the others. He'd known it was her. He would recognize her scent anywhere, and while he hadn't been able to understand her words, he knew that lilting compassionate voice well.

He had moved onto the balcony next to her to maybe steal a word or two, perhaps a kiss, but now he had ruined the moment.

"Your haircut is stunning." Literally. Corbin tried not to stare and failed. It wasn't that it looked bad, it was just so different, so much starker than what he was used to. "You look very beautiful tonight." That was true. But she was changing, changing without him, it seemed, growing bigger still in the chest, her belly swelling slightly in the black dress she wore, her lips painted a rich brown, her hair edgy and sophisticated. She wasn't looking at him in the way he was accustomed to—with soft eyes and pouty open lips, shoulders relaxed.

Instead she was angry and it showed in the set of her jaw, the proud tilt of her hair, and the way she kept her hands still at her side. She had diamonds in her ears and they flashed as she turned her head a little. There was a wariness and a reserve about her that was new, unsettling.

"Thank you," was all she said.

"I have missed you," Corbin said, feeling a little hesitant, unsure of her reaction. It seemed as if she was angry about more than his reaction to her hair. "I could not stay away, even if it is not wise."

Silent for a moment, she leaned on the railing and stared out at the city. "The primary election is over. Ethan won so there's no reason to be secretive."

How did he respond to that? As far as he was concerned,

there very much was still a need to keep their relationship a se-cret. "But just the primary, not the presidency. It still wouldn't be prudent to advertise who the father of your child is," he said carefully, well aware how close they were to fifty conservative vampires.

Her lips pursed and she whipped her head around. "You're trying to ditch out on me, aren't you? You don't want anyone to know the baby is yours . . . all that stuff you said about us being together, about you wanting to be the father, it was a crock, wasn't it?"

Corbin was startled. He leaped from his balcony to hers and dropped next to her. She flinched when he touched her arm. "Brittany."

She didn't look at him, but stared out at the night again. "Just be honest."

While she looked strong and steady, harder, with the new blunt hairstyle, her voice trembled a little. Corbin was baffled, uncertain. He tried to embrace her from behind, but she shrugged him off.

"I meant everything I said. Why would you suggest other-wise?"

"You never called or e-mailed me or tried to see me or any-thing. You never asked about the baby!"

Horrified at the wail she gave at the end of her sentence, Corbin tried to turn her to face him, but she moved out of his reach. "I was keeping my distance, like we agreed. I don't have e-mail, and I knew if I came and saw you, I would want to make love to you. Then I wouldn't want to leave you, so I stayed away.

I sent flowers," he added, because he did want credit for something. He had thought that would suffice as a gesture of his devotion, though perhaps he should have given it more thought.

Because truthfully, he had not attempted to court a woman since the 1830s. In recent centuries he had slaked his sexual needs with women of questionable moral character, but it had probably been twenty years since he'd even done that. He'd been working, not dating. He supposed things might have changed a bit in the interim.

"Whoop-de-doo," she said.

Corbin felt his jaw drop. "What es zat supposed to mean?"

"Nothing. It means nothing," she said, though clearly it meant all manner of things. "So what have you been doing for the past *eight* weeks?"

Did she really want an answer or not? Corbin hesitated, concerned he might say the wrong thing. Perhaps this distress from Brittany was the pregnancy hormones at work.

She glared at him. "Well?"

"I have been working nonstop." In fact, he had been injecting himself with drugs, trying to find the correct combination to inhibit the vampire virus. Interestingly, his aversion to daylight had decreased, as had his ability to mind-read, but other than that, he had seen no alterations in his behavior. He still needed and hungered for the blood. But he was convinced he was right at the edge of the correct combination. One or two more trials, that was all.

"That's it?"

"Yes, that's it. I've been in my lab sixteen hours a night." He moved closer to her, starting to sense a little jealousy. "My work is very important." He smiled. "But protecting you and our child is more important. I had a terrible time resisting the urge to come over here and make love to you every night."

She turned her face away from him, but she didn't protest when he took her hand, when he ran his lips over her cheek and jaw. "And I do care about the baby. So much so that I have done the strangest thing."

Her head whipped around. "What?"

He still couldn't quite believe he'd done this, but he had spent many nights worrying about the baby, worrying about his lack of experience with children, pondering some of the questions about child-rearing Brittany had raised. "I signed up for a class."

"What class?" she asked suspiciously.

Corbin cleared his throat and tried not to wince. "It es a class for first-time fathers. Baby Boot Camp."

Six

Ringo climbed carefully out of bed and stretched, watching Kelsey sleep. There was no sign of movement other than her naked chest rising and falling steadily. He almost regretted what he was about to do. Almost.

Traveling with Kelsey wasn't bad. She had been brilliant in distracting the guard back at Carrick's hotel in Vegas, and she hadn't given much of a protest when he had suggested they extend their honeymoon, see the country, that sort of shit, even though they both knew he was breaking vampire law. She didn't complain that he had her staying in flea-bag motels to save cash, and she gave amazing head.

It wasn't exactly total hell being married to her. He had learned how to block her so she couldn't get inside his head and pick through his thoughts, and she liked live feeding from humans as much as he did.

They were kind of a pair, he had to admit, and it was a damn shame that he couldn't tell her the truth about why he had married her. But she was fucking clueless, had no idea what he was up to, and it was better that way.

Ringo got dressed in the dark and went out the door, clicking it shut behind him, the last of their cash in his pocket.

Kelsey sat up in bed and pulled on the jeans and sweatshirt she had conveniently set on the chair next to the bed. The motel room had a musty odor and the sheets were damp, so she wouldn't be sorry to leave it. Gathering her prepacked messenger bag and slipping it over her shoulder, she stepped into her black and red gym shoes and headed toward the door.

Her husband was going to meet Donatelli and she had every intention of being with him when he did.

Brittany walked behind Corbin in the hallway and nearly slammed into him when he came to a screeching halt outside the hospital classroom.

"Maybe zis is not a good idea," he said, turning around, panic in his green eyes. "They will know I am not a normal father to be."

She suspected his fear had more to do with changing a diaper than the off-chance that his vampiric status would be revealed.

She tried not to smile. "Do you really want to leave? That's fine. I'll just drive myself home after my Intro to Childbirth class."

The panic changed to guilt. He shook his head. "No, no, of course not. It will be fine. I will go to my class, you to yours, and we will leave together as planned. But first I will escort you into your class."

Like she was that stupid. He was going to walk her in, then ditch out on his class and return only in time to pick her up. It was written all over his face. She could understand his fears—heck, she was freaked out about being able to handle a baby herself, and she wasn't a two-hundred-year-old vampire. But this had been his idea, and it was a good one. Clearly, he realized he could use a little guidance. They both could, and she wasn't going to let him chicken out.

"Let's go and check you into your class first. I want to meet the instructor. Then you can walk me into my class." She smiled brightly at him. It had been an incredibly awkward week, with neither of them sure how to proceed in their relationship. It didn't seem natural to leap back into bed again, not when she found herself unsure if she could trust him, doubting that he had meant those wonderful promises he had made when they were naked. She figured an easy seventy-five percent of what a man said needed to be dismissed if his penis was erect at the time of speaking. Hell, she had exaggerated herself when she was in flagrante delicto with a guy or two in the past, saying things like "that's the biggest one I've ever seen" or "no, I never tell people what we do in bed," both of which were total lies. She'd yet to see one so big it was worth special attention, and she had told her girlfriend Teresa all kinds of juicy details while giggling. But Teresa had moved to Portland and they talked only once a month, and that was then. This was now, and she hadn't lied about anything with Corbin.

But she didn't know him well enough to understand why he did the things he did. She just wasn't sure why he had made love to her so sensually, then not spoken to her for eight weeks. It made it difficult to trust. So while they had spent the week politely circling around each other, she had concentrated on learning about Corbin, trying to gauge his moods and recognize why he acted the way he did and said the things he did. She wanted to get to know him, and they both needed to accept they had done everything ass-backward yet again and try to pick forward delicately.

Corbin hesitated for only a second before his manners kicked in. "Of course, my dear, if that is what you wish." He held the door open for her.

Brittany walked into the room, noting three other men already sitting in chairs, two looking ill at ease, one looking eager and raring to go. The instructor was pulling a sheaf of papers out of his bag.

"Howdy," he said as they approached, giving them both a smile. "Are you registered for the class?"

"My . . ." Brittany pointed to Corbin. What the hell did she call him? Vampire lover? Sperm donor? Favorite mistake? "He's taking the class. I'm taking the childbirth class in the room next door, but I just wanted to introduce myself and say thank you in advance. I'm sure it will be very reassuring for Corbin to hear your thoughts and advice."

"Well, I'm glad your husband could make the class, and I'll try not to scare him too bad." The instructor winked at her. He stuck his hand out to Corbin. "Sam Adams. Like the beer."

"This is Corbin Atelier," Brittany said, suddenly nervous about leaving Corbin alone with modern American men. Mortal men. "And I'm Brittany."

Sam's eyebrow went up at her as Corbin shook his hand. "Nice to meet you both. Enjoy your childbirth class, Brittany," Sam said rather pointedly.

"Thanks." She hovered for a second until Corbin said something to her in French. She smiled, pretending she had a clue what he was saying. "Okay, sweetie." Her feet weren't moving.

"Okay," she said again, putting her purse strap back up on her shoulder, but still rooted to the floor. Corbin stared at her. "Well, I guess I'd better go."

"I will see you in two hours," Corbin said. "Unless you'd like me to walk you to your class."

"No, no, that's okay." Now that she had him in the room, she didn't want him out until the class had concluded. "Okay, then. Bye." She gave a little wave and forced herself to leave.

She had a bad feeling about this.

Corbin watched Brittany pause yet again in the doorway and wave at him. He raised his hand back and gave a sigh.

"Driving you nuts?" Sam asked. "Women react differently to pregnancy. It's normal for her to be a little clingy."

There was nothing normal about their relationship, and *clingy* didn't even begin to cover the problem. "It is just I do not have any experience with children, so she is worried. And this pregnancy, it arrived sooner than we expected." Like sooner than never.

"Ahhh." Sam nodded in understanding. He clapped Corbin on the shoulder. "But no worries. You'll learn your way around a baby soon enough. And this class will jump-start what you need to know."

"Excellent."

"Come meet the other guys." Sam moved to the front of the room. "Alright, get in closer here so I don't have to shout. I want to hear your name, what you do for a living, and the ETD. Estimated time of delivery." He grinned.

Corbin chose a seat to the left, not wanting to be front and center. A young man with multiple tattoos and a rather painful-looking lip piercing sat next to him.

"'Sup?" he said, giving Corbin a nod.

It appeared the evening was going to tax his English skills. Corbin nodded back. "Hello."

Sam pointed to the man in a blue button-up shirt. "Name, occupation, ETD."

"Dave Robinson. I'm a loan officer. My wife is due January seventeenth and it's a boy."

"Congrats," Sam said.

"Thanks." Dave beamed.

Sam pointed to the next guy.

"I'm Jason Sikorski. I'm a cop. And my wife is due February thirteenth. She's hoping for a Valentine's baby. We don't know the sex."

"Hey, surprises are good." Sam moved on to the tattoo man.

"Travis Short. I'm in landscaping. Due date December twenty-eighth." He grinned. "The wife is ready to pop."

Sam then looked at Corbin expectantly so he cleared his throat. "I am Corbin Atelier and I am a research scientist. I am not exactly sure when Brittany is due. Sometime in April. I think."

Every face turned to him, clearly appalled.

"Dude," Travis said, shaking his head.

Sam's finger came out. "First things first. It's time to get yourself informed. A hundred bucks says your wife and every female relative you both have all know exactly when the baby is due. You need to share the load with her, man, show her you're in this together."

"Well, zis was a surprise," he said, feeling the need to defend himself.

"Even more reason to get on board. She's probably worried you don't really want this baby. You been to the doctor with her yet?"

"No." He wasn't even sure if she had been to the doctor. He must have asked at one point. He was almost sure he had. She had said everything was fine, he remembered that, so he must have asked her something. Crossing his arms over his chest, he added, "I work nights. It makes scheduling difficult."

Four pairs of reproachful eyes stared at him. Corbin felt the juvenile urge to flash his fangs and scare the daylights out of them. Who were they to judge him? They did not know his situation, they did not know what he and Brittany were dealing with.

"Well, you're here. That's a start," Sam said. "I'm sure your wife will appreciate it if you pay attention. And if language is a barrier, we've got handouts. Your wife can translate it for you."

"I am paying attention and I do not need a translator. My English is sufficient." Corbin was completely offended. He had spent half of his childhood in England. He did not need a translator. Not to mention as far as he knew Brittany did not know a single word in French except for *oui*. And that he only knew because when he had whispered a very sexual suggestion to her in bed, she had responded with a resounding *oui*.

"So you guys know all about the birth process, all about the physical stuff."

Not really.

"So that's not what we're here to talk about. We're here to talk about what happens after that baby comes home from the hospital. Your wife is going to be exhausted and emotional. Excited but unsure of herself. You need to be there for her, with all kinds of reassurance regarding both her mothering skills and her appearance. She's going to leave that hospital still wearing her maternity clothes and feeling pretty lousy about that. Make sure you're considerate of how she might be feeling."

Corbin shifted uncomfortably. The problem when you had the type of relationship he and Brittany did was that you could not follow the standard rules. He wasn't sure it was his place to be telling Brittany she still looked attractive after giving birth, or if she would take that the wrong way.

This was why they needed to get married. He did not appreciate all these complications and uncertainties.

"Your other main jobs are going to be shielding her from overenthusiastic friends and family, and helping her with breast-feeding."

"Um," Travis said. "How do we help with breastfeeding? I mean, she's got to do it, man, she's the one with the goods."

Exactly what Corbin had been thinking. He could not fathom how he could assist in that endeavor.

"A lot of new moms struggle to find the right position for the baby, and if she's had a C-section, she's going to have discomfort at the incision. You can help by getting the baby and giving him to her, and helping the baby latch on."

Corbin crossed and uncrossed his leg. Was this man serious? He cleared his throat, multiple questions rolling through his head. Wasn't it instinctive for infants to feed? Didn't they just know what to do? And how did one encourage a baby to latch on, exactly? It wasn't like you could instruct an infant via a directional pamphlet.

Dave was bold enough to ask. "What do you mean, latch on?"

Sam launched into an explanation that involved repeated use of the words *nipple*, *areola*, and *lactate*. Corbin wished the floor would open up and swallow him. Never, ever, since he had been in the presence of a cheap nineteenth-century prostitute had he heard the word *nipple* used so many times and with such complete nonchalance.

Then Sam's wife entered the room with their six-month-old son. To Corbin's complete and utter horror, she sat on the edge of the desk, lifted her shirt, popped out a breast, and demonstrated exactly how little Austin ate his dinner.

Corbin wanted, quite simply, to die.

He had wished for death many times over his long lifespan, but never as fervently as he did while Beth Adams rattled off breastfeeding statistics, her baby sucking industriously, mouth fully around the entire areola, as Sam was quick to point out, finger outlining the area in question. Corbin was speechless.

Determined not to see any more of her naked flesh, Corbin glanced around for a means of escape, or perhaps a way to decapitate himself. Not finding any, he studied the pale blue carpet aggressively. How in the hell had he gotten himself into this situation?

"Sex," Sam said.

Corbin jerked upright. Yes, that was quite true. Sex was responsible. But how in the hell could he get himself back out? He was now not having sex and that wasn't fixing anything.

"We're going to talk about changes in your relationship, especially sex, after we take a break." He grinned. "And after Beth leaves."

Beth didn't comment, and Corbin didn't check to see what expression might be on her face. He was still investigating the carpet and wondering if he dashed out of the room, vampire speed, if Brittany would be angry with him. Maybe not angry, but definitely disappointed. Her fat bottom lip would stick out and her big brown eyes would go wide with hurt. He sighed, resigned, though he really had no interest in discussing post-partum sex with strangers. He wasn't even having prepartum sex. He wasn't holding out much hope for after the birth either, and at any rate, he found discussing sex in public somewhat offensive. Especially since it had been eight weeks since he'd had any.

Legs appeared in front of him. He glanced up, hoping it was nothing more than Sam with a handout. Instead it was Beth, smiling, Austin still latched on. She sat in the chair next to Corbin, astounding him with her mobility while breastfeeding. This was a woman who knew how to solicit latching on correctly. With a finger, she broke her son's grip on her, and Corbin's heightened sense of sound allowed him to hear quite clearly the lip-smacking pop sound the detachment made. He winced.

"Will you burp him for me?" Beth said.

Corbin glanced over at her in surprise. She couldn't possibly be speaking to him, the two-hundred-year-old French vampire whose experience with children was limited to walking past issues of *Parents* on the magazine rack. Yet she was. She was smiling, her round cheeks pink, her hair back in a ponytail, the soft pale flesh of her breast still partially exposed. The baby was bobbing in an upright position and she was holding him out toward Corbin.

"I do not think zat is a good idea," he said, shaking his head. "I know nothing about babies."

One-handed, she held her child, and dexterously tucked her

breast away with the other, for which he was exceedingly grateful. "This is your chance to practice."

"Perhaps one of the others," he said, sitting up straight in alarm when she shoved the baby at him. "No, no, I don't think . . ."

Left with no choice but to take the baby or leave little Austin dangling in midair, Corbin settled his hands around the baby's waist and swallowed vast quantities of saliva. "What do I do?" he asked in total panic, gingerly resting the baby's flopping feet onto his knee. The infant felt warm and soft, a bubble forming on his pink lips. His chubby legs couldn't hold him, though, and essentially collapsed, tangling the infant all up in his own appendages. Appalled, Corbin quickly used a free hand to move both limbs to either side of his own leg so the baby was sitting down on his pant leg like he was astride a horse.

They looked at each other.

The baby swung his plump arms up and down rapidly and made a humming sound, the bubble on his lip oozing down his chin, followed by a trail of milky saliva. The sour smell made Corbin's stomach flip, but it was encouraging to see Austin wasn't afraid of him. He was bouncing and smiling, showing off his slippery gums and two bottom teeth, rising up through the drool.

"So to burp him, you just need to pat him on the upper back firmly. You can do it the way he is, but it would be easier if you rested him against your chest and shoulder." Beth demonstrated with her empty hands.

Corbin gingerly lifted Austin and rested him against his shirt, grateful he'd worn a casual cotton three-button shirt, navy blue besides. He had a feeling bad things could be about to happen when he encouraged air to evacuate Austin's stomach. The baby felt intriguing, heavy and soft, fragile, yet strong enough to keep catapulting himself backward. His wispy hair smelled like shampoo, and Corbin rather liked the constant random sounds that came out of his mouth.

"You've never held a baby before?"

"No." Corbin paused and amended his answer. "Except for my little brother, who was born when I was an adolescent. But I was away at school most of the time." And Edgar had died of consumption before he had reached his tenth birthday, sending his mother into a fatal decline.

He patted cautiously on Austin's back.

"Harder," Beth said. "He won't break. You need a firm pat so he can get that air up and out."

Corbin cleared his throat and gave it a little more effort, but still exercising extreme caution. He had vampire strength and he didn't want to collapse the child's lungs or anything.

"Firm. Matter of fact. Close to him," Beth ordered, putting her hand on Austin's arm and demonstrating, tucking a cloth of some kind onto Corbin's shoulder.

Sucking in a deep breath, Corbin copied her movement, a firm but gentle pat, and was rewarded with a loud, lengthy, wet belch that came from the depths of Austin's baby belly and rattled past Corbin's ear. A little shocked, he pulled the baby back and checked him for any injuries an eruption of that magnitude might have produced. Austin just smiled at him.

"Good, yes?" Corbin asked him, charmed by that smile. Austin gave a squeal.

"Now that he's fed, I'm going to scoot on out of here," Beth said. "Let you men talk about manly things and practice diapering Austin. You did great," she told him with a smile.

"You're taking him back, yes?" Corbin asked, panicked all over again, lifting the baby toward her.

"No, no, you keep him. Sam is going to help you change his diaper."

With that she turned to go speak to her husband and Corbin was left holding the bag. Baby.

He looked around for assistance, resting the infant back on his shoulder. Travis was still next to him. "Would you like to hold him?" Corbin asked. "Since your wife is due first."

Travis shook his head, lip curling back. "No way. He's spewing."

"What?" Corbin twisted his head to try and see Austin. "What do you mean?" he asked with a sense of dread. But truthfully he already knew what Travis meant. His shoulder felt wet. Warm. Austin had missed most of the cloth.

"Sick," Travis said. "That smells curdled, man."

Corbin suddenly felt much closer to Austin and Beth Adams than he ever cared to be. "Take him from me."

"No way." Travis scooted his chair back.

Grabbing at his shoulder, Corbin took the partially damp cloth and wiped at Austin's dribbly mouth, holding him precariously with his free hand. "Is he ill?" He studied Austin and saw no evidence of fever.

"Nah, I think babies just do that. Spew. When they eat."

"Wonderful." Corbin swiped at his own shoulder.

"I'll take him," Dave said, holding his hands out with a rapt expression on his face.

Corbin turned him over gratefully. "I'll go try and wash my shirt off."

"Hurry up." Dave lifted Austin up and down, making the baby laugh. "We're talking about sex next and you don't want to miss the bad news."

"Can't wait," Corbin said under his breath, pushed his chair back, and got the hell out of there.

Brittany was concentrating on the video showing a woman giving birth. Was it really necessary for the woman to be naked? She was no prude, but come on. A robe or gown would be nice. But this woman just had all her stuff flopping around as she grunted and heaved and shook her hair like a horse after a hard run. It wasn't a pretty picture.

It was giving Brittany rather uncomfortable feelings about the birth and her ability to push a baby out of her body while Corbin Atelier and a team of hospital staff stared at her crotch. What if it altered Corbin's perception of her permanently? They had enough to sort out without him seeing her looking so mammalian.

They were supposed to be taking notes, but Brittany didn't know what to write beyond HELP, so she just sat with her pen lying on her notepad.

"I think someone is trying to get your attention," the woman next to her said, pointing to the door.

Brittany turned and saw Corbin peering through the glass in

the doorway, looking pained. He held up his watch and pointed to it. She shrugged. The class had just started.

She turned back around, but sighed when she heard the door open. Resolutely, she kept facing the front and the video, trying not to wince as the on-camera mother to be gave another guttural groan.

Corbin squatted down between her chair and the woman's next to her. "Please forgive ze intrusion," he said to the other woman, accent turned up high, charm dripping off him. "I just need a moment."

Brittany rolled her eyes when the woman smiled and said, "Sure, no problem."

"What's the matter?" Brittany asked in a whisper.

But Corbin had caught sight of the video and was staring, a look of horror on his face. "*Mon Dieu . . .*"

"Don't look!" she hissed, grabbing his chin and turning his head toward her. This was not the image she wanted him taking into the labor and delivery room. "This video is dated, very eighties, totally earth mother weird." She hoped. "Now what did you need?"

He shook his head and refocused on her. "The baby vomited on me. I'm going home to change and I'll be back to pick you up."

"They have a baby in there?"

"Yes, the instructor's child. And he . . ." Corbin gestured to his shoulder, which had a baseball-size damp spot on it.

"Just dry it off with the hand dryer in the restroom." If he left, he'd never go back, she was sure of it. She wanted him comfortable with the idea of a baby, not fleeing in terror at the first opportunity.

"Brittany." He gave her a look of total exasperation. "I smell."

Her lip twitched. "That has nothing to do with the baby, honey."

It took him a second. "Very amusing. Can you not see me laughing?" he asked, face deadpan.

She giggled and gave him a reassuring pat. "No one cares. I can't smell anything. Just go back and enjoy the rest of the class."

"But—"

"Go!" She lost her patience and pointed to the door. "It won't kill you, you know." How true was that?

He shot her a dark look, the masculine equivalent of a pout. "Fine."

"Fine." She smiled at him. "See you in an hour or so."

Muttering in French, he slipped back out of the room.

"Sorry," Brittany whispered to the woman next to her, who had turned to watch Corbin's retreat.

"What was wrong?" she asked.

"Oh, nothing major." Brittany waved her hand in the air. "But he's French," she added, like that explained everything.

"Oh. Right." The woman nodded in understanding. Then she turned back to the video and made a face. "Oh, yikes, the baby is crowning."

Indeed it was. Brittany suddenly knew how Corbin felt. She wanted to go home and pretend their child could hatch, already ten years old.

Seven

When Austin urinated on him, Corbin figured his night was complete.

"You need to keep a boy covered up at all times," Sam said with a grin.

It would have been nice to know that ahead of time. Corbin sighed and wiped his arm by rolling it back and forth on the cloth Sam had laid on the changing pad.

"Dude, you're not having any luck at all tonight," Travis said, scratching the devil tattoo on his forearm.

"Maybe zat is because I am actually touching the baby," Corbin told him, holding the clean diaper out in Travis's direction. "Care to try?"

"No way, man, I'm just trying to, you know, sit back and take it all in. Observing. Learning from watching you."

Either that or Travis was lily-livered. Austin kicked Corbin with his heel, regaining his attention. He undid the diaper the way Sam had shown him and, after a mere two tries, had it centered under the baby's bottom. Rather proud of himself, he started to fold the front up and between the legs, when Austin took a roll to the left and flipped himself right onto his round belly and off the diaper. "What the . . . ?"

"That's why you never leave a baby alone on the changing table," Sam said sternly. "And why we did this on the floor. Babies roll. You can't leave them alone for even two seconds."

Clearly. Corbin gently hauled Austin back and laid him on his back again, realizing at the last second his head was going to smack on the floor, and shoving his palm under to cradle Austin's skull until it rested on the pad.

"Good instincts," Sam nodded.

Corbin had to admit, he was impressing even himself. This was foreign to him, but it really required just some basic training and common sense. He grabbed the diaper again.

Austin did a repeat roll onto his belly, bare bottom facing up. It struck Corbin then how completely amusing and bizarre human infants were, both in appearance and behavior. As he lifted Austin yet again, his plump warm flesh wiggling in Corbin's grip as he struggled to get free, Corbin couldn't help but smile.

"You'll be still, yes?" he said, as he laid the baby back down, and drew his finger across the softness of Austin's round cheek, wanting to touch that pure skin. He came too close to the baby's mouth, and Austin turned his head and engulfed Corbin's finger with his slippery lips. Drool crawled down Corbin's skin, but the gnawing seemed to preoccupy Austin and he stopped mov-ing around. With his own fat baby hands, he grabbed onto Corbin's wrist and chewed his finger industriously.

Seizing the opportunity, Corbin got the diaper on one-handed, using his elbow to hold it in place and seal the tabs. The thing was on crooked and didn't look pretty, but it was snug and should hold. Damnation, this business was exhausting. He was going to have to stop for a pint on the way home. But it was also . . . illuminating. He thought maybe he was starting to un-derstand the devotion infants inspired in their parents. Austin was adorable and amusing and charming, and required so much care, it was no wonder parents were so vehement about their children. They had a great deal of time and emotion invested in them.

Corbin finished the job, extracted his slimy finger, and lifted Austin up. Some strange instinct compelled him to kiss the baby on the cheek, with lots of noise and eating motions, causing Austin to squeal in delight, a chuckle rising up from deep in his round belly.

If he didn't think about that horrific video he'd witnessed when he'd walked into Brittany's class, he actually felt a large sense of contentment. He could do this. Be a father. And a vam-pire. All at once.

Brittany felt ill. She had an aversion to needles, and when they'd gone straight from the birthing video to the tests and screening video, showing a giant needle going right into a woman's belly for an amniocentesis, she had gone hot with spots in front of her eyes.

There was no way. No way. She would have to be knocked out first if a doctor wanted to do that to her. Her stomach was churning, face hot, skin clammy, and she had excused herself for a drink of water.

But once in the hallway, she decided she just wanted to leave. She would read the manual at home. These videos were not instructional for her, they were panic inducing.

Sneaking into the back of Corbin's classroom, she was glad to see they weren't in a lecture-style class. The men were all gathered on the floor, bent over—she assumed with the baby Corbin had mentioned—so it wouldn't be a big deal to interrupt.

Moving forward, she noticed it was Corbin who was actually diapering the baby. His brow was furrowed and he was concentrating, completely hunched over as he tried to undo the tabs one-handed.

He looked adorable, his hair falling forward into his eyes, his shirt pulling out of his pants. Despite her precarious stomach, she found herself smiling, and reaching into her purse for her cell phone. She was going to snap a picture of him.

Then he lifted the baby up in the air and Brittany nearly puddled onto the floor. He was *playing* with the baby. Kissing his cheek.

Everything in her inflated and swelled, and she felt breathless, entranced. A little bit in love. In love? Yes, insane as it was. In love, or something close there to it. With the man who was the father of her child.

Maybe this could actually work. This thing between them, and mutual parenting.

She felt a huge sense of relief and gratitude that Corbin Atelier was the kind of man who could see the charm in a baby. Holding her camera out, she snapped a picture.

Corbin saw the flash and glanced over, his smile disappearing, replaced by embarrassment. "Brittany."

She laughed. "Busted. I caught you on camera so you can't deny it." Clicking "Review," she waved it toward him. "You like babies and I have proof."

"Brittany, don't." Corbin started to stand up, the baby against his chest.

"Too late." Amused, she glanced back at the screen, hoping the shot had turned out.

What she saw made the blood drain from her face. Oh, God, she'd forgotten. She'd just forgotten.

In the picture, Austin dangled in the air, smiling and laughing. But nothing was holding him. Corbin wasn't there.

She glanced over at him, horrified. He was a vampire.

No, she supposed she hadn't forgotten, but she had been swept up in the normalcy of what they'd been doing . . . preparing for a baby.

But he was a vampire.

And quite possibly, so was her child.

Brittany fought the panic, but all the blood rushed to her face, and she dropped her phone.

"Brittany," Corbin said, moving toward her, passing the baby to another man.

Eyes blurred by tears, she dragged herself back from the edge of a faint and said, "I'm fine. I'm fine. I just feel a little sick."

And she whirled around and ran out of the room.

"Fancy meeting you here, Columbia." Donatelli stood in front of Rockefeller Center and pulled on a pair of camel-colored leather gloves. "I was under the impression you were wearing an ankle bracelet back in Vegas."

"Maybe I've been released for good behavior," Ringo said, leaning over the railing and checking out the ice rink. A hefty teenage girl shrieked as she slipped and sat hard on her ass.

"Maybe. Or maybe you got your pretty little girlfriend to pick the key off your guard."

"Maybe." It wasn't like it was a secret. Everyone back in Vegas had to have known he left with Kelsey, and he was sure the guard would have come clean about what had happened, though he might not have mentioned to the powers that be where Kelsey's other hand had been when she lifted the key. Ringo lit a cigarette and took a deep drag.

"Your better half is quite resourceful. Though it's not as if it's difficult to get around these little inconveniences. Carrick runs a loose ship." Donatelli lifted the leg of his black pants. Ringo saw the metal cuff that had matched his own. "I'm sure I could dispense with my own punishment, but I am biding my time. I don't have any reason to leave Manhattan at the moment, nor do I want to raise ire. That is why I am not entirely pleased by you seeking me out."

Donatelli was still an asshole. Ringo blew smoke in his face and made a show of looking around. Nothing but tourists lingering and office workers rushing home from work in the dark. "I don't see anyone trailing you. No one gives a shit what you're doing, as long as your ankle jewelry stays on and you stay put. So just fucking relax."

Lifting a paper coffee cup from a four-cup carrying container on the ground, Donatelli drank through the hole in the lid. Ringo could smell it, knew it was blood. His stomach burned with hunger. He had skipped feeding last night in his hurry to find a motel and get to bed. Now he regretted it.

"I'm relaxed."

The bastard did look completely content.

He took another sip. "Would you care for a drink? Smith ended up heading home early with a date, and he never touched his blend." Donatelli bent over and lifted another of the coffee cups and held it out to him.

Ringo shook his head rapidly. He knew what was in Smith's blood drink. It would be tainted with heroin, because Smith was an addict, like Ringo had been. And Donatelli knew it.

"No, thanks," Ringo said, heart pounding. He wanted a drink. Desperately. He wanted to sink and swim into the blood, to let it careen through his body with the force of a roller coaster, setting off prickles of pleasure everywhere, emptying his mind and soaking him in a false artificial bliss. "I came because I wanted to offer you a piece of information for a price."

"In regards to what?" Donatelli still held the cup, and swirled the liquid in it around and around.

Bled Dry

Sweat formed on Ringo's forehead. This had been a mistake. Greed had driven him to take a chance, and he was suddenly afraid he'd just dicked himself over. He hadn't realized how gnawing the temptation would still be, how hard it would be to stare down Donatelli and not be reminded of their past, where Ringo had been the consumer and Donatelli the provider. Clenching his fists in the pockets of his jacket, Ringo said, "In regards to vampire procreation."

Donatelli looked mildly surprised. "You have my attention, since that is not your area of expertise."

"But it is Atelier's, who was in charge of my treatment for drug abuse."

"How intriguing. I'll bite. How much?"

"A hundred grand."

Donatelli snorted and turned toward the skating rink. "That's ridiculous. And why is that woman wearing those purple pants? That is a crime against cotton."

Ringo had been prepared for that reaction. "What if I told you that Atelier is going to become a father?"

"I would say congratulations, especially since I was starting to suspect he doesn't even have a prick. He's not known for socializing."

"What if I told you the mother is half-vampire."

That got a reaction. Donatelli shot him a startled look. "I'd say that is very interesting, but worth only five grand, tops."

"Throw in twenty more and I'll tell you who she is."

"I don't need you for that. I can just have someone observe who Atelier is visiting these days."

"Except my sources tell me that Atelier isn't seeing anyone these days. No one knows about the child. No one knows about the mother. No one but him. Her. And me." Ringo swallowed hard. He could smell the blood, thick and warm and laced with that extra tangy mix of alcohol and drugs. His hands were starting to shake.

"When is this bundle of joy due?"

Ringo shrugged. "I've said enough." He stuck his foot on the bottom of the railing, needing the support. Vampires weren't supposed to feel cold, but Ringo felt the sensation of ice water careening through his veins. He wanted that blood. "I'll be in town tonight, then I'm leaving tomorrow. Call my cell phone if you'd like to discuss it further."

Donatelli didn't reach for the card Ringo gave him, so he tucked it into the pocket of the Italian's expensive overcoat.

"You realize you have tipped your hand, don't you?" Donatelli asked him.

Ringo pushed back. "Just the first card. I've got four more facedown."

Not to mention he had lifted Donatelli's wallet out of his pocket. Ringo and Kelsey's hotel bill would be compliments of Donatelli that night. Time to move to the Ritz.

"Ever confident. Ever foolish." Donatelli smiled at him. "Stick to murder for hire. You're better at that than vampire politics."

But Ringo just smiled back. "See you around, Donatelli." He waved and cut across the sidewalk, heading toward Forty-second Street and away from the coffee cup that was calling him.

Bled Dry

Kelsey waited until Ringo had left, lifting his hand for a cab. She had been watching from the clothing storefront across the street, hidden among shoppers behind a table of turtleneck sweaters.

Donatelli was still staring at the ice rink, but she didn't want to risk him walking away, so she moved quickly. He sensed her coming behind him and turned. A smile crossed his face.

"Ah, Miss Kelsey, how good to see you again. I should have known you were hanging about. Where there is Ringo, there is Kelsey."

Her fear and revulsion fought to gain supremacy, but Kelsey stopped two feet in front of him and screwed up her courage. This man may have ordered her drained of all her blood and left for dead a few months back, but he couldn't hurt her, not here, not with hundreds of people moving around them.

"Leave my husband alone."

His eyebrow rose. "Husband? What a surprise. Congratulations, my dear. You are now attached for eternity to a drug-addicted killer. Should I send you a silver soup tureen? Linens, perhaps. Either way, may you have more success with your marriage than I had with mine."

Kelsey put her hands inside the pouch pocket of her hooded sweatshirt. "I'm serious. Leave Ringo alone."

"You aren't taking into account *he* contacted *me*. I was minding my own business, doing a little preholiday shopping and sampling the delights of the city, when he called me."

Despising the way he talked, the arrogance, the way his finger rolled around and around the rim of the coffee cup in his hand, Kelsey tensed. She knew what was in his cup, as well as the one on the ground. She knew this man was responsible for Ringo's addiction. "You don't really believe him, do you? He's trying to bilk you because we're broke and we're on the run."

Ringo thought he could shut her out of his thoughts, but Kelsey could catch random bits and pieces, enough to know that he had come to Donatelli to sell information. She also knew that he loved her, even if he didn't realize that's what it was, and she loved him in return. Unfortunately, his sense of right and wrong wasn't exactly well developed and he made bad choices. A lot of them. But she could fix this one.

Donatelli sipped his drink. "You know, I find that a fascinating strategy on your part. You're willing to risk his anger in order to protect him from me. I'm flattered that you are that frightened of what I can do to him. But I don't think he is making this story up . . . he couldn't have created it on his own, or understood the importance of it. Sorry, Kelsey, you can't make me go away. I am interested in negotiating a sale with your husband."

People thought she was stupid, a brunette airhead, and sometimes she was. Mostly she was just strange, and she knew that. But both perceptions led people to continually underestimate her.

"I'm thirsty," she said in a random, whiny voice. She bent down and pulled one of the cups out of the cardboard carrier at Donatelli's feet.

"Be my guest," he said dryly. "But one of those three cups

has a little extra something added to it. I don't think I remember which one."

Having being a drug user herself in the late sixties, Kelsey had no intention of ever going that route again and wanted to ensure Ringo didn't relapse either. She would be forever grateful to Mr. Carrick for getting her the help she had needed when she'd hit rock bottom, and didn't intend to see her husband slide backward. But she wasn't going to drink any of Donatelli's blood cups anyway.

She just shrugged and stood back up. "I'll sniff it." Prying the lid off, she delicately lifted it to her nose. "You do know that when Ringo gets desperate, he is capable of almost anything."

"Aren't we all." Donatelli had dark eyes, and they narrowed, as he clearly tried to guess what game she was playing.

"Not everyone. Like, I don't know, Gwenna, for instance. She's not capable of evil, is she?"

That got the reaction she was hoping for. "What the fuck does Gwenna have to do with anything?"

"I don't know." Kelsey blinked. "But she's in Vegas again."

Donatelli opened his mouth then snapped it shut. He gave a deliberate shrug. "Why do I care if my ex-wife is visiting her brother?"

"I don't know. But I thought it was weird that she was hanging out with the French guy that no one likes. The one who helped Ringo. She seems so quiet. But I guess they make a good couple."

Kelsey was lying through her teeth. She doubted Gwenna even knew Atelier, but her objective was simply to get Donatelli back to Vegas, so by default she could get Ringo back to Vegas, back where there were other vampires to run interference. Back where she could keep her husband away from the drug blood.

"A couple? That's ridiculous."

But he looked unconvinced and angry, grip tightening on his coffee cup. Kelsey just gave a noncommittal shrug. "Maybe they're not a couple. I guess they could just be having sex."

Donatelli's eyes flared with hatred, the cup in his hand collapsing, blood spilling all over his really pretty light brown coat. Kelsey jumped back, a red splash landing on her arm.

"Damn it," he said, dropping the crushed cup right as a woman to their left started screaming.

Kelsey turned, saw her pointing at them, at all the blood on Donatelli's chest, while she shrieked in terror. There was movement, people coming toward them. Reacting instinctively, Kelsey backed up, right into Donatelli, intending to run. But before she even realized he was doing it, he had his arms around her.

Then she was up and over the railing, free-falling down onto the ice rink. She heard the shouts, saw scrambling movement as skaters dashed out of the way.

When she landed, on her shoulder and back, with a crunch of nausea-inducing pain, she looked up at the railing.

Donatelli was gone.

And she hoped like hell he was headed back to Vegas.

That was worth breaking half the bones in her body.

Eight

Corbin gave a quick apology to Sam and the class, grabbed Brittany's cell phone off the floor, and headed out after her. He deleted the picture she had taken, glancing briefly at the disturbing image of Austin in the air with nothing holding him. The lack of a reflective image for a vampire was something he had never been able to fully explain with science.

Brittany was sitting on a bench wiping at her eyes.

"Hello," he said, sitting down next to her.

"Hi." She sniffled, her voice wobbly, mouth turned down.

"I am sorry." Corbin turned her cell phone around and around in his hands.

She sighed. "It's not your fault. I just wasn't expecting that. And I don't feel good. My stomach is upset. That's why I came in the room in the first place."

"Shall I take you home then?" He put his hand on her knee, not knowing how to fix this. He didn't even understand fully what he felt for Brittany, and he had no comprehension of how to handle their relationship. Didn't know what was expected of him, or what he was entitled to.

"Actually, I think I'll call my sister to come and get me. I want you to finish the class." She stared out the window in front of them at the dark parking lot.

There was a distance in her voice and he didn't like it. "I am trying to be normal," he said, frustrated.

"I know." She turned to him and gave him a wan smile. "And I'm trying to pretend I can be a soccer mom. I never thought I was trying to defy my childhood, but I think in some ways all I've ever wanted as an adult was to just be normal. I mean, I became a dentist. Can you get any more suburban than that? But the thing is, Corbin, we can try, but we can't change the core of who we are. You're a vampire, and in my heart, I'm still a wild child, happy-go-lucky daughter of a stripper. We can't change that, and I guess, ultimately, I don't want to. But I'm not sure being parents meshes with who we are."

Corbin squeezed her knee, his heart searing at her words. He had failed her by the simple fact that he was not the man she had expected to meet and marry. He was not the man who could give her that completely innocuous bourgeois existence. Regardless of her feelings toward him, he would always represent the loss of that dream. That made him very sad, very sorry.

But he also disagreed with her.

"The ideal parent is not based on where you live, or what

you can provide your child with. A good parent is simply one who loves his child and teaches them values and boundaries in a nurturing environment." He hadn't been watching *Supernanny* religiously for two months without learning a thing or two. Or how to articulate what he suspected he had known instinctually.

He turned to her, touched her chin, brought her gaze around to his. "We have that, *ma chérie*. If we were bad parents, we would not worry this much. But we worry, because we care. And ultimately, that is the most important thing our child needs. Two parents who would do anything for him or her."

Big fat tears spilled out of her eyes. "You're a good man, Corbin Jean Michel Atelier," she whispered.

He kissed her forehead. "Let me take you home."

"No, you should stay. You're learning a lot."

"That is true." He gave a rueful smile as she pleased him by dropping her head down onto his shoulder.

It was a comfortable feeling, her resting on him, and they sat in contentment. Silent, but together.

And after Alexis had picked Brittany up fifteen minutes later, Corbin strode back into the classroom. He had to do this. He had to show Brittany they could be *normal* parents, whatever normal might be defined as.

"Alright, men," Sam was saying. "Down on the ground."

The guys all glanced at each other, unsure what to do.

"I mean it! Down on your stomachs. Crawl. You need to get a perspective on what the world is like for a baby down there. Then we'll talk safety and babyproofing."

Determined to do this right, Corbin got down into an army crawl beside Travis, the floor hard and cold.

"It's freezing down here," Travis complained.

"Point number one. Always bring a blanket for the baby to lie on. The ground might be cold or hard or covered with nasty germs."

Corbin glanced around as his fellow classmates all crawled around the room, trying to get into the exercise, but all looking distinctly uncomfortable, except for Dave, whose enthusiasm had him zipping around the entire room. Travis had flopped onto his back.

"Is it time for my bottle and a bath yet?" he asked Corbin, and they both started laughing.

If this was Brittany's idea of normal, then Corbin was damn grateful they were probably never going to fit in.

"Why couldn't he drive you home?" Alexis demanded, peeling out of the hospital parking lot at sixty miles an hour. Brittany thought sometimes Alex forgot how strong she was post–blood drinking. With little effort, she could probably push that gas pedal through the floor, literally.

"Can you stop with the lead foot? You're going to get me killed. Not to mention the whole reason I wanted to leave was because I have a stomachache."

"Sorry." Alexis eased up on the gas. "But what a shithead, I swear, Brittany, the hell with him. You don't need to be treated like this."

Rubbing her stomach, Brittany tried not to notice that her sister smelled tinny. Like she'd just been hitting the blood buffet. Since her pregnancy, her own sense of smell had heightened, and this was a bit gross. A lot gross, actually. But it was still Alexis, her sister, and she was going to have to get used to it. She was surrounded by bloodsuckers. Regardless of whether or not she and Corbin ever got their act together as a couple, he was still the father of her child.

"Alex, calm down. Corbin is not a shithead. He was going to drive me home, but I told him to stay. The class was helpful for him, since he knows as much about babies as I know about raising alpacas—which is nothing, by the way. The instructor had his baby there and Corbin was playing with him. He likes kids, Alex, he just doesn't have any experience, and so his confidence isn't all that great. This class was good for him, and I wanted him to finish it."

Alexis was grimacing, focused on the road, hands gripping the steering wheel of her huge black SUV. Brittany had often thought Alexis was compensating for her lack of height with her beast of a car.

"If I could change one thing in life, I would have you pregnant with a normal man's baby. This just complicates everything."

That stung. Brittany knew Alexis wasn't being judgmental, she just wanted everything to be easy for her, but it still hurt, like a paper cut. Small and unintentional, but powerfully painful.

"I didn't set out to complicate everyone's life. And while I'm sure you, Ethan, and Corbin all wish we could go back in time and erase the fact that we had unprotected sex, we can't. So get over it. This is reality, and I'm trying to learn how to deal with it, and I'd appreciate you helping me instead of complaining." So there.

Alexis slammed on the brakes on the side street that led to Brittany's apartment complex. "Brit, geez, I'm sorry. I'm sorry." Flicking her blond hair out of her eyes, she shook her head vigorously. "I didn't mean that the way it sounded . . . I just want to make things easier for you, sweetie."

"I know. But there is no easier. This is it." Brittany patted Alexis's knee. Her sister looked sick, her light blue eyes clouded with anguish. "And it's not so bad, honestly, in terms of me and Corbin. I know you don't like him, but we get along. He treats me really well."

"It's not that I don't like him, I just don't approve of his research. He's dabbling in scary stuff. And he killed a woman."

"That was greatly exaggerated." Brittany found it interesting that when her sister raised doubts about Corbin, conversely Brittany's own doubts evaporated. "And he says once the baby is born and we get married, he's going to retire."

"Get married?" Alexis's look of terror warring with extreme disgust showed Brittany her sister's take on her getting hitched to an undead outcast. "That's . . . that's . . ."

"A possibility, not a given. We'll see how it goes." Brittany felt remarkably clearheaded. This conversation had been good for her. It had shown her how futile worrying was. What she needed to do was just live her life. Take charge and stop waiting for everyone else to act, while she would react. "I think there's a car behind us. You should probably start driving again."

Alexis made an incoherent sound, but she lifted her foot from the brake and started them rolling forward.

"Does Gwenna have e-mail? I was hoping I could ask her a few questions. Mother to mother."

Pulling into a visitor's spot, Alexis shook her head. "I doubt it. According to Ethan, she lives in some moldering old castle in York. No electricity. No cell phone tower. It's like the land before time. Ethan sends her stuff snail mail, or if it's important, global express. But the thing is, and do not repeat this to Ethan, but . . ." Alexis bit her fingernail and gave her a shrug. "I think Gwenna's a few cards short of a deck. Not the best person to be doling out advice."

Brittany discounted that. Alexis was such a logical, tell-it-like-it-is person that anyone who was slightly left of center struck her as weird. She saw life as black and white. But Brittany figured everyone was weird to a certain extent, and a little oddness hanging around a person didn't mean there wasn't a little brilliance in the mix as well. She wanted the comfort of talking to another woman who had given birth to a child with unique genetics.

"I don't care. I want to talk to her. Can Ethan contact her? Or would it make her more comfortable if I flew over there?"

"Good gravy, don't do that. Just sit tight and I'll have Ethan talk to her." Alexis gave her a stern look. "Promise me you won't go running off halfway around the world. I'm serious."

Brittany tucked her hand under her thigh and crossed her fingers. She wasn't making any promises she couldn't keep. While she had no intention of jetting off to Europe at the moment, she wanted to leave her options open. Her answer was deliberately vague. "Okay."

"Okay, what?"

Damn, Alexis knew her too well. "Okay, I won't fly to England immediately. Or without consulting you first."

Alexis sighed and popped the locks on the car so they could get out. "You are going to be the death of me."

"You can't die." Brittany pointed out the obvious with a smirk.

"Brat."

Brittany laughed. It was nice to know that some things would never change.

"Hey, you want to grab a beer or something?" Travis asked Corbin when they finally emerged from the classroom, overloaded with info and a new understanding of the words *big responsibility*.

Corbin had scrubbed his arm down in the men's room and checked his shirt to see if there was a visible spot from Austin's spit-up. It looked presentable, and he suspected only vampire nostrils could detect the sour scent. "Sure."

"Dave, Jason, you in?" Travis asked the others.

"I'm in," Jason said, running his hand through his short hair and rubbing his scalp. "I need a cold one after all of that. Jesus Christ. Parenting is like police work—rules, regulations, and paperwork."

"I need to get home," Dave said with a regretful shrug. "My wife hates being alone."

As he waved and trotted down the hall, Travis shook his head. "That guy's whipped."

"Seriously," Jason agreed. "And I figured hey, we might as well go out while we can, right? I mean, there won't be any grabbing a beer once the baby gets here. At least not for a while."

"You got it." Travis hit Corbin in the chest with the back of his hand. "Alright, you guys call your old ladies, then I'll call mine. Let them know what's up."

"Oh, I don't need to call Brittany," Corbin said, shaking his head at Travis's offer of his cell phone. "But you two go right ahead."

They both gaped at him. Travis looked horrified, Jason skeptical.

"Your funeral, man," Jason said.

"She went to her sister's," Corbin hedged, a little embarrassed that he and Brittany were not married. "She wasn't feeling well, so her sister picked her up."

"Yeah, but she's not going to sleep there, and she'll be pissed if she gets home and you're not there."

Corbin made a noncommittal sound and said, "Go ahead and call your wife."

Travis cocked an eyebrow. "Dude, did you two argue or something? If she's trippin', you need to deal with it. All those hormones and shit, you need to work it through, you know what I'm saying? My dad always said never go to bed wanting to kill the bitch, and that's good advice."

Corbin almost laughed. It reminded him of a conversation he had had with his own father regarding marriage. *Better to despise each other and have exceptional sex, than to get along but be bored in bed.* It hadn't made sense to Corbin at the time, and he wasn't sure it did two hundred years later, either. But apparently his father hadn't been the only sire doling out questionable advice.

"We are not arguing. The truth is that we do not live together, so she is not expecting me this evening."

"You don't live together?" Travis said, his bellowing voice ringing in the empty hallway. "You're married but you don't live together? How the hell'd you manage that kind of arrangement?"

Corbin shifted and stuck his hand in his pocket. "We are not married. I never said we were married."

"Oh. Shit. Okay. Sorry. Let's go grab that beer."

Apparently grabbing a beer in Vegas meant doing it in a dark bar with glossy seats and women dancing around poles on a pink-lit stage.

Corbin stared at the brunette critically. She looked bored, and harbored a certain sense of entitlement. For every little shake and slide, she seemed to expect money. There was no effort, no emotion. Corbin felt as bored as she did. There was nothing enticing or appealing about a woman just gyrating naked. Where was the aura of sensuality? Where was the buildup, the tease, the hint at a woman's body, the titillation? This woman was naked, yes, but she was exuding as much sensuality as a stick.

Jason was staring hard at the blonde, who had breasts that were too round to be natural. "My wife used to have a body like that. Before the pregnancy. Rock-solid thighs, flat stomach, tits high and perky." He demonstrated by holding his hands up by his pectorals. "She wore a thong all the time. Now she wears granny underwear."

"That's rough," Travis said. "But don't worry, she'll get the bod back."

"We met at Hooters," Jason said. "She was a waitress. I was a cook. She used to lean in to pick up those burger orders and smile at me. That's all it took. I was gone. I really love her."

"That's beautiful, man," Travis said.

Corbin took a small sip of his beer and frowned. He liked Brittany's thongs. She was fond of bright colors, and he liked that little scrap of fabric on her fair skin. He would be sorry to see those disappear. "What is granny underwear?"

"You'll find out soon enough." Jason drained his beer bottle.

"They're underwear that cover everything. You know, like from here to here," Travis said, his arm moving from his thighs to his ribs. White, or maybe powder blue or pale pink, cotton, nasty stuff."

Corbin made a face. "Well, I suppose it is more comfortable for the women."

"Yeah, whatever." Travis nudged him. "So how come you and the old lady ain't living together? You break up or something?"

"We've never lived together. We're sort of only partially together . . . it's complicated."

"You can tell us."

They looked so sympathetic, that Corbin found himself divulging the situation. Leaving out the issue of his vampirism, of course. And a few other things. "We have only known each other a little over four months. We had met a few times, gone out." They had met exactly three times, and had never gone out, unless you chose to count the night he had dragged her onto the roof of the casino. That had been outside, but not really *out*. All in all, they had spent approximately forty minutes total together prior to his impregnating her.

"There was an immediate attraction between us, do you know what I mean? Fireworks." That was the whole truth.

They both nodded.

"Sure."

"Oh, yeah. That's how I felt when Sue used to bend over to pick up the onion rings. Like my pants were going to burn right off."

"*Exactement.*" Corbin understood that feeling perfectly. "That is exactly how it was. And we both felt it. So we acted on it."

"And . . ." Travis pressed him.

"And I didn't speak to her for eight weeks after." Which sounded really unmannerly when he said it out loud.

"Dude."

"Shit."

Precisely. "She came to see me to tell me she was expecting our child. I was taken a bit by surprise, to say the least."

"I fucking guess so." Travis shook his head. "So you're just trying to work it out with the kid? Good for you. It's always good for the kid when the parents get along if they're not together."

"Well . . . the problem is I have complicated the matter. After she told me about the child, I, well, we slept together again. So I thought . . . but now she doesn't seem to want to, well, anything, and I don't know if we are together, or separate, or what exactly it is that she wants from me."

Their expressions were almost comical, both their eyes and mouths twisted and contorted in sympathetic horror. Corbin felt better, just getting the words, his fears, out in the open. Maybe these men, who certainly had more experience with modern women than he did, would have some advice.

"You're screwed," Jason said.

Corbin frowned. "Well, what would you do if you were me?"

"Cry." Travis grinned at him.

"Run," Jason added, and they both laughed.

Not feeling too amused, Corbin took another sip of his drink, the bitter taste sliding over his tongue. "I want to work things out. It is very awkward the way it is now."

"So talk to her," Jason said. "But before you do that, you've got to know if you want to be with her or not. You do, you go in saying, 'We should be together.' If you don't, you say, 'Let's just keep it as friends and focus on the kid.' But you gotta be honest and you can't play around."

He did want to be with her. But Brittany had pulled back. Way back. And it was obviously still bothering her that he was a vampire. "I want to be with her, but I am not sure that is what she wants."

"So ask her." Jason turned back to the dancer on stage.

Corbin looked at Travis. "What do you think?"

"Don't look at me." Travis shrugged. "I don't know dick about women. My wife, she's a good woman, and she's having my baby and everything, but sometimes I think we should have just been friends. There's something missing, and I try to ignore it, but it's there, man. That feeling like something ain't right. I don't know." He drained his bottle of beer. "It's like she's my mother or something. It's weird."

That was weird. Way too weird for Corbin to even comment on. "Maybe it's just that your relationship has changed because of the baby. She has a different focus now, other than you."

Travis shrugged, and clapped him on the back. "We're a couple of fuck-ups, aren't we? Got good women and we're screwing it up."

"That is true." Corbin sat up straighter. "Maybe we should go to our women, yes, and show them that we appreciate them."

"I'm in." Jason waved his hand at the stripper, who looked like she could drop into a nap at any time. "These chicks have nothing on my wife. Sue is beautiful."

"Maybe you have a point." Travis pulled some money out of his pocket and put it on the table. "Wouldn't kill me to think about her feelings for a change. Shit, maybe I'll even grab her some flowers on the way home."

"Good plan." Jason nodded before finishing his own beer.

Corbin was going to pass on the flowers. Brittany hadn't seemed to appreciate his previous floral offerings. But he was going to find her and talk to her. Tell her how he felt. "I am going to go talk to Brittany."

He was standing up when he sensed another vampire in the room. Turning, he scanned the room, and was surprised as hell to see Gregor Chechikov, moving up to the bar, cigarette in hand. "*Excuse-moi*, I see an acquaintance."

"Catch you later." Travis punched Corbin in the arm and gave him his business card.

Jason shook his hand. "We should do this again sometime."

That actually pleased Corbin. He no longer had friends. It would be nice to have other men to talk to once in a while. Carrick and others in the current administration tolerated Corbin, but most vampires were suspicious of him. It made for a lonely existence. When they had all exchanged phone numbers and made plans to get together in a few weeks, Travis and Jason left and Corbin headed over to Gregor.

Corbin was still three feet away when Gregor said, "Atelier." He turned. "How interesting to see you here," he said in French.

"I could say the same for you, Chechikov. It was my understanding you were in St. Petersburg." He moved in next to Gregor and leaned against the bar counter, curious. Gregor hadn't left the continent in centuries, as far as Corbin knew. He was a big bear of a man, intimidating in both looks and nature, and had been a political associate of Vladimir of Kiev in the tenth century, involved in dealings with the Ottoman Empire. Once powerful in the Nation, richer than God, or at least Donald Trump, he had suddenly retreated from the political arena, before Corbin had even entered the world of the undead. Now Gregor stayed in St. Petersburg, quiet except for the money that he doled out to various causes and factions he supported, including Corbin's own research.

Gregor gave him a slight smile. "I decided to venture out for the election."

"The primary?" Corbin found it odd. Illogical. He did not like illogical. And he could have sworn Chechikov didn't have a party affiliation.

"Yes, and then for the final election as well. It proves to be interesting, and I have never been to Las Vegas."

Corbin realized that was the extent of the explanation he was going to get. "It is good to see you," he said politely. Truthfully, he didn't like Chechikov, and wasn't really sure why not, but he had to play nice since it was Gregor's rubles that funded his research. And with virtually no questions asked. Chechikov didn't seem to care what Corbin was doing in the lab, though he had expressed mild interest in gene manipulation in one of their infrequent phone conversations.

"You, too." Gregor raised his shot glass of clear liquid and tossed it back. He set it on the counter. "Now I'm off. I am staying at the Bellagio, if you would like to have dinner one night."

Dinner? Corbin nodded. "Certainly." Even though he was thinking it was utterly bizarre to receive such an invitation. He and Chechikov were not on those kinds of terms.

Apparently now they were.

As Chechikov headed for the front door, Corbin stared at him, feeling a small niggle of concern. Something was wrong. This was not a coincidence for Gregor to be in Vegas right as Carrick had won the primary and the opposing party's candidate was set to be announced.

The bartender asked Corbin if he wanted a drink and he

shook his head absently, puzzled, staring at the shot glass Gregor had used. Old habits died hard. Glancing around to assure no one was aware of him, he picked up a cocktail napkin. Wiping the rim all the way around, he folded the napkin, and tucked it into his pocket.

He might not have another opportunity to add Chechikov to his DNA database.

Nine

Ringo was pacing, strung out from the desire to get high, anxious as hell over Kelsey. No matter that he had never intended to come back for her. Now that he had, she wasn't there, and it worried him. He had returned to their room to get her after stopping at a restaurant and tossing back two shots of whiskey. It hadn't decreased his urge for something harder, something like what Donatelli had had in that cup. Heroin.

But the alcohol had made him bold, reckless. Desperate to get rid of the urge swirling inside him, he had fed four times, straight from the source, sucking his victims hard and fast, taking more than he should have to finally feel full. It hadn't worked, and he'd left four women dazed and disoriented in Central Park. It had made him feel guilty, which had pissed him off, and when he had returned to their crappy motel room and found Kelsey gone, he swiftly shifted his anger to her.

She wasn't supposed to go anywhere without him. This was why he hated dragging her around with him, like a fucking anchor around his neck. And where was the gratitude? He could have just left her, yet he'd gone back for her, and this was what he got? Shit. He had been just fine on his own, without all these complications. Pain in the fucking ass, that's what she was, had been since the first time he'd met her. He didn't know why he put up with her, didn't know why he kept her around, why he risked his neck for her. Didn't know why the hell he was worried about her.

Because she was a freaking fruitcake, that's why, and for whatever weird-ass reason, he cared about her. And damn it, he hated that. Hated it. He didn't want to care. Or worry. Or regret that he could never be the kind of man who would be good for her.

Ringo ripped the lamp off the nightstand, its cord tearing out of the socket, and tossed it against the wall above the dresser, where it shattered with a satisfying smash. He sent the other one flying after it. And pitched the ice bucket onto the floor. He was pulling out dresser drawers one by one and stomping them into bits with his boots when the door opened and Kelsey came in. The sight of her, safe, a frown on her beautiful face, filled him with relief and renewed rage.

"Where the fuck have you been?" he demanded, splintering wood beneath his feet with a sickening crack.

Kelsey came over to him in a rush, her hands fluttering out. "Ringo, stop that. We can't pay for that."

"So. What." He reached for another one.

Kelsey grabbed his arm to stop him. "Baby, what's the matter?" She stroked his skin, her voice soothing. "I'm sorry I left . . . I hope you weren't worried. I just went to feed. I wasn't sure how long you'd be gone, since you didn't leave a note or anything."

A note? Now he was supposed to leave a fucking note whenever he wanted to go anywhere? "You should have done what I told you to do and stayed here. You never listen to me, Kelsey!"

She moved in closer, sliding her leg along his, wincing like she'd felt a sudden pain. "Shh . . . yes, I do. I listen to you. Don't be mad at me, baby. You know I only want what makes you happy. I'm sorry."

Her lips were on his ear, hands moving over his arm, his chest. Ringo stood still, breathing hard, his anger untamed, anxiety and urges rising hot and fast and sick inside him. He felt out of control, and he worked to regain a semblance of it.

"Get away from me," he said, very carefully.

"Oh!" She made a sound of pain, and pulled back, tears instantly in her eyes.

"We're leaving here tonight," he said. "We're going back to Vegas." It had been a mistake to leave in the first place. It was too soon. He wasn't ready. He had fucked up his meeting with Donatelli, shown him he was still vulnerable. If Donatelli wanted to play, let him contact Ringo. He wasn't going after him again.

"I don't want to go back to Vegas. Everyone there is going to be mad at me. I didn't give Mr. Carrick two weeks' notice."

Kelsey looked scared, her arms wrapped around her middle, hidden in the bulky sweatshirt she was wearing. That was his sweatshirt, he realized. And he hated that he liked that she was in his clothes, hated that he liked the fact that she stuck with him, and hated that she looked so damn cute. Hated that she gave a crap about that pussy Carrick and her stupid job for him.

"You should have thought about that before you ran off and married me," he said ruthlessly, tossing the still intact drawer in his hands back onto the dresser. "Now we're going back and you're just going to have to deal with it." He was testing her, certain of what she'd say. "Unless you want to call it quits right now. Tear up the marriage certificate and go our separate ways."

Her eyes widened, her expression softened. "Why would I want to do that? I love you."

Then she was a fool. But he had known that all along. And he knew, even if he couldn't say it out loud, that he loved her, too, which really sucked.

"Are we leaving right now?" she asked, slowly bending over and gathering up the wood pieces and stacking them neatly by the garbage can. "I can pack our stuff in ten minutes."

Ringo rubbed his forehead. "Don't do that. Leave it there."

"It's no big deal, I'll be finished in two seconds."

"Get up!" he shouted, angry at the sight of her picking up after him.

She quickly stood up, wincing again. "What?" she asked, confused. "What is your problem? Someone needs to clean it up."

"I'll do it," he said, yanking her by the arm toward him. "And why are you acting like you're in pain?"

She turned her head away from him. "I just had an accident. I fell down some stairs."

"Really?" That sounded like less than the truth, but he wasn't interested in talking. "Even more reason you shouldn't be cleaning up after me. Are you alright?"

"I'm fine."

"Good. Because I need to fuck you right now."

Her eyes darkened. "Why?" she asked in a breathless voice, her demeanor instantly responding to his crass words, just like he knew it would.

Yanking the sweatshirt off over her head, he kissed and nipped along her jaw. "Because you belong to me, Kelsey. And I like that."

Her arms went around his neck and she ground her hips against his. "We belong to each other."

Ringo yanked her jeans and panties down. "God help us both."

And he pushed her against the closet door—the most convenient wall—unzipped, and slid into her with a shudder. She made those sounds, the ones he loved so much, the gasping and desperate mewls, as he thrust into her over and over again. When he was inside her, when there was nothing but them and their hard, needy pleasure, Ringo almost remembered what it was like to be human, could almost touch a time when he had been normal. Happy.

Because when he pushed in, at Kelsey, she took, and never wavered in her openness to him, and he sank into that, craved that, at the same time it scared the absolute shit out of him.

She came quickly, her leg wrapped around his, her eyes dilating with pleasure, and Ringo let go, gritted his teeth, and exploded inside her. When he stopped shuddering and pried his eyes open, he realized he had pushed his hand right through the closet door. Vampire strength. He still wasn't used to it, though he enjoyed the feeling of power it gave him.

"Shit," he said, with a little laugh, and pulled his hand out. Good thing he had Donatelli's wallet. He'd have to leave some cash for the damages.

His cell phone rang in his pants pocket, which was shoved down his thigh.

"Ring-a-ling," Kelsey said, sagging against the door and wiping her mouth, a satisfied smile on her face.

That made him laugh. Sometimes she said the stupidest things.

Reaching down, he retrieved the phone, and took the call. "Hello?"

"This is Donatelli. Twenty-five grand. That's as high as I'll go. And you'll have to collect the money in Vegas from Gregor Chechikov."

Ringo jerked up his pants. "You expect me to travel all the way back to Vegas with no guarantees? How do I know you won't just turn me in?" He had been planning the trip back anyway, but it made him uncomfortable that Donatelli was suggesting it.

"Because we'll be traveling together. And if you get caught, so do I. So do you want the money or not?"

"Sure." Ringo looked at Kelsey, who was shaking her head. "But you go first and we'll follow you. I don't think my wife enjoys your company, Donatelli." Her eyes went wide at the name.

"Well, she clearly has poor taste in men. Look at who she married."

"Fuck off," Ringo said mildly.

Donatelli laughed. "I'm leaving in an hour. Someone will meet you at four a.m. in front of the Bellagio. And don't try anything, Columbia. I know too much about your weaknesses for you to win in a battle with me."

"Likewise." Ringo hung up the phone and turned away from Kelsey, who looked ready to protest. "Save it, Kels. I don't need a lecture. I'm selling a bit of info to Donatelli, that's all. We need money to live off of. Now let's pack."

"He's a bad man," she said, in that creepy voice she used occasionally, the one where she sounded vacant and disembodied.

He hated that voice. "I'm no Boy Scout either, babe."

She made no move to pull up her pants, just stared at him. "No, you're not."

Disturbed, Ringo turned his back on her and pulled out his duffel bag, sorry he'd ever taken this damn trip.

"She's sleeping, go away," Alexis told Corbin when he knocked on the door of Brittany's apartment around eleven o'clock.

"I just want to speak to her for a moment," Corbin said, trying to look charming. He wanted to tell Brittany how he felt, that he wanted to be with her, wanted a real marriage, with love and affection, where they raised their child together in tandem. He wanted and needed to tell her that. Before he lost his courage. Sleeping could wait.

"So? Come back tomorrow when she's not in bed." Alexis started to close the door in his face.

He put his hand out and stopped it. "May I step in for just a moment? Check on her? She was not feeling well at the class this evening."

"Which is why she needs to sleep. What is it about that concept you are not understanding?" Brittany's sister glared at him.

"I am not going to wake her up. I just want to see her." He wasn't sure why he was pressing the issue, but he wanted, needed, to see her for himself. In addition to his feelings of excitement about their child and their potential relationship, he had an uncomfortable fear working at the back of his brain. He wanted reassurance she was all right.

Alexis sighed. "If I tell you to go to hell and leave, you're too polite to argue, right? You'll just go quietly."

"I do not think so," he told her, surprised to find that was true. He was not leaving without a look at Brittany. The fear was expanding, pulsing, and he would disregard manners to protect her. He didn't know what danger she could possibly be in, but he had to know all was well.

"Shit. I had a feeling you were going to say that." Alexis swung the door open. "Just for the record, I don't like you. And if you wake her up, I will hurt you."

Corbin was used to people not liking him. Normally, it didn't bother him. It was the price of his work, which he fully believed in and had no intention of stopping. But this was Brittany's sister. They were going to be forced into one another's company quite frequently.

He stepped inside the apartment. "What have I done to offend you?"

"You mean besides sleeping with my sister about two minutes after meeting her, not using birth control, blowing her off, then promising her you'd stick around for the long haul only to disappear for eight weeks? Besides that?"

Corbin stared at her defiantly. What did she know about his relationship with Brittany? Those were only the superficial facts, nothing more. "Yes, besides that."

His aplomb startled her. She frowned at him as she closed the door. "Then there's the fact that you killed a woman. Not to mention you're up to your eyeballs in controversial vampire research that smacks of all kinds of moral dilemmas. I'm just imagining frozen vampire embryos. God, think of the lawsuits. I wanted my sister to marry an accountant. I wanted her to have a normal life, with a normal husband, and a normal baby. She deserves that, damn it. I've worked my ass off to give that to her, and one whoo-hoo with you and it's all shot to hell."

Well, her feelings were entirely clear. Corbin let her finish her verbal vomit. She glared at him, and he stared back. "Anything else?"

"You're weird."

If he wasn't so angry, he might have laughed. Instead, he put his hands in his pockets, hoping to retain some level of control. "I refuse to defend myself. I slept with Brittany after barely knowing her, that is true. As is the fact that she slept with me after barely knowing me. I did not use birth control, neither did she. And afterward, it was mutually agreed we would not see each other again. Those are the facts, and they are none of your business. But since you have made them your business, I will only say that if you do not like your sister's choices, it is unfortunate. But out of your control. And what you want is entirely irrelevant. What is important is what Brittany wants, and what she deserves is happiness. Support. And you are not helping her achieve either by judging her actions, disapproving, and being mean-spirited with me." Corbin took a second, his anger threatening to get the better of him. "Now I am going to ask you to overlook my weirdness for your sister's sake."

With that, he moved past the pink chintz couch and headed for Brittany's bedroom.

"Damn," Alexis said behind him. "You have more balls than I thought, Atelier."

Corbin ignored her and opened the door softly. Brittany was asleep, like Alexis had promised, and she had pulled the comforter up over her stomach and shoulders in the chill December air. He could not see her shape, which was disappointing. He had wanted to see her in her nightclothes, or maybe in her panties, to see her body, see the belly his child was growing in. He hadn't seen her bare flesh in nine weeks and the changes had to be abundant.

Settling for brushing her new choppy hair off her forehead, Corbin sighed in relief. He had been hoping to ignore the realities, but seeing Chechikov had reminded him who he was, how they would never have a normal life. Not until he found the cure and turned his knowledge over to someone he could trust. Unfortunately, he had no idea who that person might be.

It was time to head back to his lab. He had lost two nights, and he needed to test his latest vaccine. He touched Brittany's warm shoulder, smelling her pumping blood and night sweats, listening to the sound of her steady heartbeat. Suddenly he realized he could hear a second tempo. The fast fluttery heart rate of their unborn child. Corbin stood stock still, awed. It sounded absolutely amazing, mother and child not in tandem, but unified, a whole. Both his.

Mon Dieu. He felt love for their baby swelling up in him, tangible, overwhelming.

Tearing himself away from her, Corbin retreated to the living room, his own heart swelled and beating faster than normal. There was a thick taste in his mouth, a glee and ecstasy rushing through him simultaneously, along with abundant fear. He moved quickly, urgently, as he left Brittany sleeping.

"Alexis, you have to protect her."

Alexis took a swallow from the glass of blood in her hand and looked at him with a hefty dose of suspicion. "From what?"

"I care about Brittany. I care about my child." Corbin felt his hands forming fists and he took a deep breath. "And while you are wrong about many things, you are right that my work is controversial. I don't know what the future holds, but I do know that if the wrong person finds out about the origin of your sister's baby, they won't hesitate to use our child for their own purposes. There are those who would see me dead, who are merely waiting for the completion of my research to attempt to kill me, and if I cannot protect Brittany, you must do it. You and your husband."

"I will kill anyone who touches Brittany. But why would they want her baby?"

Corbin glanced back at the bedroom door. "This child will be immortal, but have no need to drink blood. I have not told Brittany this because I don't want to scare her, but Carrick knows the truth. And I'm telling you because you are the first defense between Brittany and harm."

"Jesus Christ." Alexis's face was pale. "And you wonder why I don't like you?"

"No one must know the baby is mine. They must think it is just a mortal's child. Then I will marry Brittany so I am close enough to protect her, and see that no one learns the truth."

"Brittany's agreed to tell people the baby's father is Joe Blow?" Her expression indicated how doubtful she felt that was.

"I haven't told her she should. You know Brittany. I don't think she would agree to the deception." Corbin ran his hand through his hair. "I shouldn't have come back around so soon, but I wanted to see her. I couldn't stay away. I have very strong feelings for her."

Alexis looked horrified. "Oh, God, you're like in love with her, aren't you?"

"Possibly." He wasn't entirely sure what love felt like, but he definitely had some strong emotions regarding Brittany, feelings that had only grown in the eight weeks of separation.

"I suspect she feels the same way. So I guess I really am going to have to get over it and accept you. *Crap*." Alexis set her glass down on the coffee table with a loud plunk. "I'm not sure I can lie to her."

"You're going to have to." Corbin moved closer to her. "And tell me, do you know who Brittany's father is?"

"No. For the thousandth time, no. Ethan and Seamus have asked me that already." Alexis shook her head. "All I know is that my mother met him when she was working at a club. And I remember the day my father found out. My parents were arguing and he threatened to leave her, take the two of us with him. And she told him he could take me, but not Brittany, because she wasn't even his kid." She rolled her eyes. "Nice, huh? He called her a liar and she mentioned the fact that Brittany had black hair, if he hadn't noticed, while his was a dirty blond. So he called her a whore, she laughed, and said that Italians were known for being good lovers, unlike hillbillies from West Virginia. So he left, without me, I might add, despite her offer for him to take me. You think they would have kept their voices down, since I was sitting in the next room watching Care Bears, but . . ."

Corbin sucked in a breath.

Alexis's head snapped up.

He saw the moment she realized what she had said. "Italians . . . where did that come from? I never remembered that before . . . crap, what does that mean? I always thought it was my mother who was of Italian descent. That's where we got Baldizzi from—it was her maiden name."

"It means that either your mother was lying to irritate your father, she thought the man she slept with was Italian, or the man she slept with really was Italian." Corbin's mind was racing, trying to mentally sort through his database. Did he have any Italian vampires' DNA to do a comp? He had Brittany's hair from the night they had last spent together, and he had analyzed it weeks ago, but had only begun the laborious process of matching it against potential fathers. He had started with a group of European vampires, but that number was well over twelve hundred. He had only gone through three hundred, with no match. If he could isolate that grouping to Italians only . . .

They might know the answer to who Brittany's father was.

Then again, Corbin only had twenty percent of all vampires in his database. Since they were a seventy-five percent male population, that left over five thousand potential candidates still at large.

"How many vampires are Italian?"

"I'm not sure. Maybe a hundred. Two hundred."

"So what do we do, ask them all to take paternity tests? And why does it matter anyway?"

Corbin started pacing. "It matters because who that man is plays an important role in the political pull over our child, if it were ever to become common knowledge. That man, Brittany's biological father, could either protect or harm our child, or be utterly powerless to stop those who would. And it is important for simple genetics. If there is the presence of a particular gene in her father, it means our child will have unseen power and talents."

"It all sounds so awful I'm not sure which is the worst-case scenario. And how do we find out who our culprit is?"

"Run DNA, of course. And when members of the Nation register to vote, they list their nationalities. Wouldn't Seamus Fox have access to those type of records?"

"If it's on a computer, I bet Seamus could get to it." Alexis bit her fingernail. "Hey, just an FYI, for a while I was getting strange e-mails from a group claiming to be vampire slayers. It seemed hokey, and they've stopped now, but just so you know."

"Vampire slayers?" Corbin almost snorted. "That is a myth."

"Yeah, well, those e-mails weren't a myth. And maybe slayers aren't real, but some people are delusional enough to think it's real and jump on board."

"Just what we need. Vigilantes thrown into the mix." He fished his car keys out of his pocket. "Please tell Brittany that I stopped by and that I would like to speak with her."

"Do you want her to call you or what? Because last time I checked, she didn't even know where you live."

That drew him up short. "No?" That sounded terrible. That was wrong. "Do you have any paper? I will write down my address and phone number." He didn't have a cell phone because there was no one who would be calling him, but he did have a phone in his apartment.

"It's about time," Alexis muttered as she opened the drawer of the desk Brittany kept by the kitchen door. She pulled out paper and pen and handed them to him.

The memo pad said, *Bright Smiles by Dr. Brittany Baldizzi.* A big molar with a smiley face was next to it. It made him subconsciously rub his tongue over his teeth. He had never been to a dentist.

As he wrote, he asked, "Can you ask Seamus if he can retrieve that information? I will start running the data that I already have."

"Can't you just isolate a search by nationality already? If you can't, I can ask, but Seamus and I don't really get along. He won't do backflips to help me out."

"Is there anyone you do get along with?" he asked, genuinely curious.

"Brittany. And Ethan." She shrugged. "Most of the time. Cara. Kelsey. My friend from college, Judith. My old neighbor Bob, who is renting my old house for the winter so his mother can visit from South Dakota without actually living with him."

"You have a house?" That piqued Corbin's interest. Brittany had an apartment, as did he. She wanted a house, with a yard. "Does it have land with it?"

"Like a yard? Yeah, though it's mostly indigenous desert plants. No grass. I'll probably sell it when Bob's mom goes back north in the spring. Why?"

"Brittany would like us to live in a house, that is all. Perhaps I could purchase it from you for her."

Alexis grimaced as she took the paper from him. "Wow. We'll just be one big happy undead family, won't we?"

"We can only hope." Corbin sketched her a bow. "Now, *excuse-moi*. I am off to run that search through my database and to feed."

"That's special. The Cleavers have nothing on us, I'm telling you. We're the new All-American family."

"Zat is the plan." Corbin grinned, almost able to picture it. "We will be a family." But first he had a fertile vampire to unearth and a genetic mystery to solve.

Ten

Ringo stood in front of the fountain that rose majestically in front of the Bellagio. The water was a constant hum behind him, the pool lit with spotlights as he tried not to pace, his knee bouncing up and down nonetheless. Donatelli had told him to be there at four in the fucking morning and he was on time after a hard night's travel from New York.

Kelsey was across the street at a bar, afraid to go back to her apartment in the Ava, sure that Carrick had changed the key card. Ringo had to admit it was possible, and he didn't doubt that he'd been evicted from his own apartment months before, all his shit sold on eBay by his landlord. So he hadn't protested when Kelsey had insisted on accompanying him, because the truth was he wasn't sure what to do with her. The cash in Donatelli's wallet had covered their hotel and airline expenses, and that was it.

He hadn't wanted to use the credit cards and risk pissing the Italian off before Ringo could cash in on the serious prize.

Twenty-five grand. Donatelli had told him the Russian, Chechikov, would be handing the money over to him, and he was supposed to turn over the name of the woman carrying Atelier's baby. Easy.

So why did he feel like he was standing in a big-ass trap?

The December wind was chilly to mortals, and the few tourists hanging about were wearing jackets. It wouldn't be hard to hide a knife. Ringo was doing it himself. But it would be difficult for another vampire to cut his head off in the courtyard of the Bellagio, even if it was dark and the crowd was thin.

That didn't scare him. What scared him was the unknown. The idea that he didn't understand how to play the game with these powerful bastards, who had been dicking other vampires over for hundreds of years. Donatelli was a sick mother-fucker who knew there were worse things than death, and Ringo didn't want to fall in with any of that shit.

A woman caught Ringo's attention as she wandered around the fountain, taking pictures with a digital camera. She wasn't the usual tourist bundled in nylon and fleece. Wearing a long, black and green plaid coat tied tightly at her waist, fishnet stockings, and knee-high suede boots, she stood out in the handful of people hanging around, her walk, her manners, her dress screaming of wealth and sophistication. She was model thin, burgundy velvet gloves on her hands, and a white fuzzy purse on her shoulder, dark blond hair flowing over her shoulders under a fur hat.

She didn't seem to be aware of him, or anyone else around,

and Ringo watched her, intrigued. If she were a celebrity, she would have an entourage of bodyguards, assistants, paparazzi around her. If this were a modeling shoot, there would be cameras, a director, makeup artists. But she was clearly alone, and Ringo couldn't take his eyes from her. She wasn't hot, not in the way a stripper or a Hooters waitress or a Playboy bunny was, but she was exotic, exquisite, untouchable. And mortal.

The urge to seduce her, to draw her aside, and sink his teeth into her flawless flesh rushed through him. He wanted to taste her, to feel her give in to him, to see her eyes roll back with pleasure as he drew on her, taking her into him, her sweet rich blood running over his tongue and down his throat.

But he couldn't. He had to wait for Donatelli or Chechikov's errand boy. And he was married now, ring on his finger and everything. He didn't possess the self-control to stop at a taste of her blood. He would want a full sexual joining while he fed, and that was probably wrong. Kelsey didn't deserve that kind of disrespect, no matter how she got on his damn nerves. He knew that. But that didn't stop him from wanting this woman.

Especially since she was strolling toward him, tucking her camera back into her purse and extracting a thin gold cigarette case. She lifted her head, a cigarette between her lips, and Ringo sucked in a breath. Jesus. She was so goddamn gorgeous, her thick plump lips a raspberry color, skin creamy, cheeks pink from the chill, nose long and straight. But it was her eyes that distracted him, that made him almost forget why touching her would be wrong. Narrow, an intriguing oval shape, her eyes were a pale blue, a green ring dividing blue from the darkness of her pupils.

She smiled, gesturing to her cigarette. Ringo stuck his hand in his pocket and pulled out his lighter. He lit her cigarette, smelling the thick floral perfume she wore when her head bent to inhale. Turning slightly, she blew the smoke over his shoulder. If he was expecting a thank-you, he didn't get one. Nor did she move away.

"Are you alone?" he asked, thinking that a woman who looked like her couldn't be, nor should she be. Vegas was always awake, people usually everywhere at all times, and it was well lit, but that didn't mean it was smart to wander around alone at four in the morning.

Her nose wrinkled up and she said something in another language. Then she reached into her purse and pulled out a thick envelope, pressing it into his hands.

He accepted it automatically, a realization dawning on him. "Chechikov?" he said. It made sense. She looked Russian, a hint of Mongolian around her eyes, and that could have been Russian she'd spoken. But why was a mortal hanging out with an eccentric vampire?

"*Da.*" She nodded, not smiling, not frowning. Just serious now, solemn. She took his other hand, wrapped it around the envelope, squeezing. Then she pulled her hands back and said something quickly, words that sounded urgent.

Before he could react, say something, anything, she was gone, each foot moving so far in front of the other that she swayed, her hips moving like the sprawling concrete was a catwalk. Her hand came up, and she took a drag on her cigarette as she walked away, the click of her boots loud in the quiet night.

Ringo waited until she had disappeared around the fountain and headed into the lobby of the hotel, doors swallowing her, while he wondered who the hell she was and why she hadn't asked about Atelier's girlfriend.

Then he crossed the street to his wife with a boner, an envelope, and a hefty dose of suspicion.

Brittany patted her last patient of the day, Louise Zanderman, on the shoulder as she peeled off her gloves. "That wasn't so awful, was it? You can rinse and we'll have you out of here. Nothing hard or crunchy to eat for the rest of the day. We'll see you in five months for your next checkup and hopefully no cavities next time."

Louise, a pleasant woman in her fifties, spat aggressively. "I don't understand how I have any space left to even get cavities. My teeth are nothing but fillings. And the next time I'm here for my checkup, I imagine you'll be out on maternity leave."

Startled, Brittany touched her stomach. "You can tell I'm pregnant?"

Louise smiled at her. "Of course I can tell. You've always been thin. That little bubble popping out is not a big pasta dinner. It's a baby, about five months along, at best guess."

A happy flush filled her cheeks. "That's about right. But I

didn't realize people could tell . . . it's only been in the last two weeks or so that I've really popped."

Louise ripped off her paper dental bib. "Congratulations. Pregnancy seems to agree with you—you're glowing. Do you know what you're having?"

"No." At her last ultrasound, the technician had asked if she wanted to know, but it had seemed like a decision she shouldn't make without Corbin. Of course, he had been MIA at the time, with only weekly floral arrangements to prove he still existed, but she still hadn't been able to do it. She had wanted to believe they were in this pregnancy thing together. Still did. "I said I didn't want to know. I'm happy with either a boy or a girl."

"What does your husband think?" Louise sat up. "A lot of men want a boy that first time around."

"Oh, I don't think he cares about the sex." Brittany figured Corbin just wanted their child to be born without fangs. They weren't going to be picky about a penis.

Her dental hygienist, Sandra, came into the room and made notations in Louise's chart as she said, "Yeah, but now we don't know what to give you, Dr. B. You don't know if it's a boy or a girl, and you haven't even registered at the Baby Superstore."

"The baby isn't due for four months. There's plenty of time." To drag Corbin to the store and subject him to a baby registry. Brittany threw away her gloves and washed her hands as she pondered Corbin's reaction to a breast pump. Maybe she shouldn't take him after all.

Louise stood up and pulled her purse off the hook. "Yeah,

but you need to have the shower, see what you've gotten for gifts, then still have time to fill in the gaps yourself. And what if the baby comes early? You should be having the shower in your sixth month."

"See?" Sandra looked up at her in triumph. "Told you. You need to go register."

"I'm not even having a shower." Her only family was Alexis and her mother's sister, who contacted them only once in a blue moon. Her friends had scattered around the country, and her coworkers were wonderful, and she considered them friends, but she didn't want to put anyone out. Brittany smoothed her shirt down over her stomach. If anything, she needed to get maternity clothes. The two outfits she'd grabbed a few weeks earlier were not going to cut it. And her regular pants were now out of the question.

Sandra recoiled in horror. "No shower? That's . . . that's like blasphemy! You have to have one. *We're* having one. The office staff. So go register. Now."

The hygienist quivered with indignation as she poked her finger toward Brittany.

Louise told her, "I think you'd better go register."

Brittany laughed, touched by Sandra's vehemence. "Okay, yeesh. That's sweet of you all to do this for me."

She walked Louise out and came back to get her purse. Sandra was cleaning the room as she said, "Get your calendar out so we can pick a day. Maybe we'll go to Don Juan's across the street to have it after work one day. They have good food and a party room. And you *have* to bring the baby's father."

Oh, Lord. "I don't know . . . he's French. He doesn't always know what's going on when a lot of people are talking at the same time." Okay, that was a lie. But the visual of Corbin surrounded by females cooing over packs of pastel onesies was discomfiting. That might be blurring gender and class lines too much for her traditional vampire.

"What is there to know? You open gifts and pass them around. Hey, he got you pregnant. The least he can do is show up and haul everything out to the car."

There was something to that. He had gotten her pregnant. He shouldn't be exempt from all the details parenting involved. Like baby registries.

Corbin had left a message with Alexis the night before that he wanted to speak with her. Brittany had been planning to call him around nine o'clock or so, but she was starting to think she might just pop over to his place for an impromptu visit instead. She was curious to see where he lived. And some things might be better said in person.

Like a request that he appear at both her baby shower and her next doctor's appointment. That could take some convincing, no matter how many hours he'd spent in Baby Boot Camp.

Corbin lived in an opium den.

That was Brittany's astonished assessment when she walked into Corbin's apartment. On the outside, it was nothing special, just a concrete building on the fringe of downtown, built in the seventies. But inside, it looked like an East Asia silk retailer had exploded gold and ivory fabric everywhere, with a dash of scarlet tossed in occasionally for good measure. The furniture was all carved wood, a thick solid walnut color, low slung, and filled with pillows. The art was French, gilded, portraits of somber-faced women and men, a dog thrown in here and there. Books were stacked everywhere, which admittedly didn't match the opium den theory, but added to the jumbled eccentric feeling of the crowded room. Brittany could swear she smelled vanilla, as if Corbin had just baked a cake, but when she walked past his dining area, she saw six thick pillar candles burning in a multi-armed mosaic votive holder.

The man burned candles.

She wasn't sure what she had expected, but it wasn't this. Not this homey, overstuffed intensity. Minimalism would have matched her image of him, but now that she saw his apartment, she realized how right it was for him, and how much it pleased her. Her own place was an abundance of florals and kitsch.

"Sorry it is so dark in here. I don't open the draperies during the day and at night I have excellent vision." Corbin cleared his throat and gestured to the sofa. "Would you like to have a seat?"

He had reverted to formality. Maybe it hadn't been a good idea to pop in unannounced.

"Sure." She sank onto a satin sofa, nearly slipping right off it onto the floor. "Slippery little sucker." She gripped the armrest and laughed. "I like your apartment."

"Thank you. It is convenient to have my lab right here. I connected this apartment with the one next door." He gestured to an open door at the far end of the living room.

Brittany couldn't see inside it, but she was curious if it would look like a hospital lab, sterile and computerized, or if it had a Dr. Frankenstein quality to it. "That does sound convenient."

They both went silent.

Damn it, why were they doing this again? They took two steps forward, then six back. They had had sex. Twice. With lots of moaning involved. They were having a child together. And yet they sounded like two strangers forced to sit next to each other at a wedding reception.

"Alexis said you stopped by last night," she prompted.

"I wanted to make sure you were feeling all right."

"Yeah. I was just tired, I think. And that class was too much after a long day at work." She didn't mention the needle.

"I'm sorry."

This was painful. Brittany drummed her fingers on her knee. The night before, it had felt like they were close, like they had an understanding. Now? Nothing. He was blinking at her like an owl, his eyes darting to his lab several times. Clearly she had interrupted his work.

"Well, I'm on my way to go shopping. I need to get some maternity clothes for work and I just thought I'd stop by since you said you wanted to talk to me." Hint, hint. God, she wanted him to say something meaningful. Something real. Something that wasn't polite bullshit.

"Oh, I won't keep you then." Corbin stood up and pulled out his wallet. "Here, use this for your expenses." He tried to hand her a platinum Visa card.

For some reason, that both appalled and offended her. She

shook her head and didn't take it. "I don't need your credit card. I'm perfectly capable of paying for my own clothes." She and Alex were independent professional women. They didn't need men taking care of them. And he couldn't fob off his responsibilities by buying her maternity stretchy tops.

Even as her brain told her that wasn't rational, he was just trying to help, her emotions were careening out of control. "If you really wanted to help, you could go with me. I need to register for baby gifts and it might be nice if you helped me pick out some of the choices. And we'll probably need to get doubles of some things so you can keep them here at your apartment." She glanced around, suddenly seeing the room with new, irritated eyes. It was hard to imagine a baby crawling alongside a hardback of Dante's *Inferno*, playing with Chinese porcelain. "And this place isn't exactly childproofed."

"Have I done something wrong?" Corbin asked in bewilderment, still holding his credit card. "Why are you angry with me?"

Because he wasn't in love with her. Because they weren't married. Because she couldn't give her child the nuclear family she had craved so desperately when she was growing up.

"I'm not angry with you," she snapped. "I just drove all the way over here from Summerlin in crappy traffic because I thought you wanted to talk to me, and you're just staring at me. I hate this awkwardness. Either we are or we aren't dating. It's one or the other. Pick one now and forever hold your peace because I can't do this, not when I need to have my head wrapped around parenting."

Way to be rational. Brittany sucked in a breath and tried to stay still, confident, on the sofa. It was difficult to achieve when her ass kept sliding around on the satin, but she gripped the cushion and held on valiantly. She wanted to retain her dignity when he told her he had no intention of dating a lunatic like herself.

Corbin narrowed his eyes. Frowned. Then shocked the hell out of her by saying in a firm voice, "We are. That is what I wanted to talk to you about. We are together. Zat is zat."

He squatted down before she could say anything and grabbed the back of her head. Dragging her forward, Corbin gave her a hard, possessive kiss. She let go of the couch and oozed into his arms. Damn, it felt good there, flush up against his hard chest. He made her feel so sexy, so feminine. But Brittany yanked her mouth back and sucked in a breath. "What if I say we're not dating?" Not that she would. But he needed to know she wasn't some nineteenth-century sheltered miss. They were both going to wear pants in their relationship.

Given that his hand had started to wander over her nipple, Brittany didn't think he was taking her threat seriously. He kissed her earlobe and ran his lips over her jaw. "Then I will do whatever it takes to convince you that we should be together. I will be devoted to you and our child. I will go to any store you want, read any baby book you want, and prove my sincerity to you. I will come to you every night and pleasure you for hours and hours until you no longer know your name, until you can't imagine your bed without me in it. We will be together."

His lips brushed hers. "Forever."

Okay, she was gone. Melted like wax. He did it every time with that sensual arrogance, until she was ready to rip off her clothes and do the naked mambo with him. Like now. She kissed him back. He kissed her harder, taking her mouth with his tongue, sliding and dipping inside with intrusive demanding thrusts, his taste sweet.

Blame it on increased blood flow from pregnancy, but Brittany's inner thighs fired up. She was already reaching for his belt buckle when he pulled back.

"Let's go," he said.

"Where?" she asked stupidly, breathing hard. Corbin looked utterly unaffected by the lust she was feeling. Yet he could just glance at her and she wanted it. It was so bizarre.

"To the store. We are buying maternity clothes and doing the baby registry, yes?"

"You're going with me?" She gawked at him. The baby registry, maybe, she had been hopeful, but maternity clothes shopping? Even her sister had refused to do that with her. It was like trying to find a bathing suit—a painful fluorescent lesson in reality.

"Yes." He reached for her hand to help her up. "Zat is what you do when you are together, a man and a woman, and you are having a baby. You shop. And we are together. So we will shop."

The logic was there.

But Brittany wasn't sure their unusual circumstances qualified them as a standard couple. On the other hand, normal was relative, and she was damn frightened to attempt purchasing a nursing bra all on her own.

"Baby Superstore, here we come," she said.

Bled Dry

Corbin sat on the bench outside the fitting room at the maternity shop and wondered how honest he should be.

Brittany had such a pleasing figure, long and shapely, that he would have thought her capable of wearing just about anything, but clearly he had been wrong. The black stretchy pants she had on seemed to shrink her by six inches, clung to her backside, and brought much more attention to the apex of her thighs than he could tolerate in a public setting.

"What do you think? They're very comfortable, but I think my butt looks big in these."

This was a test. Corbin felt sweat creeping down his back. "I don't care for the color."

"They're black." She frowned at him. "How can you not like black?" She twisted in front of the mirror again, trying to get a better view of her behind.

"Your feet are going to be cold." He shifted on the bench, waving away the saleswoman who had brought three more pairs of the stretchy pants in various colors. The black was bad enough. They sure in hell did not need them in pink.

"That's true. Though it seems like I'm hot all the time lately." Brittany twisted yet again, in the opposite direction.

He fought the urge to sigh. So he was bored and uncomfortable, feeling as though one wrong word might set her screaming at him. He didn't imagine she was having fun either, and she seemed to need a second opinion. This was his duty. A painful, onerous duty.

The store was stuffy and close. Brittany's pile of "maybes" was in his lap. Her cheeks were flushed, her hair askew, and he knew now why she had been avoiding the chore. For every seventeen things she tried on, she found one item that both fit and she liked. It was hell on earth, filled with mirrors and hangers and sensor tags.

It was endless. Interminable. The questions were all incendiary:

"Why do my boobs look so huge?"

"Do you think these pants are mislabeled? They're really tight."

"What's my best color?"

"Why is my nose so shiny?"

And worst of all, an hour and thirty minutes into the torture, a plaintive plea, made with big eyes and a trembling lip, "You don't like my hair short, do you? I made a huge mistake cutting it, didn't I?"

Corbin stood up and set the piles of clothes onto the bench and moved toward her. He cupped her cheeks with his hands and brushed a kiss on her soft lips. "I love your hair," he told her truthfully. If he had loved it more longer, no matter. "I love your body, I love your heart, the way you embrace life, your optimism, your passion, your tenderness, and selflessness." He rested his hand on her belly, swelling slightly beneath the cotton shirt she had put on. "I love that you are the mother of my child."

I love you, he almost added, but the words stuck in his throat. It would sound like a balm, like a token gesture if he said it now, and he wasn't sure if he even meant it exactly. He thought he did, but how was one really sure about these things?

Everything he spoke, he meant, and best to leave it at that.

She sniffled. "What the hell has happened to me? I'm never like this. But now I walk around feeling like I just got my eyebrows waxed. Stunned and watery-eyed. It's so annoying."

"I think it is called hormones." He tucked her short hair behind her ear.

She promptly popped it back out. "Don't do that. I hate the way it feels." Then she immediately made a face. "Ugh. Listen to me. I sound so bitchy and whiny."

Her words, not his. Corbin decided he needed to take control of the situation. "This is exhausting, that's all. We've done enough for today." He plucked at the pants she was wearing. "I don't like these as much as the others. Leave this pair and get the jeans." Turning, he gathered up what she'd piled on his lap. "You have four outfits here, plus you can wear some of the items together. It is enough for tonight."

She looked relieved to have him making decisions. Nodding, she headed back for the fitting room. "I'll just try on the bras then, because I have to get a couple of new ones. I'm going to suffocate in my old ones."

Corbin flagged down the saleswoman and handed her the pile. "Can you start ringing these up, please?" So they could get the hell out of there.

"Corbin?" Brittany called from behind the closed door. "I need some help."

"Do you need a different size? Pass it over and I'll get the clerk."

"No, I need you to adjust these straps." The door opened

a crack and her face peeked out. "Can you just slip in here with me?"

That did not seem appropriate in the least for him to join her inside the fitting room in full view of anyone in the store, but this was not Regency England, but Vegas in the twenty-first century. At times he had to remind himself the same rules of etiquette did not apply.

He went into the fitting room, squeezing himself in sideways so he wouldn't expose her to the room at large. Brittany was standing there in her panties and a bra with the tags dangling from it, her hands holding straps that were clearly too loose. It was nice to see she hadn't gone to what Justin had called granny panties yet. She was wearing a black thong. That was good. But it was bad that he suddenly had an erection wholly inappropriate for the setting.

"What do you need me to do?" he asked, trying not to stare at her burgeoning breasts. Her smooth thighs. Her bare, tight backside, reflected clearly in the mirror. The triangle of her black panties hugging her femininity in front. Corbin's mouth went dry and his fangs let down.

"Just adjust the little white clip thing and make the straps shorter. It's all the way in the back and I can't reach it."

She turned around, holding the straps where she wanted them, so he could see the excess length gaping. Swallowing hard, he studied the little prongs and tried to determine how they worked. The sound of her breathing, the beating of her heart, were distracting him. And he would swear on his mother's grave that he was catching the scent of arousal from her. She was *enjoying* standing nearly naked in front of him.

The thought increased his own ardor. Nine weeks was not a long time for a vampire, but it felt like forever, plus one day, for Corbin. He could not wait another minute to touch Brittany, to feel her skin, to taste her rushing, vibrant blood.

Moving the prong upward, he shortened the length of the strap, brushing his fingers over her flesh as he went to the other. He adjusted it as well, then looked at her in the mirror. "How does that feel?"

"It's better," she said, voice a little husky.

With his index finger he reached around and traced the outline of the bra, above the cotton, where her flesh was spilling forward. "You are sure it es not too small?"

"I don't think so. It feels comfortable."

Corbin flipped the straps down her shoulders. "Maybe you should try another to be certain." Undoing the back hook, he stripped it off her efficiently.

Her breath caught and she met his gaze in the mirror. "I did pick out a black one, too."

Tossing the bra over the door to dangle there, Corbin stared at Brittany reflected in front of him. "You're gorgeous," he told her, moving his hands to cup her firm breasts. He kissed her shoulder, and ran his touch down to her belly, swollen in an intriguing bubble. "I thought you were sexy before, but now, with my child inside you, I am speechless at how beautiful you are."

Her eyes drifted close as he caressed over her flesh. "Thank you. I feel really good right now . . . I've heard the middle trimester is the easiest. We should probably take advantage of that."

That sounded like an invitation to him. Corbin teased her

panties forward and slipped a finger down, down, right into her welcoming moist body. He had been right about her arousal. She was ready for him. Brittany gave a soft gasp.

"Let's take advantage of that right now," he said.

"Here?" She sounded shocked, but her hips began to move, ever so slowly, rocking herself onto his finger. "I don't know . . ."

It wasn't a convincing protest, so Corbin peeled her panties down, kissing the back of her neck. "You feel so good. I have missed you."

The panties hit the floor with a soft thump and Corbin yanked off his shirt, unzipped his pants so he could feel his body against hers. When his skin touched hers, his chest to her back, he closed his eyes, reveled in the way she felt, his senses on high alert.

He moved his finger inside her, nudging her thighs apart. Brittany's breathing was tight, stifled, quicker and quicker as he stroked faster and deeper. Her backside pressed against his erection, and he wanted her fiercely, wanted her with a primal irrational intensity. It had been like this the first night with her, and the second, and now again . . . it was different than with other women, unsophisticated, raw, reckless. He was different.

"Corbin," she whispered. "I can't help it, I'm going to . . ."

Opening his eyes to catch the view, he watched her climax in the mirror, saw how her fingers fluttered toward the wall, enjoyed the way she bit her lip to hold back her cry, watched the graceful curve of her neck as her head tilted back. Her jugular pulsed violently, her heartbeat fast and erratic to his vampire ears. A beautiful, amazing sight, and a satisfying thing to know he could make her feel that way, that he could coax her naked in a fitting room, that he, and he alone, had planted a seed in her womb and brought a child to life.

She was his.

And as he entered her from behind, sliding his aching cock into her softness, he bit her shoulder, holding her in place, keeping her locked to him, with him, together. A soft moan escaped her, and Corbin would have responded in kind except he was tasting her blood, drowning in the ecstasy of blending her with him everywhere, burying himself in her thighs while his teeth sank into her vein. He wouldn't take too much, because of the baby, but just enough to slide her taste past his lips and tongue, enough to feel their thoughts intermingle.

There weren't coherent sentences emerging from Brittany, but thoughts and feelings. He could hear, feel, sense pleasure, wonder, hope emanating from her in wave after wave.

Brittany, he murmured in his head, wanting to see if that bond between them, strangely absent in recent months, was there, intact. *Do you like the way I feel inside you?*

Yes, she answered, clearly and immediately. *I really like it. You have the most amazing cock.*

Corbin broke his bite and groaned out loud, feeling his body tighten as he thrust harder. What man wouldn't want to hear *that?* She could be lying, ego stroking, reciting a line from a pornographic film, he didn't care. Her words sent him crashing into an orgasm, his fingers digging into her thighs.

"Brittany," he groaned as he pushed forward, knocking her into the mirror, her hands and forehead slapping the glass. "Beautiful Brittany."

Her lips moved, no sound emanating, as she had another small orgasm, her body clenching his, coaxing his climax to linger. He was slowing down, but unwilling to retreat from the warmth of her entirely when a knock on the door made them both jump.

"Is everything okay?" the salesclerk asked.

"Fine," he said, his voice coming out in a growl.

"Then could you leave the fitting room, sir? It's not really good for business."

Brittany gave a soft laugh. "Whoops. We got carried away, didn't we?"

"I am helping her try on ze clothes," Corbin said with as much dignity as he could muster with his manhood still out of his pants.

"Um-hm," was the clerk's response.

Corbin licked Brittany's shoulder to heal the puncture wounds he had made and pulled back with both satisfaction and regret. They would have to continue this at home.

She bent over and scooped up her panties. "I feel ready to take on the Baby Superstore now. That was very relaxing."

Relaxing? Corbin felt tight everywhere, like his pants had shrunk. He did not want to shop for baby bottles. He wanted to take Brittany home and make love to her slowly and skillfully all night long.

"Ze Baby Superstore?" He wiped his mouth and zipped, handing her the jeans she'd been wearing from the hook on the door.

"Yes. It's so much easier to register now. All we have to do is scan and go. Piece of cake."

Eleven

Nothing was a piece of cake with Corbin. Brittany scratched her itchy stomach through her shirt and watched her bloodsucking boyfriend assess car seats. After his initial exclamation of, "Why the hell are there so many?" he had methodically started at one end and was reading the features of each seat.

Fortunately, he read quickly, his lips moving as he ticked them off down the line. Halfway through the twenty models, he looked at her and said, "When I was a boy, my nanny just held me on her lap."

"Unless you're a celebrity, that will get you arrested nowadays." She really wanted to tell him to just pick one, damn it, but she'd already tried that in the baby monitor aisle and had mortally wounded his feelings. Even worse, it hadn't made him move any faster. Apparently vampires were used to disposable

time, because Corbin moved like molasses uphill in a snow-
storm.

"I think this one is too masculine. What if it is a girl?" He
gestured to the stripped navy blue car seat.

Brittany didn't think she cared, really. It wasn't like their
daughter was going to have a gender crisis because her car seat
was blue, and besides, she didn't believe in encouraging those
kinds of stereotypes. But if it helped him narrow the list down,
she'd be down with blue. "Good point."

"Then again, on the other hand, this has the highest safety
ranking."

If he weren't so damn adorable, Brittany would be sorry
she'd brought him. But he *was* adorable. He was so sweet and
concentrating so hard, so flippin' cute, that she wanted to just
eat him up whole. How lucky could she be? She'd had unprotected sex with a vampire she barely knew from Adam and gotten pregnant, not an auspicious beginning. But not only had he
stepped up to the plate to accept his responsibility, he was giving her hot fitting room sex and debating the pros and cons of
car seats like they were sinking half a million dollars into buying a house, not spending a hundred on a carrier seat they'd use
for a whopping six months. Because he cared about their baby's
safety. Swoon.

Not every girl pregnant by a vampire was going to be that
lucky, you know.

But it still made for a long night. Thank God the store was
open until midnight. She would have previously wondered who
shopped for baby supplies at eleven at night, but now she had

her answer. Tired fathers buying formula and diapers, stressed-out mothers dashing in to pick up infant Tylenol, crying, red-faced babies in their arms, and pregnant dentists whose undead partners slept all day long.

When Corbin had narrowed it down to three models, he asked her opinion. "Which one?"

"I think this one," she said, pointing to one at random, liking its earthy tone.

"It looks more difficult to maneuver than the others," he said with a frown.

"Then this one." She pointed to the green one.

"The canopy doesn't extend as far."

"Then how about this one?" She pointed to the last remaining one, two models down from the others.

He nodded. "Good choice."

Brittany almost rolled her eyes. Instead, she just handed him the scanner. He was really enjoying adding items to their registry with the little wand. Clicking the button and capturing the bar code brought a smile to his face every time he used it. Now he wielded the wand like a saber and slashed through the air, scanning at an angle.

"There. It es on ze list."

Men never changed. They could turn anything into a toy or a weapon.

"Zap one of those headrest things while you're at it." There were only three choices, all looking very nearly the same. "Just pick the cheapest one."

To her amazement, he actually complied. "On to ze high

chairs," he said, consulting the New Parent checklist he had in his other hand.

Brittany noticed that the intense concentration of baby registry sign-up had impacted his English. He sounded fresh from Paris. Not that his vocabulary in English was lacking, because the extensiveness of that constantly amazed her. But he could never entirely shed his accent. It suddenly made her wonder if he would teach their baby French. How cool. Her baby would be bilingual. So when her child was annoyed with her that she had to clean her room, she could bitch about it in French and Brittany would never know what she was saying. Maybe not such a good thing after all.

"Who exactly is going to purchase these items for us? I still do not understand why we don't just buy them ourselves," he said as he ran his hand over a contemporary white high chair.

"Where does your money come from, Corbin?" she blurted out, suddenly curious.

He shrugged. "Family money. We were very wealthy in the nineteenth century and I was the last of the line, so it all came to me upon my parents' death. I have lived modestly, the money has grown through investments. My research is funded by an ancient vampire, so I do not spend my personal money. I am very wealthy. Perfectly capable of seeing to all the needs of our infant."

He looked offended so she put out her hand. "Chill out. I wasn't implying you couldn't. I was just curious. And the whole point of registering is so people can buy us gifts. It's tradition. People want to give gifts when you have your first child. Everyone at my office will be giving me gifts, and Ethan and Alexis will want to buy us something, and my college friends, my next-door neighbor, your vampire friends . . ."

Making a face, Corbin said, "I do not have any friends." He moved down the row. "Not these. Neither of us has this type of furnishing. We are more traditional."

Brittany felt her heart swell. She hadn't meant to remind him of his loneliness. She hadn't even realized the truth of what he had just said. Yes, Alexis, Ethan, and Cara had all told her Corbin was not accepted by most vampires, but she had figured he had some friends or comrades tucked away somewhere. She knew he was something of a loner, but that had always seemed like his choice to her. Now she understood that no matter what a certain eccentric scientist insisted, he missed simple companionship.

Going after him, she touched his arm. "Hey. I'm your friend."

Corbin smiled back at her, his thumb stroking across her cheek. "That you are. And it is a gift. I used to have friends, you know, when I was mortal. Even as a young vampire. But then, everyone died. And I didn't bother to make new ones." Corbin dropped his hand. "But I am grateful for your friendship. I did not realize how much I missed that."

I love you, she wanted to say, knowing that she did, that Corbin was different, her feelings for him unique and deep, but she clamped her lips shut. It would sound like she was trying to make him feel better, like it was a declaration brought about by pity, not true feelings. She wished they could still read each other's thoughts so he would see the truth in her heart, her head, her words written across her consciousness. But for some reason, since the two-month separation they'd had, she hadn't been able to hear him. Except for when they were having sex. And she didn't think he heard her either, which bothered her.

"All work and no play isn't good for anyone, not even a vampire. Don't worry, I'm going to be dragging you out of the house a lot." That should reassure him. She almost laughed at the look on his face.

"You are too kind," he said dryly. Then he turned to a mahogany high chair. "This one?"

"Yes. It's lovely." And matched both of their distinct decors.

Damn, they got along so well. They were like poster children for mortal-vampire parents who weren't married.

Brittany grinned when Corbin aggressively zapped with the scanner.

Everything was going to be *so* fine.

"What do you mean, your sister will be here in an hour?" Alexis looked around their apartment and tried not to panic. She was a crappy housekeeper. There were papers everywhere, bills piling up, a Wal-Mart bag full of toiletries on the breakfast bar, and various piles of laundry dotting the couch. "Brittany just asked if you could call Gwenna yesterday!"

"Actually, I invited her to visit several months ago, after you suggested that very thing. I thought you'd be pleased. This will give Brittany a chance to talk to her."

Men. "A little warning would be nice! The apartment's a wreck and so am I."

Ethan looked baffled. "I don't think Gwenna will care if we haven't run the sweeper all week."

There was no time to argue with him about female dynamics and making a good first impression. She went into action, scooping up the laundry piles and tossing them willy-nilly into the basket. "Pick up all that paperwork! Shove it in a drawer or something or at least stack it all in one pile."

Running into the bedroom, Alexis tossed the basket in their closet and slammed the door shut. Damn it. Their bed wasn't even made. She whipped the comforter over the whole mess of rumpled sheets and smoothed it flat. Tossing pillows on top, she ran back and grabbed the Wal-Mart bag, tossing her hair out of her eyes. She needed to jump in the shower.

Ethan was neatly and carefully arranging his paperwork with zero sense of urgency. She was about to use aggressive karate persuasion to encourage him along when the doorbell rang.

"Oh, shit." That couldn't be her.

"It's her," Ethan said, looking delighted. "I can sense her."

Great. Now instead of just a messy house, she was all sweaty and wearing sweatpants with a messy house, when she officially met her sister-in-law. They hadn't really talked at the wedding. Gwenna had popped in and out without ever saying hello. Alexis ditched the bag of shampoo and deodorant in a kitchen cabinet. Not that she needed deodorant these days, but habits died hard. She felt naked without it. Attempting to finger-brush her hair was futile, but she did it anyway and pasted a smile on her face.

Ethan opened the door and ushered his sister into the apartment, giving her a big hug. "Gwenna. Alex and I are so glad you came."

Gwenna hugged him back, but it was reserved, impatient. Alexis thought she looked as pale and tragic as she did at their wedding, but there was something different about her, the way she stood up straighter. When she pulled back from Ethan, her wavy blond hair fell away from her face and revealed an expression of concern, fear.

"Is everything okay?" Alexis asked, suddenly worried herself.

Gwenna came to her, hands out. She clasped Alexis's sturdy hands in her delicate ones, and looked up at her. She had pink lips, the color an almost feverish contrast to her fair skin. "Roberto is back. And he knows about the baby."

"You are back earlier than we had agreed on." Chechikov gave him a cool look over his glass of vodka.

Roberto Donatelli wasn't intimidated. "I have personal interests to see to. And no one has to know that I'm here. I left my ankle band on my man Smith. I was shocked at how easy it was to remove. Law and order in the Nation has clearly suffered under Carrick's rule." He crossed one leg over the other, admiring Chechikov's suite in the Bellagio. He was impressed with the understated elegance, furnishings done in soft blues and doeskin brown. "I imagine that someone could even get away with murder and it would go unpunished."

"No doubt." Chechikov tossed back his drink. "That is why

I am here. That is why my name is going on the presidential ballot. It is time for me to restore the Nation to its former glory."

Donatelli approved of the end, though he had hoped the means would be him, not Chechikov. But he had allowed himself to be outmaneuvered by Carrick and Fox and had left the presidential race. He had underestimated Fox's feelings for the stripper Cara, and had almost found himself without a head. He wouldn't make that mistake again. "You know I am at your disposal."

Chechikov had been a reliable ally for two hundred years, and Donatelli had benefited from their arrangement, both financially and politically.

Now Gregor nodded to acknowledge Donatelli's words. "And I appreciate your sharing the news about Atelier's progeny."

"Who is the mother?" Donatelli asked, curious. If Atelier was fucking around with a mortal, then he couldn't be sleeping with Gwenna, as that little bitch Kelsey had implied. The thought of Gwenna in bed with that radical set his teeth on edge and made his anger flare. But if Atelier had an Impure plaything, he couldn't be involved with Gwenna. Two women was not the Frenchman's style.

"Ah, but that is interesting. Your little informant did not share the name with my wife, but it is of no matter because I have been doing a bit of investigating since I came to Las Vegas. It seems that Alexis Baldizzi-Carrick, first lady of the Nation, has a sister who is an Impure. Who is pregnant."

"If it was that easy to find out about the sister, why did we pay Ringo Columbia?"

"It was a thank-you gesture, that is all. We would not have connected the dots without your informant."

"But how do you know Brittany Baldizzi's child is Atelier's?"

"She was seen in the company of Atelier two nights ago attending classes at the hospital—childbirth classes. Very, very careless of him. I'm surprised he isn't showing more discretion."

That was surprising. Atelier wasn't stupid, nor was he social. "Maybe the child isn't his. Maybe he is playing up to Carrick for special favors."

"By going to childbirth classes?" Gregor scoffed. "No, the baby is his."

"That doesn't explain his carelessness."

"Perhaps he fancies himself in love with the girl." Gregor smirked.

Donatelli didn't return the grin. He knew all too well how idiotic a man could act when he allowed himself to feel emotion for a woman. That was why he was in town, risking his own neck, at that very moment. He had never been able to control his feelings toward Gwenna. Not since the first day he'd laid eyes on her nine hundred years before. She made him insane, with want, with greed, lust, anger. Love.

"Perhaps. And speaking of love, may I offer my congratulations on your marriage? Your wife must be absolutely charming to have coaxed you down the aisle, Gregor." Roberto had caught a glimpse of long legs and flowing hair heading into the bedroom of the suite when he had entered, but he hadn't seen her face.

Chechikov shrugged. "Sasha was something of a gift. And she'll serve me well as we hit the campaign trail. A Master Vampire with a mortal wife—everyone will assume it is love." His eyebrow went up in a way that made Donatelli's skin crawl. "I'm a very romantic kind of man, you know, Donatelli. Did I ever tell you about my days serving the Prince of Kiev and how it was my duty to crush rebellions in the countryside?"

"No." What the hell was the old lunatic talking about? Donatelli shifted in the plush club chair.

"I was known as the Black Bear, and men shook in fear when they saw me riding in with my warriors, as well they should have. We would kill them all, one by one, as a lesson for the next village, the next man who dared to defy the Prince, and after the men were all dead in the dirt, I took their filthy toothless women, one after the other, then let my men have them as well. If that isn't romance, I don't know what is." He smiled, eyes unfocused, as if he was remembering with fondness his youthful exploits.

Donatelli kept his expression impassive, even as his stomach flipped over. He had never known quite how sick Chechikov was. And while Roberto had done what he had to to survive—had lied, manipulated, used violence and mind control, and subjugated others—he had never raped a woman. Never would. Every man had his moral boundaries, and that was Donatelli's. Murder he could stomach if it was justified; humiliation, torture, sure. But rape crossed the line.

"Now you'll have to settle for the presidency. Not nearly as exciting."

"True. But the power is the same, and the power is what I enjoy."

Didn't they all.

Corbin was high on the power of the scanner and the growing rapport between himself and Brittany. They were comfortable with each other in a way that had been missing previously, and it was pleasant, fun to be with her, while they made decisions about innumerable baby products, and laughed together at the ludicrousness of black leather jackets for infants.

They had registered for approximately nine thousand baby products, which led Corbin to wonder how human beings even managed to sustain themselves as a race if that much effort and expense went into their first year of life. But he had to confess, after the initial stress of too many options, he had enjoyed picking products out, and had even found himself with a sudden inexplicable attachment to the stars and moon nursery theme, picking the pattern whenever it was an option. Brittany had teased him about it, but she hadn't protested, and had let him register for the whole bedding set, draperies, and wallpaper border. He thought perhaps it was his need for his child to appreciate the night, his father's world. Or maybe he just liked the yellow stars. He wasn't sure. He just knew he was grateful to be a part of the minutiae regarding his child, knew that suddenly everything felt important and wonderful and hopeful.

It was all those complex, myriad, and amazing feelings coursing through him that prompted Corbin to say to Brittany in the car, "Spend the night with me."

She glanced over at him, leaning against the passenger door. "I have to go to work tomorrow. It's already really late."

He noticed then that she had circles under her eyes from fatigue, and she was leaning out of pure sleepiness. Even more reason he didn't want to take her home. It would make him feel better to watch over her, ensure she was safe. He had work to do, and needed to feed, but he liked the idea of placing her in his bed, hearing her breathe while he was in the next room.

Raising his eyebrows up and down, he shot a grin at her before refocusing on the road. "I do not have designs on your person, *ma chérie*. I have already had that delight once tonight. But I am not ready to part from you. Does that make sense to you? I would just like you near me."

It was the right thing to say. Her expression softened. "Oh. I do know what you mean. And I did buy that sleep shirt from the maternity store . . ."

"Then it's settled. We're much closer to my apartment anyway." Pausing at a red light, he asked her, "Do you think it's a girl or a boy?"

"I don't know. I don't have any sense one way or the other."

"I think it is a girl," he said. There was no reason why he felt that way, he just did. And it was a new feeling to realize that for the first time in a long time, a great deal of his thoughts revolved around someone other than himself, and that he and Brittany shared a focus, shared the secret of their child. "What shall we name her?"

"God, I have no idea. There are a million choices." She sighed, a good content sigh. "A girl would be nice. But so would a boy. I just want our baby to be healthy."

"She will be." Corbin couldn't guarantee that, any more

than the average father to be, but he didn't want Brittany to worry. He didn't want to worry. He only wanted to discover who Brittany's father was and test his vaccine, which he was sure was ready. Action was better than sitting back waiting for disaster. "And I am fond of the name Renee."

"That's a nice name," Brittany said in a voice that indicated she'd name their child Monkey before she'd choose Renee. "I was kind of thinking of the name Coco, though."

Corbin was horrified. "That is a dog's name. It is not dignified. And I thought you said you had no ideas, no preferences."

"It worked for Coco Chanel."

That did not make it any less of a poodle's name. "What about Chantal? Marie?"

"Does it have to be French?"

That took him aback. *Mais oui* was his first reaction. But he supposed that was a bit inflexible. "It would please me, but it is not a requirement. It is a decision we should make together."

"We have plenty of time. And we should pick a boy name, too, just in case you're wrong." She patted his leg. "It can happen, you know. You being wrong."

Was she calling him arrogant? Corbin frowned. "Occasionally. But not very often."

She laughed as they pulled into his apartment complex. Looking at the area in the dark, Corbin realized it was a bit shabby, not the safest neighborhood, lingering on the fringes of a crime-ridden neighborhood. But he had chosen it for its proximity to downtown and the casinos, and crime didn't bother him. He'd yet to meet a mortal man, gun or no gun, who was a match for his vampiric strength and speed.

Yet it wasn't the place to bring Brittany to at midnight. Nor should he be raising a child in this area, not when he had the means to move.

Parking the car, he turned to her, and took her hand. His expression must have been serious, because her laughter died. "What? What's wrong?"

He caressed her fingers in his. "Marry me. Let's buy a house and really start a life together."

Her eyebrows shot up. "Just a few hours ago we agreed to officially be dating . . . now you want to get married?"

"Yes." When put that way, it sounded a little less than rational, but his conviction did not change. "And if you recall, I have always wanted to get married."

"You're insane. You're more impulsive than me. And I swear, that's why I like you so much."

Corbin liked to think he was intuitive, not impulsive. He was a scientist. He did his work slowly and methodically, yes, but he also went with what modern slang called the gut instinct. It had served him in research, and he was certain it was right once again.

They *had* to get married.

"I don't want to do something crazy . . . I need to think . . ."

Knowing when to retreat, he kissed her forehead. "That you consider it is all I ask. We are good together."

And they would stay together. He would do anything to ensure that.

Twelve

Maybe they *should* move in together.

Brittany lay in bed beside Corbin, knowing she needed to get up, go home, shower, head to the office.

But she was still sleepy, languid, warm under the comforter. And Corbin had just returned to bed for the day, and he was already asleep, his breathing steady, mouth slightly open. She liked being next to him and didn't want to leave. It had been very nice to be waking up, dozing in and out as he had stripped down to his boxer shorts, climbed under the sheets, and given her a soft kiss. Just like it had felt comforting, safe, to go to sleep knowing he was working in the next room.

It felt right.

Maybe they could modify his marriage idea to cohabitation. It would be good to have several months together in that kind of

intimate relationship before the baby arrived. Brittany was willing to take the plunge. She'd even give up her apartment, go
halfsies with him on a house, or a condo, because if they moved
in together, she would put her heart, her energy, her resources
into making it work. That was the way she was, and she liked
the picture of her and Corbin sitting on their patio, watching
their baby play in the sandbox.

The one thing she couldn't see herself doing was marrying
him. That scared her and she wasn't sure why. Maybe it was because she was afraid to fail. Maybe it was because marriage had
never brought her mother happiness. Maybe it was because in
twenty years she'd be sagging and Corbin would still be gorgeous.

Or maybe it was because she was an idiot.

All were credible possibilities.

And the bottom line was if she had doubts, she shouldn't
marry him. Living together, though, that was different. That
could work.

Trying not to disturb him, Brittany rolled to her left and
shimmied out from under the sheet. It felt like her stomach had
grown just since the night before, and the baby was making that
fluttery ticklish sensation beneath her belly button. "Good morning," she whispered to Coco Renee, or whoever she would wind
up being, pressing her hand over the movement.

Brittany wandered into the other room, yawning. First thing
they would have to fix when they moved in together was the
food situation.

"Jesus." She blanched when she opened the fridge, hoping
for OJ to miraculously appear, and instead found herself face to

face with bags of blood. She should have known better. She never went in Alex's refrigerator anymore.

"Note to self: Get two fridges for new house." And what the hell was that noise?

Brittany heard a chirping beep over and over, coming from Corbin's lab room. She glanced toward the door, curious in spite of herself. But strolling into a room full of viral test tubes didn't seem like a hot idea. On the other hand . . . maybe she could just poke her head around the corner. If anything were toxic, Corbin wouldn't leave the door open.

A quick glance inside showed a room very normal in appearance. It looked like an office, with cabinets and laminate countertops running around three walls. There were test tubes and a refrigerator—she so did not want to know what was in there—but everything else seemed to be tucked away into the cabinets. Corbin was neat in his work space. It was one of the three computers that was making the noise. It seemed to be some kind of alarm alert, like Brittany's reminder chime that went off the morning she had a doctor's appointment.

What did Corbin have on his night's schedule? Sample collection at eleven? She remembered how she had seen him using pleasure to daze a woman while he withdrew her blood, and she hoped like hell he'd stopped using that particular method. Science be damned, she wasn't going to tolerate his lips on anyone else if they were going to make this work.

What exactly did Corbin do all night?

The question rolled around in her head, set her imagination racing. She doubted his research would make any sense to her, but then again she'd gotten a bachelor's degree in biology, and had gone to dental school. She knew her anatomy and physiology, and had a rudimentary knowledge of pharmaceuticals in general, and a vast knowledge of analgesics. What exactly was involved in Corbin's vaccine?

Glancing back toward the bedroom, she couldn't see him because of the angle of the door, but Corbin wasn't making any sound.

This was nosy and wrong. What if he had porn on his computer screen? What if he had financial data listed? What if he got e-mails from obsessive women who wanted him to bite them again?

But if it was any of the above, wasn't she entitled to know?

Brittany chewed her bottom lip. Alex would have poked through his entire hard drive in the time she'd been standing there debating. She moved forward, tugging her sleep shirt down.

It wasn't porn. A reassuring beginning.

The screen showed a row of numbers, and the beeping seemed to indicate Corbin needed to do something to continue on with whatever analysis or program he was running. Nothing particularly interesting. But it was what was sitting next to the computer that suddenly caught her attention. A plastic bag marked BALDIZZI, BRITTANY with a bar code underneath. And inside that bag was one of her dark hairs, still long from before she'd cut it.

What the frick was that? Why did he have her hair and when had he taken it? The thought that he'd picked a hair off her pillow after they'd made love sat wrong. And if he was running tests on her for something, drugs, DNA, whatever, he could have mentioned it to her first. The bar code was labeled BB1977. Which she realized was the same damn code sitting right on Corbin's computer screen. He was running her DNA through some kind of software. It wasn't a spreadsheet she was seeing, it was a search.

Next to her number was another code—RD1021 and an explanatory paragraph that spouted a whole bunch of words and numbers, the end result of which was the claim that, given all points of comparison, the specimen matched to within a 0.4 percent margin of error, establishing a positive paternity.

Oh. My. God. Corbin had found her biological father. RD1021 was her father, whoever the hell he was.

"What do you mean? Who's Roberto?" Alexis asked stupidly, her hands wrapped in Gwenna's tiny ones.

"How could Donatelli know about the baby?" Ethan asked, looming behind her, his voice tight and angry.

"Donatelli?" Oh, crap. The last man in the world Alexis wanted to catch wind of her sister's situation. That pig would sell his mother for a quick buck. That is, if she hadn't died about a thousand years earlier and Donatelli wasn't a vampire.

"Yes, he knows. And he's here, in Las Vegas, to investigate. I don't think he knows your sister is the mother, but he knows there is a baby, the Frenchman's child, and that he will be a special opportunity for bargaining with Atelier."

"Bastard." Alexis squeezed Gwenna's hands, anger flaring. "I'll kill him before he touches my niece or nephew."

"How do *you* know Donatelli knows?"

Uh-oh. Big brother was suspicious. Alexis knew that tone from Ethan and it wasn't a happy one. She let go of Gwenna and put her hand on his arm, feeling the taut, tense muscles.

Gwenna's cheeks went pink and she looked at the floor. "I can still read Roberto's thoughts if I try. He is open to me even if he doesn't realize it. Normally nothing tempts me to listen, but two days ago, I felt sudden, intense anger from him—directed at me." She tucked her hair behind her ear, her long, lithe fingers fluttering a little.

She reminded Alexis of a delicate bird, a white crane, or a tiny hummingbird. As they stared at her, she shifted uncomfortably, her movements self-conscious.

"I haven't done anything to invoke his ire—not in several hundred years. I was surprised to feel that kind of anger. I thought we were past that, so I listened. It seems he had someone tell him that I was having, well, a love affair with the Frenchman. Which is ridiculous, of course," she added in a rush. "And I think he knows that, but it still made him jealous. While I was gleaning this from him, I heard that he knows Atelier has impregnated an Impure, that there will be a three-quarter vampire child. As I said, he's here to see how that information can serve him."

"Why didn't you tell me you can still hear his thoughts?" Ethan asked through gritted teeth.

That's what he took from that extraordinary revelation? Alexis almost rolled her eyes. "Who cares? The point is, she can, and what she heard sucks. That impregnated Impure happens to be my sister."

"Who told him?" Ethan put his hand in his hair and closed his eyes, like he was gathering his thoughts or his patience, maybe both.

The answer came to Alexis out of nowhere. "Ringo. Ringo and Kelsey. They left right after we found out Brittany was pregnant. And Ringo was there, in the apartment, with them when Brittany told Corbin. He must have overheard." Even as she spoke, she became more and more convinced that was what had happened. Who else could have known?

"But how did Ringo contact Donatelli? He's in New York. Or was."

"Maybe they went to New York. They've been gone for two months. You should have sent someone to find him." Like she had told him. Alexis didn't think it was cool that Ringo had tried to kill her husband, got punished, then walked away and no one bothered to haul his butt back to Vegas. That kind of leniency rubbed her nerves raw as a prosecutor.

"It didn't seem like a big deal to just let him go. I figured Kelsey would slow him down, peck at his conscience."

"You're too nice. Someone breaks the law, lock them up and throw away the key. Otherwise, there's no point in even having the laws in the first place."

"She a lawyer," Ethan told Gwenna. "Don't let her scare you."

Alexis smacked him. "I'm serious. You need to reevaluate this with your cabinet after the reelection is behind you. This is the first step to lawlessness, if vampire crime isn't cracked down on."

Ethan studied her. "Maybe you'd like a job?"

"Are you serious?" Alexis thought that through.

"Yes, I'm serious. I have no experience with that, and the Nation has a criminal tribunal, but perhaps we need to clean house."

"Sweet. I'd love to do that." It was the only way she liked to clean—firing useless bureaucrats sounded much better than dusting. "But what do we do now about Donatelli and my sister?"

"He won't hurt your sister," Gwenna said. "I'm sure of it."

Alexis was not reassured. "Maybe not until the baby is born, but what about afterward?"

Gwenna smoothed her hands down the front of her jeans. It amazed Alexis how thin and petite Gwenna was. That khaki blazer had to have come from BabyGap.

"Roberto is out for money and power. He won't kill anyone."

Um, someone needed to give up the delusions. "He broke my arm the last time I saw him. He had a knife in Kelsey's chest. I don't trust him as far as I can throw him, Gwenna."

"You're still protecting him," Ethan accused.

Face turning a mottled pink, Gwenna frowned at him. "I am not! I just know him. And he is capable of a lot, but hurting a pregnant woman or a baby is not his style." She turned to Alexis. "You have to believe me, Alexis. I have my eyes open wide when it comes to Roberto, but I think we should discuss this with him. Pay him off. Money talks with him, and if he already knows the truth, it's better to go on the offensive than the defensive. He can be reasonable."

Alexis had spent too many years in criminal justice to think that someone capable of one crime wasn't capable of an even bigger one. It wasn't as big of a leap for a morally bankrupt person as most people thought. "If you trust him, why did you hide your daughter from him?"

Gwenna gasped, all color leeching from her cheeks.

Way to foster a relationship with the in-laws. But Alexis thought it was a legitimate question.

Ethan's cell phone rang and he dug it out of his pocket. "It's Seamus. Let me grab this."

As he moved across the room, Alexis sighed. "Look, that didn't sound right . . ."

"It's a legitimate question. And the truth is that I was young and foolish, and did whatever my brother thought was the right action to take because I had never made any decisions on my own. I was heartbroken and convinced Roberto had seduced and abandoned me, that I was nothing but a momentary diversion to him. I didn't even know how to get in touch with him at the time the babe was born, and Ethan assured me he was missing. My daughter only lived twenty-five years, during which time I never saw Roberto. When I met him again hundreds of years later, he remembered me, professed love for me. And he did, in his way. I married him, but I never told him about our daughter, because it hurt to speak of her, and there are some things you don't say to Roberto, do you understand? He would never have forgiven me, so I kept quiet. It was fear, yes, but not the fear you imagine."

"I'm sorry." Alexis didn't know what else to say. Her social skills basically sucked. Brittany would know how to be comforting, but Alexis was better at kicking ass. "You don't have to say anything else; it's none of my business."

Gwenna smiled. "It's not for you to be sorry. I want to be honest, and I want you to understand. I left him because I know that he is lacking in morals, that he has flaws that cannot be ignored, that he can be cruel and violent. I don't kid myself. But he does have lines he will not cross, and trust me, he won't hurt the baby."

"We have a spot of trouble," Ethan said, returning his phone to his pocket, expression grim.

"Wonderful. What now?"

"The opposition has just announced their candidate for president. It is Gregor Chechikov."

"Gregor?" Gwenna started. "I thought he never left Russia anymore."

"So did I. But he is here in Vegas, and ready to hit the campaign trail. With his new mortal wife."

"What's so special about this guy?" Alexis asked, annoyed that everyone else had about a millennium of knowledge she didn't possess. She needed to sit down and read the CliffsNotes on vampire history.

"Let's just say he's not a nice guy. I've never had the misfortune to run across him personally, since he has stayed out of politics for the last several hundred years, but he is something of a vampire legend. A cult figure for vampire arrogance and population growth."

Alexis didn't like the sound of that. "So people will actually vote for him?"

Ethan nodded, lips pressed tight together, shoulders taut. "And he has a very real chance of winning. Which means I will have no governmental power to protect Brittany and the baby. Or even Atelier's research, for that matter."

The blood she'd had for dinner soured in her stomach. "That's it. We're putting her in a vampire witness protection program. We'll change her identity and move her to Alaska. Christ, Ethan. How hard would it have been for him to use a condom?"

Mothers had probably been asking that about their daughter's defilers since the Egyptians.

But Brittany was a big girl who had made her own choices and Alexis hated it.

It took Brittany all of three seconds to decide to go wake Corbin up. He could sleep later, she needed answers now.

Leaning over him, she touched his arm, intending to gently shake him awake. But the minute she made contact, Corbin's hand shot out and grabbed her arm in a steely grip and twisted it up and away from him.

"Ow, Corbin!"

His eyes had sprung open, and the second he saw it was her, he let go. "I am sorry. Are you all right? It is a reflex, instinctive, from my days as a soldier. And perhaps it is a vampire trait."

Sitting up, he rubbed at her arm, kissing it, looking sleep warm and tousled. "What is wrong? Did you need me for something, *ma chérie*?"

Brittany allowed herself half a second to enjoy the way his tongue felt traipsing across the inside of her palm, then she gently extracted her hand. "Your computer was beeping, making all kinds of a racket. I didn't want it to wake you up, so I went to see if I could stop it." Okay, that was kind of a lie, but her nosiness wasn't the issue at the moment.

"You didn't touch anything, did you?" he asked, pushing the sheet completely off him.

"No." Maybe she had touched the plastic bag, but geez, she wasn't stupid enough to start clicking buttons on his computer. Okay, she had just said that's what she'd gone to do. Which she hadn't. She'd gone to be nosy and see what was in there. Not that she needed to explain herself. He needed to explain himself.

"Good." He sighed in obvious relief.

"Why is there one of my hairs on your desk? And is that my DNA on your screen?"

Yeah, that was guilt. He looked down at his feet, hands on his bare knees. "I have run your DNA, yes, to isolate the vampire gene. It is just better to have some rudimentary knowledge of your sequence before the baby is born."

That sounded like half an answer. "Why? And didn't it occur to you that you could have asked for my cooperation? Discussed this with me?"

"No, that did not occur to me." Corbin stood up, bare-chested and gorgeous, damn him.

His boxer shorts clung high on his hips, bunched up, before dropping down to cover his thighs. "Brittany, I have made every decision for the last two hundred years entirely on my own, with no thought to anyone else's opinion. I am not used to discussing what I view as inconsequential. You will have to forgive me, and I will have to try to adjust." He brushed a kiss on her lips, his hands on her shoulders. "We will have to remember that it will take time to learn how to be together. Especially for me."

That was all fine and good, but the weightier question had yet to be asked. "Who is RD1021?"

"What?"

Brittany felt her panic rising like a balloon in her chest. Did she really want to know who her father was? And why the hell was it any of Corbin's business, or his decision to uncover that truth? "In your database. It's bad enough that you were analyzing my DNA without telling me, but you had no right to conduct a search for my biological father without asking me how I felt about it."

"Brittany . . ."

He reached for her, but she pulled away, putting her arms over her chest. "Maybe I didn't want to know. Maybe it's irrelevant to me, and I've been fine without a father. And now you've taken that decisiosn away from me. RD1021 is my father, and now I feel like I have to know who that is." It had been easy to walk around not caring who her father was when there was no possibility of ever learning his identity, but now she had to know his name, and that scared her. The reality was he could be a jerk, dead, insane, creepy—and that DNA was in her, and in her child.

"There was a match?" Corbin said.

About to answer, she suddenly realized she was standing in the room by herself. "Corbin? Where the hell are you?" And could he piss her off any more?

"Sorry," he called from the other room. "I'm in the lab. I cannot believe there was a match so quickly. This is fantastic."

Said he. Brittany fast-walked into the other room in her sleep shirt, glancing at her watch. She was going to be late to the office in about another twenty minutes, but she needed answers. Like who her father was and why Corbin looked like he could turn a vampire cartwheel. He was grinning.

"This is good, very good."

"Why?" Brittany went up to where he was leaning over the computer, using the mouse to click on something. She touched his shoulder, squeezing hard. He didn't seem to understand she was annoyed. "Can you please tell me what is going on? Why do you care who my father is?"

He didn't answer, just kept clicking and scrolling and scanning with his eyes, at one point his finger running down the screen.

Brittany went from annoyed to dangerous female. She inserted herself between the computer and him, knocking his leg out of the way and bending over to face off with him. "I want answers, Atelier, and I want them now. Why did you do this search? Why does it matter who my father is?"

Corbin looked startled. "For the child, of course. Because your father may be politically powerful or he may be inconsequential. That matters in regard to what he can do for our child."

Brittany leaned back, not sure what to make of that. "I don't care about getting our baby into a paranormal Princeton. I'm not going to make contact with a man I've never met just so he can grease wheels for our kid."

His fingers drummed on the armrest of his office chair, and he stared to the right, not looking at her.

It hit her that he was lying. Just flat-out lying to her. She knew him well enough now to see it in the subtle shifting of his mouth, his lips flat together, the way he wouldn't meet her eye. The stiffness of his shoulders. She shook her head, rubbing her temples. "Why else does it matter? You'd better come clean with me right this minute or I'm walking out this door and not coming back."

Swinging his head back, he stared at her. "You cannot!"

"I can and I will." Even with tears stinging the back of her eyes, she managed to keep the tremor out of her voice. "I deserve respect, Corbin. I'm not afraid of being alone. I never have been. I would rather be on my own than in a relationship that isn't honest."

She gave him a minute to decide. He tried to see around her to the screen, but she moved to block his view.

"Damn it," he said, falling back against the chair. "Do not do this."

There was no point in responding to that. Brittany just waited.

He gave a sigh of extreme irritation. "All right then, listen to me. You have to understand that I thought it was safer not to divulge all my concerns to you initially."

Okay, so he'd chosen to lie to her. Not an auspicious beginning. "What concerns?"

Clearing his throat, he finally looked at her. His expression chilled her insides, a shiver rippling over her in a waterfall effect.

"If our child has the genetic conclusion I think he will, then he will be immortal, but will not need to feed."

Immortal? Brittany tried to process that. But Corbin wasn't finished.

"When the birth of our child becomes general knowledge, there will be those who want him. For research. To figure out how to reproduce such genetics again. Because a man who is immortal, with all of the strength of the vampire, and none of the vulnerabilities of needing blood and night dwelling, represents a new race, and ultimately power. Do you understand? That is why I stayed away from you. I did not want anyone to know that the child was mine. I thought I could enter your life publicly later in your pregnancy, letting everyone assume I was not the father, and I could marry you to protect our child. And who your father is could assist us in protecting our child, as well as give us clues to gauge exactly what the child's abilities will be."

Brittany shook her head, trying to process what he was saying. It was incomprehensible. The implication of what he had just presented to her . . . "Our child is in danger and you didn't bother to *tell* me? Why didn't you let me know what we're dealing with here?" She jerked her hand through her hair, frustration and fear colliding. "My God, I feel like such an idiot. I've been worried about baby registries! I've been picturing moving into a little adobe house with a playset in the yard. How could you let me think everything was fine, was normal, when it's not? God, I'm like Bubble Brittany! No clue what's going on. How could I possibly protect our child if I had no idea what was going on?"

Pushing away from the desk, she let the tears go. She felt sick. If her child was in danger, she had no idea how to deal with that. "Does anyone else know what you just told me?"

"Carrick and your sister do."

"Oh!" Betrayed by her own sister.

"And I imagine Carrick's sister and Seamus Fox understand the implications."

Great. Everyone knew what the hell was going on but her. "I'm leaving." She needed to get away from him. She felt like a total fool, lying in bed that morning thinking all kinds of delicious thoughts about houses and making love to Corbin every day . . . falling in love. It was all an illusion and she was angry and scared.

He grabbed the hem of her T-shirt, pulling her back. "Hey. Do not leave like this. We need to talk."

"About what? How you're a jerk?" And to think, she'd actually thought he wanted to marry her because he had *feelings* for her. Instead he just wanted to act as bodyguard. Talk about delusional. Now she knew how her mother had found herself in so many lousy relationships. It was very easy to see what you wanted to when you cared about a man.

"Now be reasonable."

When tugging didn't get him to release her shirt, she smacked at his hand, feeling slightly hysterical. Where were Alexis's karate chops when she needed them? "Kiss my pregnant ass. You're a lying, bloodsucking bastard."

His jaw dropped. "Brittany . . . I do not know what to say. You need to understand I did this for your protection. What was the point in you worrying about something you could not fix? I wanted your pregnancy to be free of stress."

How thoughtful of him. She wasn't buying it. "You didn't tell me because you didn't want me to say no to marrying you.

You decided you were right, so in order to convince me to go along with your plans, you just didn't tell me."

Score. His eyes shifted and he let go of her shirt. Guilty as charged.

And damn it, that hurt. Eyes blurring, Brittany moved away from him. She needed her pants. And a ride. Shit.

"Brittany . . ."

Not wanting to hang around for a load of crap, she brushed at her tears and started for the door. She was going to break down and she did not want to do it in front of him.

"Wait, Brittany, don't go. *Mon Dieu.* I know who your father is."

That stopped her. She turned around. He didn't look so good, eyes locked on the computer screen. His face was ash white. That didn't bode well. Heart hammering in her chest, she touched her stomach. "Can he . . . help us?"

Corbin shook his head slowly back and forth. "No, *ma chérie*. He cannot help us." He turned to her, expression grave, stunned. "Your father is Roberto Donatelli."

Thirteen

Nag, nag, nag. Ringo glared at Kelsey. "Whatta you want me to do? Turn myself in? Fuck that. They want me, they can come after me."

He'd married her. He'd come back to Vegas, he had gotten them twenty-five grand. But it wasn't enough for her. She wanted him to apologize to the tribunal for leaving? No chance in hell. Next she'd ask him to get her stupid secretary job back.

"But if you turn yourself in, they'll be nicer." She bit her fingernail and paced the floor.

They were staying at the Hilton, where Elvis had slept. It wasn't glitz, but it was still pretty damn nice as far as he was concerned. Yet not one word of appreciation from her. All she could do was complain—about losing her job, about his dealings with Donatelli, about his chain smoking.

"Ain't nobody going to be nice to me, babe. Get that through your ditzy head." He lit another cigarette in defiance, even though there was still a haze lingering in the room from his last four.

The silly bitch yanked the smoke right out of his mouth. He was so shocked he didn't even try to stop her. But as he watched her grind it out, his temper climbed. "Oh, you're really pushing it now."

"Listen to me." She met his gaze unflinchingly and didn't quail when he moved toward her. "You're losing your grip. You need to back up, Ringo, and get control of yourself."

It was so different from her usual quirky self-love talk, which went in all those circles he could never understand, he hesitated. "What are you talking about?"

"I mean you're about to crack. You know it. I know it. You need to stop denying it and deal with what happened with Kyle."

"What do you know about it? You don't know anything. You know his name, and the rest of it is none of your damn business." How dare she bring his brother into their shit? This wasn't about how Kyle had died, this was about her turning into some kind of schoolteacher, lecturing him about right and wrong.

He needed some air. He headed for the door.

She stepped in front of him, spreading her legs apart in her tight jeans, hot pink T-shirt riding up. Nothing tough about her appearance, but her face looked pretty damn determined. "I'm going to ask Mr. Carrick for my job back."

It was the one thing she could have said that would piss him off even further. "You don't care how I feel, do you? You don't give two shits about how it makes me feel to have my wife crawling on hands and knees back to that sanctimonious prick begging for a job. Like he ever kept you around for your secretarial skills. Please. You want your stupid bimbo job back so bad? Fine, I don't give a shit. Do what you need to do." He flicked his hair out of his eyes and moved around her. "Blow him for all I care. I'm sure you have before."

"Ringo."

"What?" He turned around, hand on the doorknob.

Her hand slammed across his cheek with impressive velocity, and his head snapped back, teeth sinking into his tongue. "What the fuck!" His face stung, eyes filling with water from the impact. For a stick, she packed some force.

"That's for making me sound like a whore."

"Whatever." Blinking hard to clear his vision, he patted his pocket to make sure a good-size wad was there, and walked out the door.

He jumped on the Monorail and twenty minutes later he was knocking on Donatelli's suite at the Venetian. Bastard was intriguingly predictable. He'd gone right back to his old room.

A bodyguard that Ringo had worked with back in his days on Donatelli's security force opened the door. Ringo just nodded to him and strolled on past.

Donatelli was watching HGTV. A home makeover show. God, what a weirdo.

"Columbia. Can I help you?" Donatelli turned the volume down two notches and glanced at him impassively, leg crossed over his knee. "I don't imagine you're here to return the money you stole from my wallet."

"How much for a pint?" His hand shook, so he stuck it in his pocket.

The man who had made him a vampire, and turned him into a heroin addict, smiled. "For you? I'll give it to you for nothing. Consider it a wedding gift from me."

Ringo should be humiliated by that self-satisfied smirk on the Italian's face, but he was too thirsty to care. "Thanks."

Donatelli stood. "Have a seat by the window. It's a beautiful night."

Ringo followed, hating himself for doing this, hating Kelsey for driving him to it, hating Donatelli for being so damn accommodating.

Their butts were barely in two chairs facing the skyscape when the bodyguard was there with two large goblets of blood, one clear glass, one an aquamarine color that turned the blood a deep, rich purple color. He was given that one, and Ringo leaned back, closed his eyes, smelled the tangy aroma before tipping the glass, letting it fill his mouth.

It was gone in two swallows. Ringo shuddered as it slid through him, fanning out over his eager, quivering body. He opened his eyes and stared at the Vegas night. All the lights glowed hot and white against the dark of the sky. The colors blended and shifted, fuzzing in and out, and he stared at it, mesmerized. Relaxing.

Everything was going to be okay. He was okay. Licking the rim of the glass, he said, "How about a double?"

"Sure. And then there's something I'd like to discuss with you. A job."

"A job?" Ringo blinked, his head feeling heavy. Donatelli must want him to kill someone. He was good at that. Never made a mess.

Kelsey would be mad at him. But he was his own man. He could do whatever he wanted. And at the moment, he'd literally kill for another drink. "I can do a job for you, no problem."

Donatelli smiled. "Fill Mr. Columbia's glass up again, Williams."

Amen to that. Ringo held his goblet up.

Oh, wonderful. Her father was Donatelli, a psychotic political power monger who tortured, pushed drugs, and gave bad speeches. This was just the cherry on the sundae of her day.

"Are you sure?" Duh. Of course he was sure. She was sure, having seen the results on the screen herself. If Donatelli was RD1021, there was a 99.6 percent chance he was her father. Which meant he was. Damn it.

"Yes, I am sure."

Good thing he wasn't going to sugarcoat it for her. Brittany's face felt hot, a coppery taste in her mouth. For a second she thought she was going to faint, but she remained standing, a sudden wet sensation under her nose distracting her as she wiped at it. "I'm bleeding!"

Corbin whipped his head around and jumped out of the chair, actually hitting her leg with it. "What happened?"

"Nothing, I don't know." She swiped again, more scarlet

blood on her finger. "I have a nosebleed! I've never had a nose-bleed before."

He patted his boxer shorts, as if a hanky might appear, then did his vampire speed trick, returning in two seconds with a wet wash-cloth. "Pinch your nose slightly. It's just the pregnancy. Increased blood flow. Nosebleeds are common in the second trimester."

"How du you nowb?" she asked, words thick from squeezing her nose shut. Closing her eyes, she fought a rising panic. Her father was a loon. Her mother had slept with a nutcase. The man she was falling in love with wanted to marry her only to protect their child from evil vampire forces. And she was going to die from a nosebleed.

"I read one of those baby manuals. What to expect when you are birthing an *enfant* or something like that."

Somehow she didn't think any book was titled that, but it wasn't the time to quibble. She let go of her nose and gave a test sniffle. It seemed to have stopped bleeding as quickly as it had started. "Does Donatelli know he's my father?"

Corbin shook his head. "I doubt it. If he did, he would have raised the issue during the election. He would have approached you long before Carrick did."

He went back to the computer and started clicking again, moving files.

"What are you doing?"

"I'm deleting this match. In fact, I'm deleting your DNA results altogether from my database. I do not want Donatelli or anyone else to know that he is your biological father."

"Why not?" she asked, even as she knew the answer.

"He'll want the baby, Brittany. He'll want to raise the child, groom him for power. You are carrying his grandchild. He'll see the possibilities and want to act on them."

Damn it, that's what she'd been hoping he wouldn't say. "No, Corbin, no. No, no, no. We can't let him do that." The thought of that man with her child—influencing her, keeping her from a normal, nurturing life—made every cell in her body vibrate in protest. It made her want to dissolve into a full-fledged hysterical panic. But she couldn't. She needed to act, and it seemed there was only one obvious solution. "Shit. I just need to leave, don't I? I need to change my hair, my name, start over somewhere else. Hide from him. Never let anyone know."

Corbin stopped clicking and deleting, and slowly rubbed his forehead. "*Mon Dieu*. Brittany." He turned to her and his face was hard, eyes agonized, a rich cobalt blue. "Maybe that would be the smartest thing to do. At least temporarily. If anyone asked, Alexis can just say her sister had moved to California or something. And then you can go to Atlanta or Boston, somewhere far from California. Hell, maybe Europe or India and get lost in the crowd."

Wet washcloth wrung between her hands, Brittany nodded. "I'll have to tell Alexis and Ethan, but no one else."

"I'll destroy all evidence of the biological connection. I will move my other files, then destroy this hard drive. It will take me a few hours."

"Can you stay awake?" She knew how hard it was for vampires to function during the day.

"I'll have to." He nodded. "It will be fine. Everything is fine.

You go and pack and I'll pick you up tonight. We can leave immediately."

That stopped her. Her mind had been racing ahead, mentally picking a replacement for her dental practice until she could sell it, trying to decide where she'd want to live, what her name might be. How she would need Ethan's help to establish a new identity for herself. An identity by herself.

It had never occurred to her to take Corbin with her.

While part of her wanted to fling herself into his arms and let him fix everything, her pride, her independence, and mostly, her maternal instinct told her Corbin couldn't leave with her.

"I was planning to go alone."

He stopped clicking on things long enough to stare at her, mouth wide open. "Alone? No, I am going with you. I will protect you. Watch over you and the babe at night when you cannot."

Brittany made note there was no mention of love or devotion or how he couldn't picture his life without her.

But regardless of that, even if he did love her, which he clearly didn't, he still couldn't go with her. It was dangerous, she sensed that. Felt it instinctively. "Corbin."

"Yes? Explain this to me. I cannot let you go without me."

"You have to. No one knows you are the baby's father, remember? That is the key to our success. No one knows about the baby. Or if they do, they will assume the father is mortal. That was your plan all along, and it was a good one, even if you didn't tell me. If I leave, alone, no one will think twice about Alexis's half-mortal sister moving to another state. No one will bother to check to see if I went where I said I was going. No one will care. If you leave with me, everyone will want to know where you went. And they will start to put two and two together and wonder if we left together. If vampires start asking questions, they might find answers we don't want them to. They might get suspicious. They might eventually find us."

He shook his head. "But . . . I cannot just let you go off into the night by yourself. I cannot."

"You have to." She swallowed the massive lump in her throat. "I know you want to protect us, and this is the best way. The same reason you wanted to marry me before is the same reason you can't marry me now."

It was a solid minute before he answered her. She could see the agony on his face, but she knew by the set of his jaw he had made the right decision.

"You are right." He shook his head. "I hate it. I despise the idea of letting you go without me, but you are right. Brittany, I am so sorry that I have brought this all upon you. It is all my fault."

"Hey, I was there that night, too." And while she was terrified, she wasn't sure she'd undo anything. She was having a baby, the child of the man she loved. That was worth any sacrifice, any inconvenience. And she would battle the devil himself to protect her baby. "Recriminations are a waste of time. I admit, I'm very angry that you didn't disclose the danger of the situation to me, and it's possible I'll have a hard time getting past that, but it has nothing to do with my rationale here. We both know this is what we have to do. And I promise to let you visit if it's safe, and I'll send you updates and contact info through Ethan and Alex."

At that, he stood up, and she realized that her words of reassurance had just undone her previous logic. In two seconds, he was on top of her, expression fierce and passionate, pulling her tight against him.

"There has to be another way, damn it."

Brittany closed her eyes and let her face rest against his chest. "You know there isn't another way." She wrapped her arms around his middle and breathed deep. Touching him calmed her, and she savored the moment, knowing this might be the last time she was this close to him. "We have to think about the baby. That has to be our priority."

Hands in her hair, he said, "Just promise me . . ." His voice cracked. "Promise you will tell our child who her father is when the time is right. Explain that I would have been there for her if I could have."

Brittany felt the tears rise all over again at the pain she heard in those words. Pulling back, she blinked hard. "Hey. Don't worry about that. You are the father and our child will know all about you. I promise you that."

"*Merci*. I appreciate that." He stared at her, eyes wandering over her face, hands on her cheeks. "I love you."

She hadn't expected him to say that. It shattered her composure. "Don't . . ." If he was exaggerating to make her feel better, it wasn't working. If he was sincere, then it only made her feel worse. It was better to leave it unsaid, to not know what they were giving up.

"Yes. I must say it." He brushed his lips over her forehead. "Know that even if there were no baby, I would love you. And I would marry you just for being you, if I could."

"Corbin." She was sobbing now. She felt relief, glee, that he felt what she did, felt the pressure of her hurt dissipating, yet it only made her regret, her pain, her understanding of her future loneliness increase tenfold. It would be impossible to move on, to forget him, knowing he loved her in return. "I love you, too."

The kiss he gave her was passionate, but tender. She opened her mouth for him, almost cried at the sweetness of his tongue sliding across hers. It was a good-bye kiss and they both knew it.

Brittany couldn't stand it. If he kept touching her, she wasn't going to be able to leave. Breaking the kiss, she pulled away and wiped her cheeks. "I should go."

"Go to Ethan. He'll help you make arrangements. Do what you need to. I'll finish this up then I'll come over. Do not leave until I get there."

"Okay." Brittany suddenly realized she had no car. "I didn't drive here. You picked me up."

"You can take my car. I'll find a way there tonight. The keys are on the kitchen counter." He gave her hand a last squeeze. "I'll see you tonight. I'll be there before midnight, all right?"

She nodded, and went to get dressed. By the time she was dressed and flipping him a good-bye wave, he was back at the computer, popping CDs in and out of the drive, working on all three computers at once. It amazed her he was that technically savvy. He always struck her as resistant to modern amenities.

And she wasn't sure if she was glad he had the capability to decipher who her father was or not. Walking down the hall and out the front door of the apartment building, she knew she'd certainly been blissfully ignorant not knowing her biological origins. On the other hand, now that she knew Donatelli was her father, she was better prepared to protect her child.

The morning was hazy and chilly. Crossing her arms and rubbing, she tried to remember where Corbin had parked his BMW the night before. All the rows looked the same, many of the sedans a similar black or blue.

She didn't see the man until he was standing in front of her. Then she jumped and gave a little shriek of surprise. Corbin had said this wasn't the best of neighborhoods, but her thoughts of muggers died when she realized it was Ringo. His hair was longer, and his eyes bloodshot, his hand twitching in a disturbing tick.

Instinctively, she knew he wasn't there for a social call on Corbin. Turning around, she started to move back to the building.

"What's your hurry?" he asked, blocking her path.

Oh, God. Brittany couldn't believe this was happening. Maybe Ringo just needed money. He looked high as a kite. A skinny, creepy, dangerous kite.

"I just realized I forgot my cell phone." It was a total lie but she wanted to feel out his intention before she panicked. Maybe she could just give him what he wanted. Maybe it had nothing to do with the baby.

"That's a shame. But you weren't going to be able to call for help anyway."

Ringo grabbed her arm before she even saw him move. "What do you want?" she asked, trying to yank out of his hold. He was too strong. She couldn't even make his arm move with her violent attempts to jerk herself away.

"I want money."

"Oh." She sighed in relief. "I have a hundred in my purse, and if you go upstairs, Corbin can give you some, I'm sure."

But he shook his head slowly, a small laugh rolling out of his mouth. "No, that's not what I mean. I need money, so I'm doing a job. You're the job, sweetheart."

Okay, no use holding back on the panic. It was there, full force, and it propelled her into action. Brittany kicked him in the shin and opened her mouth to scream.

Ringo slapped his hand over her mouth, his vampire strength so intense Brittany felt her lips start to bleed from being ground against her teeth. "Be nice. I'm not going to kill you. I just have to take you to someone who wants to talk to you. Now will you be good? Keep your fucking mouth shut?"

She nodded her head, sucking in air when he let go of her. "Where's Kelsey?" she asked, as he dragged her across the parking lot.

It didn't make any sense, but in her head she kept thinking if Kelsey was okay, then somehow she would be okay, too. If he could care about a woman, he could care about her unborn child.

But his face darkened. "We had a bit of an argument."

Wonderful.

"Which car is yours?" Ringo demanded, ripping the keys from her hand.

"The blue BMW." Brittany tried not to cry. Now Corbin wouldn't even notice she was missing with his car gone. In her head she called to Corbin, hoping like hell their mind-connection still had some kind of power.

Otherwise, she was screwed.

Fourteen

"What do you mean, she called off work today?" Alexis asked the receptionist at Bright Smiles. It was six o'clock, Alexis had just gotten up for the night, and Brittany should be doing her end-of-the-day bullcrap in her dental office.

"I mean, she called off work today," the receptionist repeated dryly. "I guess she's sick."

"Thanks." Alexis hung up and dialed Brittany's house. No answer. She tried her cell. Nothing. She frowned. "Ethan!"

"What?" her husband answered, voice still sleepy.

"Do you have Corbin's phone number or address?"

"In the address book on my computer."

Two minutes later she impatiently waited for Corbin to pick up the phone.

"Allo?" he said.

"Where's Brittany?"

There was a pause. "Alexis? Brittany should be at your apartment by now. Have you called her cell phone?"

"She's not answering. Why didn't she go to work today?"

"You mean you haven't spoken to her at all? There was no message from her?"

"No." Alexis started to feel annoyance and a nagging little worry morph into serious fear. "Was she supposed to call me? What's going on?"

"Brittany was planning to ask for some assistance. That is all I wish to say at the moment."

Every time she thought she might actually learn to like him, he had to go and piss her off. "Ethan and I need to talk to you and Brittany. Get your French ass over here."

"I will be there in a few hours. I have an issue or two to resolve here first. Brittany and I intend to meet at your apartment around eleven."

That wasn't good enough. "Gwenna is here."

"Gwenna Carrick?" Corbin sounded surprised. "Why?"

"She has something she needs to share with you and Brittany."

"Perhaps I can get there sooner."

She thought so. "Good idea." Even though she meant to play it cool, she couldn't help voicing her suspicion. "Are you two planning to elope?"

There was a pause. "No. That is not what we are planning."

The words should have been reassuring, but instead they scared the crap out of her.

Brittany had spent her whole life in Las Vegas, and had frequented her fair share of casinos and bars in her teens and early twenties. But she had never been inside a suite at the Bellagio.

She would have been impressed with the luxury and the amazing décor if she hadn't been tied to a chair and scared out of her everlovin' mortal mind.

There were two guards posted on either side of the door. A woman lounged on a divan reading a book, her long legs crossed at the ankle, her expression bored and disinterested. And three men staring at Brittany, each in a club chair that matched hers. One was Ringo, and he looked half-asleep, a glass of blood in his hand that he continually sipped from. She briefly wondered if a vampire could overdose on drugs, because he looked perilously close to a coma. One of the other two was Donatelli. Her father. He gave her encouraging smiles, alternated with inquiries into how they might make her stay more comfortable. Would she care for a pillow? A drink? A bite to eat? It was irritating to listen to him being so civil, when she was strapped down like cumbersome luggage on a car top. But the annoyance she felt at Donatelli was nothing compared to the fear she felt when she looked at the third man. He was huge, with a thick beard, broad shoulders, and fat, hairy hands. His appearance wasn't the only reason he terrified her. She wasn't real thrilled with the sick smile on his face. He was enjoying her fear. And his eyes were dead, empty. Insane. He didn't speak, so she tried not to look at him.

She concentrated her attention on Donatelli, who was doing all the talking.

It appalled her to look Donatelli in the face and admit to herself that he was her father. That he had oozed oily charm and suckered her mother into bed, and she was the result of that illustrious encounter. What was worse, though, was the realization that he knew she was pregnant. There was no hiding it. And it was clearly the reason she'd been brought there, because Donatelli's overly casual questions all focused on the baby and Corbin.

"So when are you due?" he asked, crossing his leg.

She didn't answer.

"Come now, no need to demur. I can see that you are at least four or five months along. April? That is a pleasant month to give birth. Lots of walks in the spring sunshine. Good for you and the baby."

Moving her head to flip her hair out of her eyes, she kept her mouth shut. She didn't know what he wanted or why, and she didn't want to give him whatever information he must be seeking.

"And Atelier will be there when you give birth? That is so charming."

It wasn't hard to stay quiet. She had no interest in making chitchat with him.

What she wasn't prepared for was the big, boorish man to suddenly stand up and smack her cheek with the back of his hand. He moved so fast she couldn't even try to shield the blow, and it stung like hell, ripping tears out of her eyes and an involuntary gasp from her mouth.

"Show some respect and answer."

Brittany flinched, but he only returned to his seat. The woman on the couch gave a casual glance up before turning the page of her book.

"I'm due in April," Brittany said quickly when he made like he was going to stand up again, hand raised. She was actually due in May, but Donatelli had guessed April, and it felt safer to lie.

Donatelli sat forward, elbows on his knees, a frown on his face. "Really, Gregor, that was not necessary."

"She gave you an answer, did she not?" Gregor's accent was thick. Russian.

"I'm sure she's willing to be reasonable, aren't you, Brittany?" Donatelli asked, giving her a charming smile.

"I can be reasonable." In her head, she screamed for Ethan, hoping he would hear her cry for help. She was afraid to call for Corbin, fearful of what would happen if he showed up and the men in front of her forced Corbin to hand over his research. Besides, her mental connection with Corbin had been silent since their second separation, after she had told Corbin about the baby. She didn't understand why, but they could only hear each other during sex.

Alexis had never been able to hear Brittany's thoughts, but Ethan could. Once he'd even heard her cry out from an amazing orgasm the first time she'd been with Corbin, and Ethan had been miles away from them, which had been really damn embarrassing. But surely he would hear her fear now if he had been able to hear her pleasure then.

"We know Atelier is the father of your baby. What we need to know is what he plans to do with your child."

"Nothing."

"So he has told you nothing about his plans?"

She shook her head, confused. What did they think Corbin was going to do with her baby?

"Alright, that's fine. Perhaps he hasn't been forthcoming with you. You are a surrogate. No need for him to share everything with you."

Brittany frowned. A surrogate? Why would they think that? She glanced at Ringo, who had heard her telling Corbin he was the father of her child. He knew she wasn't a surrogate. Why would he lie to Donatelli? But he clearly had, and his face revealed nothing. His eyes were hard, glassy, going in and out of focus.

"I've done everything I was supposed to," she said carefully. "I've taken vitamins, I've been to the doctor, I've gone to childbirth classes. What do you want?" It wasn't hard to put a tremor into her voice. Her fear was legit.

"Why did you do it? Having a baby isn't the easiest way to earn a dollar." Donatelli asked, "Did you really need the money that badly? Is your dental practice failing?"

Brittany was a good liar. Much better than Alexis, who was incapable of hiding her feelings. "I . . . I . . . got into some gambling debt." She glanced at her lap, as if she were ashamed. "I owe fifty grand, and I didn't want my sister and her husband to know. Atelier offered me a hundred to have his baby."

Donatelli whistled. "Gambling. So like a woman to be weak. What is your game?"

Bled Dry

It had been years since she'd played, but she said, "Blackjack." She knew the rules to that, could answer questions about it.

"We'll give you a hundred and twenty-five thousand if you give the baby to us."

The shocked gasp she gave wasn't faked either. "But it's his sperm. His kid."

Gregor stood up and came at her. Brittany tried to shrink back, but his thick hand grabbed a handful of hair on the top of her head and yanked her back so she was staring straight up at him, the pain making her wince. "Maybe I'll just bury my own sperm in you. What do you think of that?"

She thought she was going to be sick. Her stomach roiled and she was sure she was going to vomit right into his salt-and-pepper beard. It wasn't hard to believe him. He looked like he could rape her and enjoy it.

There was a torrent of Russian from the woman on the couch. Gregor broke eye contact with Brittany and turned around. She breathed deeply, trying to calm her stomach down, clamp down on her terror, hold on to her nerve.

"Your wife doesn't seem pleased with that idea," Donatelli said in amusement.

"My wife does not speak English. But she is still a jealous little minx." He let go of Brittany's hair with a jerk and moved toward the woman. "Sasha."

But the woman was up off the couch, flouncing away, her hair bouncing down her back, her little backside swaying. Her chin was tilted indignantly. Brittany wanted to throw something at her. Like a boulder. Or a grand piano. How could she just sit there and let her husband tie up a pregnant woman? Of course, she had to be a heartless bitch to be married to a beast like Gregor.

"That is why I'll never get married again," Donatelli commented as Gregor followed Sasha out of the room. He crossed one leg over the opposite knee. "Now are you agreeable to our terms?"

"What do you want the baby for?" With Gregor gone, she felt emboldened. Donatelli didn't seem nearly as threatening.

"Sasha has always yearned for a child."

That woman wasn't raising her baby. No way, Russian José. "What do you have to do with all of this?"

"I'm the middleman. The negotiator. As you can see, Gregor has poor social skills."

"The answer is no."

He grimaced. "That is the wrong answer. I will continue to ask the question until you give the right answer."

"No. I may not have intended to keep this baby, but it is still a baby. It belongs with its father."

Donatelli sighed. "All these goddamn ethics are so exhausting. I'm trying to be reasonable. Spare you the rod."

A high-pitched moan floated out from the next room. Brittany couldn't prevent a grimace. She so did not need to hear that at the moment. It was Sasha, giving an exuberant cry of pleasure, which was seriously gross, considering that her husband was just about Satan with facial hair.

Yet Ringo actually stirred and glanced toward the door, naked longing on his face, and a good-sized tent in his pants.

Blech. She didn't need to see that any more than she wanted to hear Sasha and Gregor getting it on.

Which was getting more disgusting by the minute, a nice rhythm building to the groans and yelps. Sasha did the Russian version of an "oh, oh, yes, oh, oh, aahh," over and over. And over and over. You know, if Brittany wasn't mistaken, there was actually some faking going on there. Having pulled that a time or two in her life, she recognized the signs. Sasha's voice was too even, too rhythmic, too poised. Gregor was silent, which made her wonder where his tongue was, which made her stomach flip again.

At least Donatelli seemed unnerved and uninterested. But he also held his hand out to her. "Sleep, Brittany."

She tried to resist, tried to close her mind to him, but she felt herself falling under, into darkness.

"If she is not here, where is she?" Corbin asked, staring at Alexis, who was wringing her hands together.

"I don't freaking know! That's what I'm telling you," Alexis shouted at him. "No one has seen her all day. She's not answering her cell phone and she's not at home. I went over there. Her car is in the driveway, but she's not there."

"Did it look like she'd been packing?" he asked. Brittany was probably just en route to Alexis's and had stopped at the grocery store or the bank. Though he found it odd that she had not called Alexis. She knew she needed Ethan's assistance to get new identification.

"Packing? No, not at all. It looked like she hadn't been there all day, and her bed was made."

"That is because she spent last night with me." Corbin set down the bag of maternity clothes he had brought over. She had forgotten them in his apartment. "She took my car to drive home. It was gone from the parking lot, so I know she left. Where are Ethan and Gwenna?"

"Gwenna hasn't gotten up yet. She sleeps late. And Ethan went to talk to his security team, to see if they can figure out how to track Brittany down. I just know something is wrong."

So did he. Corbin felt cold, stark terror slide over him. Brittany should have been there. Or she would have called. Unless she had chosen to disappear on her own. But no, she wouldn't do that without saying good-bye to her sister.

"Alexis, Brittany and I were planning on her leaving tonight. She was supposed to go home, pack what she needed, withdraw all her available funds, and come here. She was supposed to ask Ethan to establish a new identity for her so she could leave tonight and start a new life under an assumed name."

"What! Why?"

Corbin grimaced. The truth still appalled him. "Because my DNA search on Italian men resulted in a match. Brittany's father is Donatelli."

"Jesus Christ!" Alexis went pale. "Corbin, the reason we wanted to talk to you is because Gwenna came here to warn us that Donatelli is back in Vegas. And he knows about the baby. We think Ringo told him."

Corbin went very, very still. He tried to squelch the anger, the fear, the self-recrimination, so he could think rationally. "Then it is very possible that Donatelli has Brittany right now, no?"

Alexis nodded, than took off for the bedroom. "I'm going to wake Gwenna. She can read Donatelli's thoughts."

It would be an interesting move, for Donatelli to take Brittany. He obviously could not know he was her father. And if his other information was accurate, he would know that the baby wasn't due for months. So why would he take her? It struck Corbin as bold and aggressive, not adjectives he'd normally associate with Donatelli.

Alexis came back into the room with Gwenna, who was a pale wisp of a woman, shadows under her blue eyes, silvery blond hair uncombed. "She's with him. I can hear quite clearly his curiosity, his impatience. Something is bothering him. He's worried someone else is being too rough with her and he is debating how much he can interfere."

"*Mon Dieu.*" If Donatelli thought someone else was being rough, Brittany was in serious trouble. "Who is with them?"

"I don't know." Gwenna shook her head. "I'm sorry. And I don't know where they are either."

"Do you think he would go back to the Venetian?"

"I don't know."

"It's worth a try," Alexis said, her mouth closed tightly, lips a pale white line.

Corbin was about to ask for a weapon when the front door opened and Ethan came in with Seamus Fox and Kelsey, the errant secretary.

She was crying, her blood tears streaming down her pale

face. She came right over to him. "Ringo's using drugs again, I know it. He went to Donatelli."

"I'm sorry," Corbin said automatically, patting her back when she launched herself into his arms. He looked over her shoulder for help, no clue what to do with her. The others were in a serious discussion, heads bent.

A thought occurred to him and he pulled back to look at Kelsey. "Where is Donatelli? Do you know?"

Kelsey gave a sniffle and wiped at her tears. "I think he's at the Bellagio. With the Russian guy. That's where Ringo picked up his payment."

"The Russian guy? Chechikov?" Corbin was stunned. The man he had given access to all his research, including the potential for cloning, was working with Donatelli?

"Yes, that was his name." Kelsey nodded, her lip curling up. "And his mortal wife, who looks like a slut if I ever saw one. A supermodel slut."

"His wife?" Corbin turned to Ethan and Seamus. "Did you know Chechikov is in town?"

"Unfortunately, yes. He's here to run for president. Though I had no idea he was hiding a mortal wife up his sleeve, the tricky bastard."

"President?" Corbin ran his fingers through his hair, unable to comprehend how idiotic he had been. "That wife is the least of our worries. If he is with Donatelli, then they have Brittany. It is Gregor that Donatelli worries will hurt Brittany." Corbin clenched his fists. "You know his reputation. He would not hesitate to hurt her. And I am very sorry to say that it is Chechikov who has been funding my research all these years. I give him biannual reports on my progress. With the right research team, he has the framework in place to reconstruct my antidote, at least to a point. Without my latest series of controls, though, it will take years. Unless he steals my most recent data."

His head was pounding. He just couldn't let that research fall into the wrong hands. Chechikov had played him for a fool. He intended to take the research, take the office of the presidency, and clone vampires. So he would have total control. Corbin was not about to let that happen, nor was he going to let any harm befall Brittany or his child.

"I need to go find Brittany. Can someone go to my lab in my apartment and start destroying my files? I cannot let Chechikov or Donatelli find my research."

"I don't have the technical skills for that," Ethan said. "But I'll go with you to find Brittany."

"I can destroy files," Seamus offered, stepping forward. "Just tell me what you want saved."

"Put everything on a ThumbDrive. There is one sitting on the desk. Then destroy everything on all three computers. Obliterate it. So no one can retrieve anything. Put all the paper files through the shredder." It was painful to say that, but he knew it was necessary. He had created the means to do the very opposite of what he had intended. It was his responsibility to destroy it.

He wanted the ThumbDrive, though. The files would give him the ability to re-create his vaccine. Giving up that choice he had created, the chance to be mortal again, wasn't an option he was comfortable with. Not yet, not when he knew he had the cure.

And he might need the genetic database with regard to their child.

"Just give me your apartment keys and I'm on the way," Seamus said, hand held out. "Kelsey, I'll drop you off at your place in case Ringo comes home."

Corbin gave him the keys. "*Merci.* Now I am going to get the mother of my child and I will kill anyone who has harmed her. Does anyone have a sword I can borrow?"

"I do," Alexis said.

Why didn't that surprise him?

"Oh, Christ," Ethan replied. "You had to ask her that?"

"I'll take it." Corbin was skilled with a sword thanks to boarding school. He would relish sticking someone today, given his current mood.

Brittany had been in the chair for twelve hours. She knew because there was a platinum clock on the wall opposite her that showed how excruciatingly long she had been held captive. It had been an hour since she had woken up from Donatelli's little mind sleep, and while they had let her use the bathroom, Gregor had also smacked her twice, shaken her, and, most recently, bitten her wrist and snacked on her blood.

He was trying to terrify her and it was working. She was pee-her-pants afraid, though at least her bladder was empty. Calling for help in her head didn't seem to be effective, because no one was answering, and given that a guard had actually stood in the doorway of the bathroom while she had used it, she didn't see how she could possibly escape. At this point, she figured Gregor could rape her, maim her, whatever, and she would live. But she was scared that somehow in his psycho mind games he was going to inadvertently hurt the baby. She could tolerate anything done to her, but she was going to go ballistic if anything happened to her child.

It was past 8 p.m., so she suspected that while she had been in a forced slumber, the vampires had been daysleeping as well. Now they were up for the night and she very possibly had hours before Corbin realized she wasn't going to show up at her sister's. God only knew what Gregor might decide to do to her in the interim. He was definitely enjoying her discomfort.

Sasha at least had disappeared. Ringo had stepped out for a cigarette. And Donatelli looked distinctly unhappy.

He shifted in his seat, tugging at his suit jacket. "Enough of that, Chechikov. Leave her be."

But the Russian only laughed, wiping her blood off his lips and licking his fingers one by one. "I am just playing with her."

The two men stared at each other, and after a minute, Brittany realized they were speaking to each other in their heads. She moved her thighs restlessly, making the leather on the chair squeak. She was thirsty, hungry, and getting a cramp in her leg. The baby was fluttering around in her belly in what felt like frantic somersaults, scaring her more than she already was, which she wouldn't have thought possible.

There was no obvious escape from the situation, yet she knew without a shadow of a doubt that Donatelli was the more rational of the two, the one who might be sympathetic, or at the least, unwilling to risk destroying his future prize. He wanted her child, and he wanted to keep her alive, which was different from his psycho pal. It had occurred to her that Gregor didn't need or want her alive. He wanted her baby and he had no interest in waiting for her to give birth. It wasn't a live child he wanted—it was her child's DNA. The genetic sequence, nothing more. He would treat her baby like a blood sample. Extract, use, discard.

That would have to be over her dead body. And while she was just a free-spirited suburban dentist who happened to get knocked up by a controversial vampire research scientist, she had no intention of bursting into tears and giving up. Something had happened to her since that day in her doctor's office, since her OB had said she was pregnant. She had morphed from happy-go-lucky to warrior woman. She'd protect her child with every last breath in her.

What she needed to do was play it smart. If Donatelli was feeling uncomfortable with Gregor's cruel behavior, she figured he would be downright furious if he knew the truth about her genetics.

And as luck would have it, Gregor and Donatelli appeared to be arguing. Gregor threw his hand up and gave a loud "Bah!"

Turning around, he slapped her again without warning, causing her to bite her tongue. Brittany winced, blinking hard against the pain, biting her lip to prevent a cry from slipping out. She wasn't going to give him the satisfaction. But Gregor didn't stick around to watch her suffer. He went out the door, slamming it behind him, making the walls shake precariously.

Donatelli shook his head in disgust before giving her a shrug. "Listen to me. Accept the money, Brittany. It is really your only choice. The money or death. Either way he'll have what he wants."

She ignored that. "Did you live in Las Vegas twenty-seven years ago?" she asked, swallowing hard, her mouth dry except for the blood from where her teeth had lacerated her tongue.

"What? I don't remember. I might have. I spent a few years in the seventies and eighties here. Why? Didn't you hear what I just said?" He frowned at her, hands on the knees of his black pants.

She didn't see herself in his features at all, except arguably her dark hair. It was odd to gaze into his face and try to find her own, but she saw nothing that proclaimed he was her father. Yet he was. "My mother knew you. She was a dancer at the Kareless Kitten Klub."

Donatelli smiled. "The Kitten? No kidding. I actually remember that club rather fondly. I spent many a night there."

"My mother's name was Gina Shoemaker. But chances are she went by Gina Baldizzi, which was her maiden name. She was very tall, with long legs, and jet-black hair." Brittany glanced toward the door, wanting to make sure Gregor wasn't returning.

Donatelli looked annoyed. "So?"

"So you slept with her."

His eyebrow went up. "Did I? And she shared this with you? That's a curious mother-daughter conversation."

"Oh, she didn't tell me. Corbin did."

"What the hell does Atelier know about it?"

Brittany leaned closer, straining her hands in the painful rope ties. She whispered, terrified someone would hear her. "You know that I'm an Impure, don't you? That's what makes my baby so special to all of you."

Donatelli stared hard at her. "So you know what we want."

"Yes, I do. But before you let Gregor take what he wants, let me tell you that this child, this three-quarter vampire, is your grandchild. You had sex with my mother, Gina Baldizzi, and *you* are the reason I have vampire blood. You're my father."

He sat up straight, his head shaking. "What? You are lying to me. That is . . ."

"Impossible? Why? How many vampires were hanging around the Kitten in the same time period?" And how many clubs could have been named something as ridiculous as the Kitten?

"My mother may have been a good-time girl, but I don't think she was doing half the Vampire Nation. You were probably the only vampire she ever slept with." Keeping her voice steady, she drove her point home. "Besides, Corbin ran a DNA test on me, and you, Roberto Donatelli, were the match. You are my father."

Her heart was pounding viciously as she waited for his reaction. He looked appropriately stunned and suspicious, but she could also see that he was considering believing her.

"Perhaps I remember your mother. Perhaps we had sex once or twice or twelve times. Perhaps I am your father. Why are you telling me?"

"Don't play stupid with me. I'm telling you now because I'm tied to a chair and I know that your Russian friend wouldn't hesitate to kill me or my baby. So I'm telling you if he does that, he will be killing your daughter. Your grandchild. Your future."

He studied her, for so long that she started to lose hope. It was a risk, telling him the truth, but it was her only opportunity for escape unless Corbin or Ethan came for her. But finally he nodded. "You could be my daughter. You are smart enough. And I would be a fool to risk anything happening to you, at least until I can verify the DNA myself."

Wow, that was heartwarming. But no more than she had expected, and she was pleased he could see the logic in protecting her.

"And I do remember your mother, actually, because I wasn't normally fond of brunettes. But her legs were amazing and she was willing to try anything . . . a wonderful combination of attributes." He stood up and moved toward her. "Though I imagine you'd rather not hear about that."

"I could do without it, thanks." But in a weird way, she was grateful he remembered her, that she wasn't just a nameless number in a long string of women he had seduced.

Donatelli leaned over, stared at her face, searching. "You do look like her. Yet you seem stronger, more stable." He started to untie her hand bonds. "How is your mother these days?"

"She died fifteen years ago. A drug overdose." Brittany tried not to recoil as his chest brushed near her face, the rustle of his suit and crisp dress shirt ringing in her ears. He smelled like a deep rich cologne and her stomach turned again. He didn't seem the least bit put out or distressed that he had a daughter he'd known nothing about.

"I am sorry to hear that. Who raised you then?" he asked, tone mildly curious, conversational.

"My sister, Alexis."

"Ah, yes." He got one hand free, and lightly massaged her wrist where the rope had burned her flesh. "Carrick's wife. No wonder she is such a fierce defender. Forced into adulthood too soon. It is a shame your mother never mentioned you to me."

Somehow Brittany couldn't bring herself to regret that.

"I could have provided for you in some fashion or another. As far as I am aware, you are my only child. I find the concept fascinating. I would have liked a hand in influencing your upbringing."

She just bet he would have. Boarding school for political power mongers' offspring maybe. She could have chummed around with daughters of dictators.

Undoing the other bond, he pulled back, and Brittany stared up at him. "I don't care about the past. All I care about is the future of my child." She didn't want to beg, so she locked her chin up, narrowed her eyes. "Protect me and your grandchild."

"Oh, I will." His voice was still casual, unconcerned, but she heard the determination in his voice, saw the conviction in his dark black eyes. "I have no intention of letting Gregor harm you."

Relief made her sag her shoulders a little, suck in a deep breath.

"Now stand up. I'm going to get you out of the building before the lunatic gets back."

Brittany stood, her knees and hips groaning with stiffness. Donatelli startled her by quickly retying her wrists in front of her. "In case we happen upon our friend." He stripped off his jacket and draped it over her bonded hands. "And in case we happen upon any mortals."

The fabric felt warm on her skin, and she realized she was cold, and exhausted. She wanted to do what she had always done, shrug her shoulders and assume everything would be alright, that Alexis or someone else would take care of it for her. But for the first time in her life, she realized that, ultimately, she was the one who had to take care of herself, and that for her child, she was the "it" person. The one who had to fix everything. She couldn't trust Donatelli. He was a means to an end, nothing more.

"Where are we going?"

"Somewhere safe."

"I want you to promise me you'll tell Corbin where I am."

He sighed. "Fine. Now do you want to stay here or not?"

"No." She followed him out the door. The danger ahead seemed much less threatening than staying and hanging with the slap-happy Russian.

Fifteen

"He's moving her," Gwenna said suddenly from the backseat of the car. "He's debating where to take her."

Corbin was already regretting that he had decided to drive. The traffic was typical for Vegas at night. He was crawling at about twenty miles an hour and he had only a miserable two miles to travel.

"I'm getting out," he said. He could have been there already if he'd run. Throwing the car into park, he started to open his door.

"I'm coming with you," Carrick said. "But you should leave the sword. Just take a knife instead." He flashed Corbin a wicked-looking hunting knife with a jagged blade.

"You carry the knife. I will take the sword. Nothing wrong with extra protection." Besides, it was December and he had thrown on a winter coat. There was no difficulty in concealing the sword. And he preferred its steel smoothness, its light, skillful drama. It was a classic weapon, whereas that knife was brutal, rough, inelegant.

"How about no one takes any weapons?" Gwenna asked as she jumped out of the backseat right after Alexis did. "Can't we just discuss this rationally with Roberto? Let me talk to him."

"No! You're not to say one word to him," Ethan said, pointing his finger at her.

Corbin did not have time to argue with either of them. He abandoned his car, earning lots of honks and finger gestures from other drivers, and took off running down the Strip, dodging groups of giggling women in their twenties, drunken couples leaning on each other and exchanging sloppy kisses, and men attempting to hand him flyers to bawdy shows.

He had done everything wrong. Everything. He had kept himself too isolated, he had forgotten to pay attention to the movements of those in power, had allowed himself to be self-absorbed and ignorant of the climate of the Nation. Now it was Brittany who was paying for his distraction. Brittany and his child.

Brittany? he called, feeling a sense of desperation. The Bellagio was a massive building with thousands of rooms and he had no idea how to find her.

There was no response, but suddenly Ethan was running alongside him. "I can hear her, Atelier. She sounds scared, but calm, and she answered me. He's taking her onto the roof."

"Why is she answering you but not me?" Corbin was stupidly devastated. It was an emotion totally inappropriate for the situation, and while he was grateful they knew where Brittany was headed, he wanted to be the one she called for, needed. Not her brother-in-law.

They jogged past the Bellagio's fountain, going off in its elaborate water display to the strains of Sinatra. "I don't know. Who cares?"

He shouldn't care, but he did. "You are right. That is good. We can find her easily on the roof."

Glancing behind him, he saw Alexis was right behind them, not even breaking a sweat, but Gwenna was nowhere to be found. "Where is your sister?"

Ethan swore. "Christ, I don't know. Let's hope she just couldn't keep up."

They were on the elevator in five minutes.

"Get off on the floor beneath the penthouse suites," Ethan told him. "We'll walk up the stairs from there."

When they reached the last turn of stairs before the rooftop, an EMERGENCY EXIT ONLY sign glaring at them, Corbin sensed vampire, knew Brittany and Donatelli had to be right ahead of him. Cautiously, he cracked the door open and saw Brittany with her hands tied in front of her, shorter hair sticking straight out in the wind, her stretchy top clinging to her swollen belly.

Closing his eyes for two seconds, he fought the fury, the guilt, the agony of wanting this to end positively. Then he shoved open the door and said coldly, "Move away from my woman, Donatelli."

Brittany turned and her face reflected relief. *"Corbin."*

Donatelli showed no surprise, his stance leisurely, unconcerned. "For once we are on the same side, Atelier. But there is no time to discuss this. We need to get her out of here."

Brittany was shivering, her teeth chattering, and he wanted nothing more than to pull her into his arms and comfort her. He settled for extracting the sword, removing his overcoat, and draping it over her shoulders. "Everything is fine, *ma chérie*," he whispered to her, easing her back away from Donatelli, who made no move to stop him.

Her big, black eyes stared at him over her shoulder. *I love you*, she said, her lips moving silently, as if she wanted to tell him quickly, privately, in case she never had another chance.

That nearly undid him. But he looked away from her, not wanting to let Donatelli out of his view. The Italian looked bemused.

"Now I understand," he said. "There is no debt, is there, Brittany? You are not a surrogate. You and the Frenchman are lovers. Very, very clever of you." He smiled at her. "I am impressed. I did notice his scent on you, but I thought it was because you are carrying his child."

Corbin really wasn't sure what in hell Donatelli was talking about and he didn't really care. He just wanted Brittany home, safe, with him. "Whatever you are planning, Donatelli, it ends here. She is leaving with me, and you will have no further contact with her."

"Actually, she's leaving with me," Chechikov said from the doorway, Gwenna held tightly against him, her head squeezed under his armpit.

Donatelli lost his cool insouciance. "Gwenna! Damn it, Gregor, let her go."

"You betrayed me," Gregor returned. "You were taking the girl off for yourself. That makes me very angry. Return her to me, and I'll return this one to you."

Donatelli's fists clenched, and there was suddenly sweat on his forehead. He glanced at Gwenna. Corbin held his breath, holding his sword loosely, ready to strike if Donatelli turned over Brittany. But Donatelli just shook his head. "I can't do that."

"Then I'll kill Gwenna." Gregor held his own sword in his free hand and he raised it menacingly.

"No!" Donatelli moved toward them, as did Carrick, but Gwenna startled them all by grabbing the sword and yanking it to her neck.

"Don't bargain for me, Roberto. It's not worth it. I have no issue with dying. In fact, I've wished for a very long time that I were dead." She tried to look up at Gregor, tried to force the blade closer to her flesh. "Go on, kill me. I welcome it."

The tension emanating from everyone was palpable. Corbin was impressed with Gwenna's courage, but also alarmed at the look in her eye. She looked serious. Gregor seemed to understand that as well.

When she said, "I'll slice my own head off before you can touch Brittany," he backed away, letting her go as he realized his bargaining chip was no longer worth anything.

"Give me the girl, Donatelli."

"No." Donatelli was in front of Brittany, and he put his arm behind him, waving at her to scoot back.

Corbin expected him to rush Donatelli, or grab Gwenna again. Instead, with no hesitation, he swung out with his sword and sliced Donatelli straight across the chest with so much force that blood arched everywhere, blinding Corbin and sending Donatelli crashing backward into Brittany, who screamed.

Wiping his face, Corbin launched himself in front of both Brittany and Donatelli, trusting Ethan and Alexis to get Brittany off the roof. And while it might not be the smartest move to go on the offensive with Gregor, he suspected Chechikov's desire for the child was greater than his anger at Donatelli. He would step over the Italian and go right for Brittany.

Which Corbin didn't intend to allow. He raised his own sword and attacked.

Brittany knew she should stop screaming, but she couldn't seem to turn the volume off. There was just so much blood, it was everywhere, wet and thick, smelling sweet and putrid all at the same time. Donatelli had collided into her, knocking her down onto her butt, and now he was lying on the roof in front of her, his chest looking like he'd had a date with open heart surgery. In the dark ages. He was gored from end to end and she gagged, taking deep little breaths so she wouldn't vomit the bile that kept crawling up her throat.

But he was a vampire. He would heal. And he had prevented Gregor from striking her. She suspected she had been the monster's target—that he had intended to just swing out and kill her, then cart her body off in the melee. Easier to haul off a corpse than a kicking and screaming live person.

Alexis pulled Brittany back, away from her father, but that

Erin McCarthy

didn't seem right, to just abandon him, so she fought her sister. Her spindly arms were no match, though, for vampire strength, and Alexis kept hauling her, despite her protestations. It was when Alexis had her a good five feet back from Donatelli, and she had stopped kicking long enough to look up, that she realized Corbin was engaged in battle with Gregor.

"Corbin! Jesus!" she shrieked, trying to break free from Alexis, whirling toward Ethan for help. "Stop him! He's . . ." *No match for Gregor*, was what she was thinking. Corbin was a lot of things, including sweet, cute, intelligent, and downright fierce in bed, but she didn't think he could go head to head with a burly Russian double his size.

But the words died on her lips when she noticed that Corbin *was* a match for Gregor. Holy crap, he was a sword stud. He was doing that French musketeer thing, whirling and jabbing and clanking, moving with skill and confidence, and looking kind of, well, hot. Really hot. Hello. Yet he was still in mortal danger, regardless of the fact that he seemed to be holding his own.

Someone should rescue him, because she was going to croak if he got hurt. Not that he could get permanently hurt, because he was a vampire, but shit, what if Gregor cut off his head? Even a vampire could die if someone really wanted to kill him. She winced as Corbin stumbled backward from a particularly brutal blow. "Oh, geez, Alex, do something."

"He's fine," was her sister's reply. "He has everything under control."

"But shouldn't we . . . can't we . . ." Shoot a rocket at Gregor and launch him off the roof? There was an idea.

250

Alex rubbed her arms gently. "Sweetie, no. This is Corbin's fight. Men don't want to be rescued. Hell, *I* don't want to be rescued. Now come on, let's go."

Leave? Was her sister nuts? "I can't leave until I know he's okay."

"You'll just distract him. He wants you safe."

Crap. She knew Alex was right, but she couldn't leave. Gregor was so strong and Corbin was . . . kicking his ass. Gregor was huffing and puffing, while Corbin hadn't even broken a sweat. He held the sword loosely, yet whenever Gregor charged him, he was always right there with a block and a stab. Gregor's chest was blooming scarlet from all the hits he'd taken.

"The baby, Brittany. Think about the baby."

At the same moment, she saw Corbin glance over at her. "Brittany!" he yelled, appalled. "Get out of here!" Shoot, she was distracting him.

"Okay!" She moved toward the stairs. "But what about Donatelli?" It seemed rude to leave him there after he had tried to help her escape.

"Gwenna's got him. She and Ethan will haul him out."

Actually, Donatelli was walking on his own, and he and Gwenna were arguing.

"What the hell is the matter with you?" he demanded. "What were you thinking to grab that sword? I almost had a goddamn heart attack."

"You can't have a heart attack," she told him sharply, her arm around his middle, supporting his weight. "And you should be ashamed of yourself for kidnapping a pregnant woman."

"I had no intention of hurting her. And this is what happens when I don't have you acting as my conscience."

Gwenna bristled. "That was utterly exhausting, given your many misdeeds, so I retired. It's called a divorce. And you haven't changed one bit in the two hundred years since." They moved slowly toward the door.

Brittany exchanged a look with Alexis. Gwenna was a bit more of a pistol than she had expected. And Ethan looked like he was choking on a nut. His face was completely red. "Can you move a little faster?" he demanded. "We'd like to get Brittany out of here before Gregor throws down his sword and charges us. Maybe we should leave Donatelli here."

"Don't let me burden you," Donatelli pronounced coldly, letting go of Gwenna, and stepping aside, a sour and stubborn look on his face.

"Oh, for crying out loud." Gwenna yanked his shirt. "Just get your bloody arse down these steps. Ethan, you be quiet or I'll be tempted to box your ears. You have absolutely no reason to despise Roberto as much as you do."

Donatelli and Ethan both looked startled, but Ethan was quick to retort, "You've gone daft! He's been a bloody thorn in my side for nine centuries. He broke Alexis's wrist. And he just hired an assassin to have me killed last fall!"

Scoffing, Donatelli limped down the stairs, holding his ribs under his blood-soaked shirt. "I knew he couldn't kill you. It was just politics, nothing personal, Carrick."

Gwenna glared at the men. "And you both wonder why I

choose to hide in a pile of rocks in York? It's so I don't have to deal with either one of you."

Alexis turned to Brittany, looking bewildered. "Something weird just happened. The three of them just had some kind of power struggle and I think Gwenna won."

But Brittany was barely listening. As they went through the doorway, she was glancing back over her shoulder, checking on Corbin. He and Gregor were circling each other. Corbin had a feral grin on his face as he strode to the left, eye always on Gregor, his wrist spinning his sword like he was working the table at a hibachi steakhouse.

There was just no way she could leave.

Doing a totally stupid girl move, she ran back up the stairs, out onto the roof, and slammed the door shut behind her.

"After everything I've done for you, this is how you repay me?" Gregor said to Corbin, moving slowly, his breathing hard and labored.

"If I had had any idea zat you wanted to use my research for cloning, I would never have taken your money." Corbin should have realized that no man shelled out hundreds of thousands of dollars without having a personal stake in it, no matter how rich or odd. Yet Chechikov had fooled him with his recluse status, his complete disinterest, his eccentric and random distribution of funding. "And I have lifted my sword because you took Brittany and my child."

"You're a scientist. You, more so than anyone else, understand the implications of that baby. You can't keep him hidden, you know. I am going to win the election and then I will find your child. It would be much smarter to work together with me. I promise not to harm the baby if you conduct all your research on my behalf. Together we can rule the Nation."

Corbin shook his head. "That's your dream, not mine. And there is no more research. I destroyed all the data this afternoon. I am the only vampire who understands our genetic makeup, who can facilitate both a return to mortality and a population explosion, and it is gone. All of it." Which wasn't exactly true, but he was keeping that information to himself.

His words sent Gregor into a rage. "You French fool! I'll kill you and take your baby and do the damn research without your goddamn pathetic little concerns."

When he charged him, Corbin was ready, knowing Gregor had more strength than he did, but that his asset was agility and technique. When the Russian came at him, Corbin spread his legs, arched his sword, and with every ounce of strength he had, sliced the blade deep into Chechikov's throat and neck, pushing backward to drive it deeper. Gregor stumbled, blood spraying, hands clawing at his neck, and with a tremendous heave, he managed to repel both Corbin and the sword back. But the momentum of his own massive push, the give of the sword leaving his neck, sent him catapulting backward, where he tripped and went over the side of the building with a roar of fury.

Dropping the sword, Corbin jogged to the edge of the roof

and glanced down. Chechikov was falling fast and hard, and he heard the faint thump when the Russian collided with the top of a semitruck parked at the food delivery entrance of the casino and hotel. With any luck, Corbin had succeeded in driving the sword deep enough to cause death, or to injure him enough that he would bleed out on the truck before healing.

Unable to resist, he spat over the side to reflect his disdain for Chechikov. "Bastard."

"Corbin, are you okay?"

He turned to find Brittany careening across the rooftop, holding her belly as she ran at breakneck speed. "What are you still doing up here?" he asked in horror. "You were supposed to leave with Carrick!"

"I couldn't leave until I knew you were alright."

Offended, he bent over to pick his sword up. "You did not trust me? You thought I could not handle the Russian? Perhaps I am not man enough?"

"Oh, good grief, chill. That's not what I meant. I wasn't questioning your masculinity, I was just worried."

"You should have worried less about me and more about our child." He was appalled that she had stayed when she should have taken herself straight to safety.

Not answering, she peered over the roof edge. "It's too dark to see anything. Is he dead?"

"We should be so lucky." Brittany was making him nervous, leaning like that, so he grabbed her arm and pulled her back. "It is possible, and if you return home with your sister, I could investigate the situation."

Her jaw dropped. "Why does it feel like we're fighting with each other?"

"I am not aware that we are doing any such thing," he said stiffly, even as he realized he was being unreasonable. But he had spent the entire evening terrified for her safety, and now he found that she had deliberately risked herself and their child because she thought he could not survive a battle with Gregor. It had his nerves shredded, his pride injured, his relief that she was safe so sharp, he felt as though he could actually taste it.

"Fine. Since we're not arguing, you won't say a word when I tell you that I'm going to the Ava and I'm going to eat something, and then sleep for about twelve hours in Alex's apartment. If you feel like discussing anything with me, you can do it in the morning."

Hurling his overcoat at him, she whirled around and tossed back over her shoulder, "Oh, and by the way, I told Donatelli he's my father so that he would have an interest in saving me from Gregor. It worked, but now I have no idea what he'll do with that information."

Wonderful. Just *fantastique*.

Using his coat, he wiped the blood off his sword, and followed her down three flights of stairs to the elevator, suddenly feeling like a naughty schoolboy.

Arms folded over her middle, she stared up at the elevator numbers and gave little huffs and sighs of impatience.

Corbin could not tolerate the ridiculousness of their silence. "Brittany." He wrapped his arms around her, bloody sword under his coat and all. "I was terrified they would harm you. I am so glad you are safe." Leaning into her, he breathed deeply the scent of her body, her hair, and kissed her temple. It was calming to hold her, and he closed his eyes, pulled her closer. "I love you. It amazes me how much."

"I love you, too," she whispered, stroking her fingers lightly across his arms.

"I do not know what I would do if something happened to you."

"Nothing happened to me."

"I know. And nothing will as long as I have breath." The elevator dinged at the first floor. "Now let's find your sister so you can go home and relax. I have to check on Chechikov."

Turning, she frowned. "Don't do anything stupid."

"What stupid? What are you talking about? I'm just going to see if he is dead." He covered the sword with his overcoat as they stepped off the elevator, knowing the Bellagio security would find it fascinating that a pregnant woman had shown up on their elevator cameras standing next to a sword suspended in midair. They would probably wonder if the building was haunted.

"Don't provoke him. You won. Leave it at that. There's no reason to pick another fight with him."

There it was again. That implication that he could not win in a battle. He tried not to lose his temper. "Go with Alexis and sleep. I can handle Chechikov."

She shook her head with a soft smile. "Boys."

Kissing her forehead, he put a hand on her tight belly. "Girls." He saw her sister pacing anxiously by a seating group of sofas in the lobby. "Now there is Alexis. Go."

"Fine." She went with a wave and a last admonishment. "Be careful!"

"Yes, yes." Corbin picked his way through the casino and out a back door marked for employees. It took several minutes to find the loading dock that Chechikov had dropped down onto. Fortunately, there wasn't a lot of activity in that area at night. The truck seemed to be parked in the loading dock waiting for the next shift to unload. Putting his coat back on, Corbin jumped up on the fender, and leaped onto the roof. He could see Chechikov lying on top and knew immediately he was still alive. He could hear his heart beating, the noisy rattle of his labored breathing as he moved in closer.

The neck wound was healing, but his eyes were glazed with pain, his arm bent at an odd angle. Corbin did not want to kill him, because he was certain that would not sit well with the tribunal. Also, he was not entirely sure how Brittany would react to that. But he knew leaving Gregor to recover would be dangerous. There would be nothing then to prevent him from abducting Brittany or the baby at a later date.

"Atelier," Chechikov said, struggling to sit up.

"Chechikov. I see you have suffered no permanent damage from your clumsy tumble," Corbin said, feeling not a single ounce of pity for him.

Gregor gave up the effort and fell onto his back. "Rot in hell. Go and leave me alone to heal. You won't kill me, I know you won't. You are too soft, like Carrick. Even like Donatelli." Gregor closed his eyes briefly, then opened them and locked gazes with Corbin. "And when you have forgotten all about me, and you're living your charmed, self-important life, with your pretty little mortal girlfriend, I'll come for her. And when I'm done with her, after I've raped her over and over, taken her blood, broken her bones, forced her into submission on her knees, my cock in her mouth, she'll wish she were dead. But I won't kill her. I'll play with her, torment her, until I'll leave a knife out or maybe a gun and she'll kill herself rather than have to suffer one more minute. And the whole time she'll wonder where is my lover? Why won't he save me? Corbin, Corbin . . ." Gregor mocked, his voice a high-pitched imitation. He sneered. "But you'll never find her, not until her body is filled with rot, and the vultures have pecked out her eyes."

Corbin wanted to kill Gregor, take his head off with one slick swipe of his sword. He could do it, and Gregor wouldn't be able to defend himself. But that was too good for the bastard. So he sat down next to Chechikov, calmly, coldly, and listened to him hiss and spit his threats, his vile promises. Corbin said nothing, but stared out behind the Bellagio at the labyrinth of Dumpsters and employee parking lots, the reality behind the illusion of the casino, and waited.

And when he saw that Chechikov's neck had healed sufficiently, and he was starting to move restlessly on the truck, testing his healing bones, Corbin reached into his overcoat and pulled out his portable lab kit that he carted everywhere. The kit in which he had stored his triumph, his vaccine. Loading a syringe, he plunged the needle into the vial and withdrew the clear liquid.

Gregor was coughing, but still managed to say, "What the fuck are you doing, you French pussy?"

Corbin turned and ripped Gregor's sleeve up. There was a plump, rich vein hovering right at the surface of his inner elbow. Waiting for him. Perfect. This was the best solution, the most logical way to protect Brittany and the baby.

So he pricked Gregor with the needle, and injected him with the vaccine that would suppress his vampirism virus and essentially return him to mortal.

"Have a nice, long recovery, Gregor," he said, tucking the syringe back in the carrying case. "And stay the hell away from my girlfriend."

He walked away with Gregor's groans of agony ringing in his ears.

Sixteen

Ringo only vaguely remembered entering the Ava, Carrick's casino. He had been flying at the Bellagio after he had picked up the girl for Donatelli, but it was vague after that. He thought maybe he had slept, and he'd woken with a serious erection and an anvil of guilt pressing down on him.

So he must have decided to look for Kelsey, and when he hadn't found her at the Hilton—in fact, had discovered she'd paid their bill and checked them out—the Ava had seemed the logical place to look next. But he had gotten distracted by the blackjack table, and the fact that he had cash in his pocket from the job.

It wasn't with a lot of surprise, though, that he saw his wife slide into the chair next to him, her lips in a straight, angry line. She always had a way of turning up.

"Hey, babe," he said, giving her a smile. She really was pretty, his wife, her hair glossy and smooth, complexion flawless. "I was looking for you."

"Obviously very hard," she said.

Was that sarcasm? Kelsey didn't do that tone with him. Ringo didn't like the frown on her face so he nudged her with his knee and smiled.

"This is where we first met," he said, throwing his hand out so far, he accidentally hit the woman next to him. "Sorry." He leaned back toward Kelsey. "Isn't that romantic?"

"How much did you have?"

Six, maybe seven glasses. He wasn't sure, really. And it was better not to piss her off when he was feeling friendly, horny, ready to make nice. "Not much. And that was an accident."

With a sigh, she glanced at the table. "I have a room upstairs. Are you going to come to bed?"

Hell, yeah. "Deal," he told the dealer.

The card was flipped. "Over. House wins."

Ringo saluted him. "Have a good night." He lifted his cigarette out of his ashtray and smiled at Kelsey. "Lead the way, babe."

She didn't speak to him the whole way to the elevator, and her silence bothered him. Kelsey wasn't the silent type. "Okay, I screwed up, is that what you want me to say? I'm sorry. Really, really sorry."

As they waited for the doors to open, he threw his arm around her and kissed the top of her head. "Give me a break, Kels." He loved the way the lights bounced and swam when he was on a trip, and he could have sworn there was a halo of light around Kelsey's head. A fucking halo. He tried to lick it, but there was nothing there.

"What are you doing?" she said, swatting at him.

He laughed, feeling good, so damn good, he didn't even understand it. "I love you, you know, you make me crazy, but shit, I love you. It's like you and me, we're both such fuck-ups we belong together."

With a small smile, she said, "I resemble that."

That made him laugh again, loud and full, and he gave her a nudge forward when the elevator opened. "What floor's our room on . . ."

Ringo's laughter died out. In the mirror in front of them on the back wall of the elevator, he couldn't see either one of them, just the potted plant on the console table behind them. Just the plant and his brother Kyle.

"Holy shit." Ringo swung around but there was nothing there.

Looking forward, there was Kyle again, watching him steadily, carefully, not smiling. The elevator doors started to slide shut, bumping into him.

"What?" Kelsey asked.

Shaking his head, Ringo moved forward, letting the door close. He blinked hard. "Shit. Bad trip."

That was all it was. Nothing more.

When Brittany woke up, she noticed two things immediately. She had slept for fourteen hours, since the clock in the guest room at her sister's apartment read 2 p.m., and Corbin was sitting in a charcoal-colored overstuffed chair next to the bed, watching her.

"*Bonjour.* How are you feeling?"

"Stiff. Thirsty." She smiled up at him, stretching her arms over her head. "But fine. How are you? All in one piece still, that's good."

"Yes, all in one piece." Reaching a long arm, he brushed her hair back off her face. "We need to talk."

That sounded ominous. "Okay." Propping the bed pillows behind her, she sat up and fixed the straps on her tank top. He looked serious, and tired. He probably hadn't even been to bed yet himself.

"Gregor is no longer a threat."

"He's dead?" Brittany wasn't sure how she felt about that. There should be remorse, pity for a man who had become so twisted, but she had a hard time dredging up any sympathy.

"No. Not dead. But taken care of." He moved over to the bed and sat on the dove gray sheet next to her thighs. "I do not want you to worry about him."

Well, that was illuminating. If he thought she was going to leave it at that, he had forgotten what century they were in. She wasn't the delicate little miss who couldn't take the truth. But before she could argue the point, he continued.

"And Donatelli, in order to save his own ass, and to protect both himself and you from Gregor, has joined your brother-in-law's political campaign. He understands that he is to have no contact whatsoever with you or the baby."

"What?" Brittany didn't consider herself up on vamp politics, but she'd been forced to learn enough to know that Donatelli had previously been Ethan's opponent, and he had lobbied for population growth, something Ethan didn't support. "Why the hell would he join Ethan's campaign? Why would Ethan let him do that?"

"Because Gregor is still running against Carrick, and he has something of a celebrity status in the Nation. Sort of like an Oprah of the vampires. With Donatelli on his side, he had the potential to win. But with Donatelli switching camps, going over to a sworn enemy, everyone will be suspicious of Chechikov. And together, Carrick and Donatelli make a powerful statement of unity. Everyone—Impures, ancients, conservatives—is happy."

Everyone but her, that is. She was more confused than happy, but it wasn't her arena. It wasn't her political battle. If Corbin and Ethan thought it was the right step to take, she would have to trust them. Her concern was her child. "So since Donatelli knows about the baby, there isn't much use in me running off and hiding, is there?"

Corbin shook his head, his green eyes troubled. "No. I see no real value in you cutting yourself off from friends and family who care about you and can help you with the baby."

But not him? Brittany's heart started to pound. Corbin didn't look right. "What about us? Where do we go from here?"

"It is still dangerous, I will not shield you from that this time. We must be cautious, vigilant, where the baby is concerned. I have not yet decided which is better—to live in Vegas, where you have friends to protect you, or to start anew somewhere else, where no one will be watching you."

"If it's not clear-cut, I'd rather stay in Vegas. It would be lonely raising a baby in a new place." And since she was getting no sense of whether he had meant he would go with her or not, she couldn't assume he would be helping her.

"I understand. And I will protect you, of course, if that is necessary." He ran his finger down her thigh. It was an odd gesture, like he wanted to touch her, claim her, but hesitated to take all of her.

He made a pattern on her knee with his fingertip. "And after the baby is born, I could turn you. That way we can be together, forever. All of us."

"Corbin!" She hadn't expected him to say that, knowing how he felt about immortality. Yet it immediately was a tantalizing concept, a carrot of eternity dangled in front of her . . . forever with her child and her lover. It was a happy thought for a simple moment. But reality intruded. What he had suggested was wrong, unnatural, and given the expression on his face, he knew it, too. That was not the way to raise a child.

"You know we can't do that, as much as I would like to be with you, as much as it hurts to say no." She put her hand over his, wanting to touch him, wanting to soften her words, and the ache in her heart. "We have to do what's right for the baby. With you immortal, and me mortal, working together, we can ensure the baby is both safe at night, and being raised in a normal manner, in the day."

"You think being a vampire is abnormal? You think we cannot be good parents if we are immortal?" His voice rose in indignation.

Brittany fought back the lump in her throat that kept rising. "You know what I mean . . . every vampire I know was raised by mortal parents, during the day, with schools and friends and birthday parties. I can't imagine what it would be like to be raised only at night, in a world filled only with adults, who don't eat regular food and can leap off buildings. No children, no playmates, no sunshine in the park. That has nothing to do with us and the kind of parents we will be. It just wouldn't be right to force our child into that kind of abnormal, isolated life."

The image of raising her child in the darkness made her want to weep. It meant being apart from Corbin, at least during the day, but she would sacrifice that for her baby. "With you immortal and me mortal, our child gets the best of both worlds."

His eyes were dark, troubled. "Except for her parents together. We cannot give her that."

Tears made him blur in front of her. "Corbin . . . don't say that. We can and will be together. Just like we talked about before. We'll get a house, we'll live together."

"Of course we will," he said. "But it will be but a pale shadow of a normal life. I can never give that to you."

"Normal is what we make it. We'll have the same amount of time together that a lot of couples do . . . some work swing shifts from each other so they don't have to pay for day care, other women have husbands who travel. This is no different."

He nodded, even as his eyes told her otherwise. There was defeat there, sorrow. "You are right. Of course. It will be no different."

Without warning, his fist bunched in the sheet, and he tore it down, off of her. "I want you."

Men could so easily shift their emotions to sex, it was astonishing. But Brittany could use the touching, the distraction, the feel of him inside her, the promise of being together. "What do you want me for?"

"For everything." He kissed her, lips hard and aggressive. "For forever."

"You have me," she told him, putting her arms around his neck, pulling him closer to her. She loved the way he smelled— like rich, confident, and sophisticated man—and she liked how his smooth, polished control always disintegrated in bed with her.

In two seconds he had her tank top off, and her bare nipples beaded in anticipation as the cool air hit her skin. She was forced to lift her backside off the bed as he immediately went for her panties, dragging and tugging them down.

His mouth was hot and urgent, his tongue thrusting deep into her as he undid his pants. Brittany fell back on the bed, gripping the taut muscles in his biceps. He pulled his mouth off hers long enough to ask, "Is it okay on your back?" His fingers, hands that had known two hundred years of life and had held that sword so confidently, fluttered carefully over her belly, over their child.

The position didn't feel uncomfortable, and she liked the way he rose up over her, the way she could see every inch of his face, his expression, when he filled her. "It's okay."

That was all he needed to hear. His pants disappeared, and he entered her, his body covering hers, his urgency and desperation and love pressing on her, in her, and Brittany gasped in pleasure, at the intimacy of being connected to him, their child between them.

Before she could match his rhythm, or adjust her hips to meet his thrusts, he flipped over and pulled her on top of him, his hands cupping her breasts, thumbs toying with her nipples. Gripping the sheets, she leaned forward and moved on him, wanting him to recognize, to know, to see, what she felt for him. That some way or another, they would make it work. It did work, because they loved each other, and wanted a future.

The slick pressure on her clitoris as she rode him was agonizing, delightful, and the way he watched her, the way his eyes opened wider, the way he got a feverish wild look of pride, like he thought she was amazingly sexy, made her gasp, grind harder, deeper. And when she couldn't take any more, when her emotion and passion overwhelmed her body, she came with a cry, locking eyes with him.

"Beautiful," he said, cupping her cheek.

She sucked in air, tried to collapse on his chest, body still trembling, but he rolled her onto her side, and pulled her leg over his, opening her completely for him. Her breasts brushed his bare chest, and he kissed her at the same time he pushed his erection into her. They were touching from forehead to feet, entangled together, locked in an intimacy so primal, so elemental, so extreme, that Brittany felt tears in her eyes. As he dug his nails into her naked thighs and exploded, a curse ripped from his lips.

"I love you, *ma chérie*," he said. "I love you. For me, there is only you."

Brittany hung on, her emotions perilously close to the edge, skittering toward what, she wasn't sure. Closing her eyes, she cried, "I love you, too."

It would always be like this, Corbin knew. Brittany had gotten up for the day after their lovemaking, while he had gone to sleep for a few hours. Now she was tucked back into the queen-size bed in Carrick's guest room, and Corbin was up, roaming, ready for the night.

There was nothing to be done. He should be grateful they had what they did. That they were together, such as it was. That he would have a family, however spliced together. But it wasn't gratitude he felt. It was anger, sadness, a creeping, debilitating sort of bitterness that crawled around the edges of his heart and made him want to throw things.

Instead of chucking Alexis's vase sitting on a low table in their hallway, Corbin went into the living room, where Ethan was working on his laptop computer. He undid his wristwatch, and pulled it over his hand. That watch hadn't come off his arm in forty years, but now he tossed it onto the table in front of Carrick.

"I am returning this. I consider my punishment over, my retribution fulfilled."

Ethan looked at him. "You can't do that. It's not your right to decide that your punishment is over. It's mine, and the tribunal's."

"I injected Gregor with my vaccine," Corbin told him. "He

will essentially be a mortal, whether he realizes it yet or not. And I suspect he'll try to hide it—at least until the election is over."

Almost dropping his computer, Ethan stood up. "You can't just do that either!"

"I can and I did. He was a threat to my child, to Brittany, to the Nation. To our entire way of life. I neutralized the threat. And I do not regret it. I just thought you should know, as a courtesy."

Corbin turned on his heel and headed for the door.

"Where the hell are you going?"

"To Paris."

Or as close to it as he could get in the desert. When he was on top of the faux Eiffel Tower at the Paris Hotel, he sat down on a lit iron rung and looked at the Vegas skyscape. His parents had been exiles in England during the Terror, and he could still remember how his mother had longed for France, wept for the memory of Paris, expressed her impatience in all things that weren't home. He knew that feeling, that frustration now. He wanted home. Paris. A family. The sun.

He wanted what he had had, what he could have with Brittany, if it were different.

The gift of immortality was one he had never asked for, one he had never wanted. He had been turned against his will, and had always regretted the change in his destiny. He still didn't want eternity. What he wanted was Paris. Coffee and baguettes. The heat of the sun on his arms, the cold splash of the Seine on his face. Brittany and his child and a finite amount of time to make the most of his existence, to squeeze his worth into a half-century, and to never have to face an endless, gaping yawn of a future.

They could make it work as such. They would make it work. But it broke his heart that he would never see a school play, never watch his daughter on the soccer field, never see her chubby little legs pumping hard on the playground at noon, cheeks flushed with heat. He would have two hours a day with her, at most, and while he walked the night, she would be tucked into her crib, eyes closed to him.

Corbin wanted to sink into obscurity, to be a nameless number in the mass of humanity, who mattered only to his bride and baby. That wasn't his calling, his destiny. He had a different life, and he would live it.

But on his terms.

"What if I told you . . ." Corbin said, leaning over the railing, his words trailing off.

"What?" Brittany asked, sitting in a patio chair on Alexis's balcony, fighting the urge to stand up and go to him. Corbin was acting strange, storming into the apartment and demanding to speak to her. Alexis would have told her that was par for the course with Corbin, but she knew him. Something was bothering him, something that had him edgy and brusque, and it was different than the way he had been the night before.

She wanted to hug him, to comfort him, but she didn't want

to distract him from whatever he needed to say. There couldn't be any more withholding of important information from her.

He turned slightly, stared straight at her. "What if I told you I could be mortal again?"

Forget not standing up. She almost leaped off the balcony. "What!"

"What if I told you that, if you wanted it, I could give you that normal life, with a house in ze suburbs, and a husband who is home for dinner every night and attends all ze soccer games?"

"The vaccine?" she asked, pressing her hand to her chest because she had the sudden fear that her heart might actually catapult out of her body.

He nodded. "Yes. It is finished. And tested. On Gregor Chechikov."

"*That's* how you took care of Gregor?" Holy crap and then some.

"Yes." And he looked a little smug over that fact. "I have a clean conscience. I protected my family and the Vampire Nation, yet I did not kill him."

"Jesus. And you know he's mortal now?"

Corbin nodded. "I saw him. Apparently he wishes to keep it a secret from the general vampire population, but he is recuperating from the injuries sustained in the fall. His wife is tending to him. He is very angry, and he is very much mortal." Corbin gave a slight smile. "She was feeding him chicken broth while he swore at her."

"My God . . . you did it. You can reverse vampirism." Tears

popped into her eyes and she swiped at them impatiently. "What are you going to do with the vaccine? And how do you know that Gregor can't just make himself a vampire again by being drained?"

He turned completely around to face her and leaned back against the railing, crossing his ankles. His black Italian shoes were gleaming and new, pants pressed, shirt expensive. "Even if someone were foolish enough to drain Gregor and give him their own blood, I am confident it will not achieve the same results. And I destroyed my lab. It's dangerous information to have so accessible to the wrong people, as we both discovered. But . . ." He patted his leather jacket. "I did not use it all on Gregor. The formula is encoded on a ThumbDrive, and it will stay there for now, until I determine what is the best course of action to take. But I have enough, right now, to return myself to mortality."

"Is that what you want?" She couldn't let him do it for her, or the baby. It had to be what he wanted, even though she had the urge to jump up and down and shriek with joy that he could be with her, every day, all day, that he could age with her, and share in all the moments of pride and worry and pleasure that raising children could bring.

But she didn't want to influence him, wanted him to be sure that he was doing it for the right reasons, for himself. The fact that he might do it for her and the baby spoke volumes about the depth of his character, his caring, his compassion, but it wouldn't be right to use that to her advantage.

"Yes, it's what I want." Corbin gave a short laugh. "*Ma chérie*, it is all I have ever wanted. I want to be a mortal man. I want to see my child grow up. I want you. I even want to die one day, an old man, knowing that I treated each day as a gift, each moment as a treasure."

Then he went down on one knee. "Will you do me the honor of being my wife, through good times and bad, in sickness and in health, until death do us part? Not for the child, but for us. Because of our love, our friendship."

Brittany was speechless. She was blubbering, tears just streaming all over the place. She managed a ridiculous, choked out "Oh, Corbin!" but nothing else.

He gripped her hand a little harder. "Is that a yes?"

Nodding her head up and down, she gave a short, sob-smothered laugh. "Yes. I'll marry you."

Rising elegantly, he sketched her a bow. "*Ma chérie*, you make me the happiest of men."

He was so damn hot when he pulled out those nineteenth-century manners. "And I'm the happiest chick in Vegas. But I have to ask . . . are there any side effects to the vaccine?"

"Not that I'm aware of." He pulled her into his arms. "Why? Would you not have me if I grew large nose hairs or turned a strange chalk white color?"

She laughed and settled against his chest. "Don't be ridiculous. I meant, I don't want anything awful happening to you. I don't want you to suffer. I don't want it to kill you. If there is even a chance, it's not worth the risk."

"I am confident that the drug inhibits the virus, that is all. Minor side effects may be possible, but nothing alarming."

Feeling ridiculously, sickeningly happy, Brittany squeezed her arms around him tighter and teased, "What about your sperm?"

Erin McCarthy

"I'm sure I'll have plenty to keep you busy for years." He gave her a French kiss, in every sense of the word.

Brittany pulled back and sighed. "Oh, la, la." Then she smacked his arms, shook him a little. "Promise me you'll give this some thought. Be sure this is what you want. Mortality, that is. You're locked into marrying me and can't retreat from that offer, but mortality is totally your choice."

"I have thought about it."

"Just wait until the baby is born. Be sure." She didn't want him to have any regrets. "You're choosing between life and death here. That can't be an easy decision."

"It was an easy decision for you," he pointed out. "I offered to turn you, and you immediately refused."

"That was different. I wasn't giving something up. You will be giving up immortality."

He shook his head. "I am not giving up immortality." Caressing her belly, he said, "You and I, our love, it will live forever in our child."

There were the tears again. She was a freaking water faucet. On, off, on again. "What will happen to our child, if he is immortal, and you and I die? If you stay a vampire, you can be with him forever."

Corbin's jaw locked. "All children live beyond their parents. That is natural and normal. But our child will have Alexis and Ethan to go through eternity with her."

"It sounds like you've made up your mind already."

He shrugged. "I will think about it. I will wait. But our marriage cannot wait. You will be Mrs. Corbin Jean Michel Atelier as soon as it is possible."

"I'm a dentist," she reminded him. "I get to be Dr. Atelier."

"Technically, I have that title as well, since I went to medical school in the 1860s. We will both be Dr. Atelier. But you're the beautiful one."

"And you're the hairy one." Brittany felt silly, giddy, delirious. She kissed his jaw, his neck, his collarbone.

"I am most certainly not hairy."

"Show me." She peeled at his shirt, his belt buckle.

"Right here? Right now?"

"Yep."

So he did.

Seventeen

"Why black and gold?" Alexis was saying to Ethan, as she peeled her shoes off and flopped on the pink suede couch Corbin and Brittany had picked out when they had bought their new house.

Their decorating tastes had collided so that their living room was Bombay meets the Cotswolds, with a splash of Vegas glitz thrown in. Atrocious by some standards, but perfect for them.

"Why not purple and gold?" Alexis continued.

"Because New Orleans already uses that for Mardi Gras," Ethan told his wife dryly.

"But what about purple and black? Green and black? Yellow and chartreuse? Black is so morbid. Even for a vampire inaugural ball."

From the chair on the other side of the coffee table, Corbin listened to the discussion with only half an ear. He was too busy staring at his daughter, who was astonishingly perfect, from the tip of her soft, distended head, to her wrinkled red and peeling toes.

"It's black and gold and that is just the way it is," Ethan told her, leaning over Corbin's shoulder to tickle Ava's tiny fingers. "Hello, gorgeous. Did you stay awake to see your Uncle Ethan in his triumph? Everyone else has to call me Mr. President or President Carrick, but you get to call me Uncle Ethan, what do you think of that?"

"She's awake because Corbin won't lay her down," Brittany said, giving a yawn. "She's four days old and she has him wrapped completely around her finger."

"She's not sleepy," Corbin protested, holding Ava on his knees. "Her eyes are wide open, staring at me. Her beautiful big brown eyes just like her mama's. Isn't that right, precious?" He looked down at his daughter and she blinked back at him, her little button nose wrinkling a little. His heart had that unmistakable sensation of skipping a beat, as it had with regularity since the minute he had first laid eyes on his baby in the labor and delivery room. Ava Coco Renee Atelier had come into the world screaming, red-faced and angry, her lusty cries echoing in the room, and he knew in that moment that she could spit up on him, throw tantrums, wreck her car at sixteen, and he would never do anything but adore her.

It was awe-inspiring and frightening and glorious.

"If you would like to sleep, Brittany, go ahead, *ma chérie*. I will stay up with her."

His wife yawned again. "Maybe I should. The little beast will want to eat again in two hours anyway. Better sleep while I can."

"She is not a little beast, are you, darling?" he asked Ava, her barely there eyelashes brushing up and down as she blinked. "You're just hungry, aren't you, and Mama is tired. We'll let Mama sleep and you and I will entertain your aunt and uncle, yes we will." He ran his thumb over the softness of her cheek. "You are perfect, you know that, don't you?"

"Oh, my God," Alexis said, grinning. "Listen to you. She does have you wrapped around her finger. And what on earth is she wearing? Her shirt says, *Daddy drinks because I cry*. Okay, that's funny in a warped sort of way, though I cannot imagine that either one of you bought this."

Corbin winced at the white T-shirt his daughter had on.

Brittany gave a laugh. "Hardly. The onesie is a gift from Corbin's friend Travis. The Baby Boot Camp graduates stopped by with their congrats earlier."

"Brittany thought it would be a nice gesture to have Ava in the outfit Travis sent to the hospital." Personally, Corbin wanted to burn it.

"Nice," Ethan said.

"Okay, I'm off to bed," Brittany yawned. "Night. Bye, baby." She ran her hand over Ava's downy hair, then waved to all of them. "Congrats again, Ethan. I knew you'd win the election."

When the bedroom door closed behind her, Alexis lifted her eyebrows. "Geez, Corbin, Brit looks drunk. She's swaying on her feet."

"We've hardly slept at all in four days. Maybe a few hours each. You know how hard her delivery was." During which he had felt like a helpless idiot. But mortal. Wonderfully, vulnerably, weakly mortal. It was amazing.

When his daughter had left the hospital, he had walked beside the wheelchair carrying his wife and baby, right out into the spring sunshine. It was the finest moment of his long life.

"If you ever need us to babysit her at night, we'd be good at that," Alexis said with a grin. "Since we're up anyway. It would give you both a chance to get a good night's sleep."

"Thank you. Maybe in a day or two." Right then he figured he would stay awake looking at Ava until he absolutely could not keep his eyes open another second. But he supposed eventually he was going to have to sleep.

"How was the ball?" he asked Alexis. "Was there a good attendance?"

"It was a madhouse. It seemed like every vampire in the western hemisphere was there offering congrats. Everyone except Gregor, who of course, despite his adeptness at hiding it from the Nation, is not really a vampire anymore anyway. He gave his concession speech after the election and has been lying low at the Bellagio. Man, I don't know what we would have done if he had won."

"He wouldn't have won," Carrick said confidently.

"And Donatelli?" Corbin asked.

Ethan rolled his eyes. "I despise him. Bloody bastard gets on my nerves." Then he frowned. "Beg pardon, Ava. I'll have to watch the language now that she's around. But anyway, Donatelli was there, reveling in the glory of our win. Damn irritating. Shit. Darn irritating."

"You're just annoyed because he danced with Gwenna."

"Yes, as a matter of fact, I am. She had no business waltzing around the room in his arms."

"Will you relax? She only did it because he cornered her and she didn't want to make a scene. Hey, maybe we should set Gwenna up with one of your friends."

"I don't think so!"

"Why not? She could use a boyfriend."

"No."

"Yes, I think it's a great idea."

Corbin interrupted their good-natured bickering to say, "I am grateful to Gwenna for befriending Brittany and reassuring her about Ava's future. They've become good friends."

"It's good for Gwenna, too. I think it's helped her pain heal," Ethan said. "And she needs friends like Brittany more than she needs a bloody boyfriend."

Alexis snorted. "Stop being such a big brother."

Corbin let them resume their circular argument as he watched Ava stretch her plump arms out to the side. Eight pounds six ounces at birth. A ten on the Apgar score. Latched on first try. Yes, she was definitely perfect.

And this was happiness, past and present and future, fleeting yet permanent, a drop in the bucket of time, yet eternal. Immortal.

The bedroom door opened and Brittany came back out.

"What es ze matter?" he asked. She looked sleepy, her eyes squinting against the lamplight.

With a shrug, she just gave a smile. "I just forgot to do this." Bending over, she kissed him on the lips. "I love you."

"I love you, too."

"Aren't they cute?" Alexis asked Ethan.

"We're cuter, babe," he told her, and dipped her back to a rousing kiss.

"I'm covering your eyes, Ava," Corbin told his daughter, even as Brittany draped herself across his back. "Your aunt and uncle are being inappropriate."

"Hey," Alexis protested, pulling her mouth from Ethan's. "If it wasn't for our lust, she wouldn't even exist. You would have never met Brittany if I hadn't been living in the Ava."

"Wrong. I met Brittany first, so Corbin met her because of me, not you or your lust for me," Ethan told her. He frowned at Corbin and Brittany as Alexis whacked him on the arm. "And I still can't believe you named our niece after a casino."

"It's your casino," Brittany said. "Doesn't that make it better?"

Corbin smiled back at her. "Should we tell them why we named her Ava?"

"If you're going to tell me she was conceived in my casino, I could do without that information."

"It's not that scandalous. We named her Ava because we couldn't agree on anything else, because it's pretty, and because we did *meet* at the Ava. And actually, just as an FYI, she was conceived in that chair you're sitting in," Brittany told him.

"Christ!" Ethan leaped out of the chair.

Corbin laughed. "She is joking, Carrick."

Though we have done creative things on that chair, Brittany said.

"Not that we need to share that, *ma chérie*," Corbin said, a little surprised.

"Share what?" she asked him.

"What you just said," he replied.

"I didn't say anything."

"Yes, you did."

"Did not." *Give it a rest.*

"Pardon? Give it a rest? That's a bit harsh."

Brittany sat up straight. "I didn't say that out loud."

Are you sure?

Positive.

Corbin looked at her in astonishment. "I can read your thoughts again."

"I can hear yours, too."

Brittany had tears in her eyes and she sniffled. "Everything is right, isn't it?"

Corbin held his daughter, kissed his wife. "Yes, it es. Everything es just right."